FALLING ANGELS

FALLING ANGELS

Melissa M. Garcia

iUniverse, Inc.
New York Lincoln Shanghai

Falling Angels

iUniverse books may be ordered through booksellers or by contacting:

iUniverse
2021 Pine Lake Road, Suite 100
Lincoln, NE 68512
www.iuniverse.com
1-800-Authors (1-800-288-4677)

ISBN-13: 978-0-595-37710-7 (pbk)
ISBN-13: 978-0-595-82090-0 (ebk)
ISBN-10: 0-595-37710-6 (pbk)
ISBN-10: 0-595-82090-5 (ebk)

Printed in the United States of America

For my family and friends who helped
even when they had no idea they did.

"A feast is made for laughter, and wine maketh merry,
but money answereth all things."

—Ecclesiastes 10:19

PROLOGUE

———————— ▼ ————————

She stomped down the narrow sidewalk toward the street with a grimace on her face. Dropping herself on the curb, she attempted to scrape off the flakes of dried blood from her knuckles and under her nails.

She didn't look anything like the eight-year-old angel that her parents had dropped off that morning. She had scratches on her hands. And on her face. Her new pink, striped shirt and matching shorts her mother had bought specifically for her first day of school were now brown. Her pigtail braids had come loose where the little pink balls had attempted to control the chaos.

Her eyes were red. Her face was red—not from tears, not from pain—but from anger.

Grinning, he sat down on the curb next to her. The angel and the devil sitting side by side.

He ran his fingers through the unruly black hair that hung to his shoulders.

He didn't look at the little girl sitting beside him. Instead his eyes patrolled the empty street in front of the school. Not a soul in sight.

She had fought well, he thought. For a girl. He found it amusing. Then he realized he was just so damn proud of her.

"Let me see your hands," he demanded.

She was still angry. He noticed the tightness in her face; the stiffness in her shoulders. But she relented and shoved her small hands toward him. They were bruised, but the blood on her hands belonged to Julie Clark, not her.

She didn't wince when he checked her fingers. She didn't complain of the pain that must have come from hitting a girl in the face. She was a strong little girl. Stubborn. Obstinate. Passionate. He liked that about her.

There was no hint of a fragile little girl.

"You did good. Don't worry about your dad. I'll talk to him. He'll be proud that you defended yourself."

At least he hoped so. Her parents had disagreed with sending her to the public school in the first place. Her mother knew it was a bad idea. It would only cause her to become ordinary like the other public school kids. Or unruly like him.

He pulled a cigarette from his tattered pocket and lit it. He blew the smoke away from her. She hated when he smoked around her. But he did it anyway. Not to annoy her. No, he would never do that. He did it only to prove that he always did what he wanted.

He wasn't a bully. He never cared enough about the other children to spend time bullying them. He attended the school to be close to his only friend. He was there to take care of her, to watch over her, like she had done for him.

But his torn and dirty clothes and his malnourished and frail body had made him an easy target at the school. The teasing hadn't lasted long. He refused to be teased. He refused to back down.

The other children didn't see a normal eleven-year-old child when they looked at him. He was hardened from having survived the mean, cold streets for years.

He was a criminal now, promoted from homeless and hungry. The younger children ran from him, not wanting to catch his glare. The older children ignored him, knowing one day he would no longer be there. Even the teachers and counselors knew he was past saving.

She looked back at the quiet school. The rest of the children were in class. She should have been, too. Instead she sat in silence next to her best friend.

She glared at the cigarette in his mouth. He winked at her and smiled. She knew better than to ask him to put it out, although he knew she was about to. Unconsciously, he brushed a strand of golden hair away from her face.

She finally smiled at him. "Do you think I broke her nose?"

He pulled the cigarette from his lips and looked back toward the empty street. It was hot. Even the breeze couldn't cool him down.

"Yeah, I think so."

He remembered the blood and tried to hide his smile. It was strange to him how a child could cause so much harm and the only thing they could do was send her home.

"Good. She deserved it."

"What did she say to you?"

She shrugged, yet he waited for an explanation.

"She said I should go back to private school where I belong."

"Yeah, she's probably right."

Her eyes narrowed on him. He could feel the heat from her anger.

"I don't want people telling me what to do."

He put his hands up in surrender and smiled at her. Her parents had lost that argument. He wouldn't rehash it.

"I didn't need your help, you know," she said.

"I know."

Again, he found himself hiding his smile. He didn't want to be the next victim of her powerful right hand.

He had watched the fight between his best friend and Julie Clark from a distance. He wanted to watch and still be able to keep an eye out for the teachers. He had no doubt she would win. She was small, but her determination was as strong as hell. And he knew firsthand that she had a right hook that could knock a grown man to the ground.

He had watched the two girls pulling each other's hair with some amusement. But when he saw Julie's friend rush in to help, he knew it was time to get involved. He believed in fair fighting. Two on one would have been interesting, but it wasn't fair.

All he had done was hold the girl's hands behind her back as she screamed for him to release her. Julie was already on the ground holding her nose, blood seeping through her fingers. He regretted missing his friend's well-placed punch to Julie's face. More so, he regretted losing his surveillance.

They were both suspended for fighting. She would be fine. She was still a sweet little girl from a respectable and wealthy family. A little scuffle on the playground wouldn't change anyone's opinion of her.

But he was accustomed to his own fights, his own violent outbursts. Her fight would be blamed on him, the troublemaker. The school was already plotting to discard him with the daily trash. Finding the switchblade on him hadn't helped.

"Can I have a cigarette?" she asked.

"No," he snapped.

He didn't want to get into another argument about his smoking. He flicked the cigarette into the street and watched it bounce into the gutter. The heat floated from the asphalt. He liked the heat.

"I'm a tough girl now," she said proudly.

"No, you're not."

He refused to think of her as tough. If she were tough, she wouldn't need him to protect her. It would give him pride to know he could protect her, shelter her from all the bad in the world—the bad that often found him.

"You're too pretty to be a tough girl."

"I want to be a tough girl," she insisted.

"Nice girls don't argue," he challenged.

"My dad says I can be whatever I want."

"You can be whatever you want. But you can't be a tough girl. You're too sweet, too smart, too...rich."

"What about you?" she asked.

"I don't have a choice. I can either be a fighter, or I can end up dead."

She didn't respond. She watched him while he debated lighting another cigarette. He looked down the empty street. Church bells rang in the distance.

"You don't have to wait with me," she said finally.

"But I will. At least till your dad comes." It was his responsibility, the only one he took seriously. He didn't want to go home anyway. It was always so cold in that tiny run-down apartment.

"It might be awhile," she said, looking out at the deserted street.

"Then I guess I'll be waiting awhile."

"What if he doesn't come until tomorrow?" she teased.

"Then I'll wait until tomorrow. I'll wait until the end of time for you."

"Liar. You'll leave the first time a pretty girl walks by."

He shrugged. "Yeah, probably. But I won't ever be that far away."

"Just remember, I may not wait for you to come back."

She looked down the street and watched her father's black Mercedes approach.

CHAPTER 1

▼

Tuesday, November 2, 2004
5:28 PM
Washington DC

At the same time a young man was being shot to death in Southern California, I was holding an impromptu batting practice across the country.

The crack of the bat echoed in my ears. I searched my trusty Louisville Slugger, checking for any splits in the wood. It was beginning to look old. It had seen a lot of action. There were new scratches and a few dents, but I was pleased to see it was all still in one piece.

Maybe I should have joined the baseball team in high school instead of trying out for football. I probably would have been pretty good. Baseball coaches probably didn't yell as much. I hated being yelled at.

I tightened my old gloves and took another long look at the bat. One more swing and then I had to get moving. It was getting late and a cold breeze was chilling the air. I brought the bat behind me and took another major-league swing.

The sound of crushing bones made me smile. The bat still had some power in it. I ignored the screams. Yeah, I could have made the majors.

I zipped up my jacket. Rain would be coming soon. Snow would be waiting around the corner. I hated winter. It was just too damn cold here. Not like LA.

I looked down at the mess at my feet.

"First rule. If you make me repeat myself, you ain't leavin' this alley," I said calmly. "Your name?"

The crumpled heap moved slightly and muttered, "Marcus."

The distant cry of traffic loomed down the empty alley. As I expected, the screaming was ignored. No one wanted to play hero in this neighborhood.

"Now, Marcus, that wasn't so hard, was it?" I said, laying the bat down.

The man clutched at his swelling ankle but didn't respond. His head rested on the hard, cold concrete; his eyes closed. He smelled like a wet dog; he looked worse. His nappy hair hung down, covering most of his bruised face. These bruises weren't from me.

He seemed young, but I knew you could never tell the age of someone who survived on the streets. I watched him fight the pain with little more than a grimace. He was determined to not let me see his pain. He reminded me of a younger me.

I searched the pockets of his jeans and found nothing. I grabbed the backpack I had caught him with. His eyes finally opened, glaring at me.

"Hurts like a motherfucker, huh?" I laughed.

I dug out a wad of cash. I counted $154, pocketed it, and continued my search. I threw a pick on the ground.

"You're one stupid crook. If I was a cop, you'd be in handcuffs right now." I glanced at him and smiled. "I bet right now you wish I was."

"I wasn't stealing nothin'. I don't know what you're talking about. I'm only a kid."

"How old are you?" I asked as I pulled a nine millimeter from the bag.

"Sixteen." The kid attempted to wipe the sweat from his face but only succeeded in spreading grease and filth.

"Don't move. So you're young and stupid." I took the bullets out of the pistol and tossed it in a nearby dumpster. It was useless to me.

I learned a long time ago that guns were ineffective on criminals. We don't care about dying. We all end up in the ground sooner or later. Some of us can't wait to get there.

As a kid, I used to carry a gun. And when some asshole pulled a gun on me, my thought was to die like a man.

Only once had someone fired. The three bullets missed me completely. Some said I was lucky. I never thought so. I would have done anything to feel that lead pierce through my flesh, to feel the blood rush from my body in gushes and spurts. To feel alive for just a split second before death engulfed me.

"Who do you work for?" I asked.

"No one," the kid insisted.

I granted the kid a hard kick to his kidney and he screamed in pain. Both his ankles were possibly broken, and now he was going to be pissing blood for a month. He looked up at me with desperate eyes. I waited for him to beg for his life, but it never came. I wondered if he had lied to me about his age.

"Tell me who you work for, or I move the bat up to your kneecaps. Your ankles will heal. But once you lose a kneecap, you'll spend the rest of your life in a wheelchair." I threw the now-empty backpack in the dumpster.

The kid spit, wiped his mouth, and stared at me. This kid was no amateur. I was just like him at sixteen. Too skinny and too dirty. But stronger than hell. His arms revealed his heavy workouts. His eyes showed regular abuse. The threat of the bat wasn't cutting it.

I drew my knife and held it to his face. He tried to focus on the large blade. I could take his eye out in one swift move.

"Remember rule one? Don't make me repeat myself." I placed the tip of the blade under his right eye and watched it waver. Pain is always a worse threat than death.

"Louis. His name is Louis."

"What is Louis's last name?" I said pulling the blade slightly away.

"He doesn't have one."

Because I don't like making idle threats, I always make it a habit to follow through. Since Marcus wanted to play games, I ran the blade along the kid's cheek.

The crimson drops burst from the cut as the kid shrieked in pain. Not a man's scream, this time. His hands attempted to grasp at his face, but I stopped them.

"What is his fucking name?" I asked again.

"I only know Louis. I don't know his last name. He hangs on Thirty-Fourth Street. He runs these streets. He told me to steal the car. That's all I know."

Committing the name to my list of enemies, I wiped the blood from the blade on the kid's torn jacket and put it away. The kid's new screams would bring the police in a matter of minutes.

"You tell Louis that the cars on these streets belong to me. If he wants one, he needs to talk to me first."

Taking one more look at the kid, I put the bat back in my gym bag, followed by my gloves. I don't normally beat up on kids. But Marcus had committed the cardinal sin: trying to steal what I already had my eye on. He would pay. Louis would pay. And the Porsche would be mine by morning.

Sirens screamed in the distance. I pulled out my cigarettes. Only one left. I would have to stop for more. Hopefully before the rain started. I looked up to the graying sky.

"I'm gonna give you a choice. A choice I was never given."

My bag rang. I snatched the cell phone from it.

"Speak," I barked. Marcus didn't move.

I lit my last cigarette. It did little to keep the cold away.

"Luc, it's Mattie."

My stomach plunged to my feet. The tension and anger dissolved.

"Hi, sweetheart." My voice was sweet now. Gentle.

More sirens. I didn't look at the kid.

"What's up?"

"Spencer's gone." She stated it simply. Charlie barked in the background.

I didn't understand. Her voice wasn't normal. Pitchy. Strange.

"What do you mean?"

The sirens grew louder. Closer. I slung the bag over my shoulder and sprinted down the alley.

Disappear. Blend.

"He's gone. He disappeared. I don't know…" Her voice trailed off.

She was crying. I couldn't remember the last time I had heard her cry. She didn't cry when she fell from her tree house. She didn't cry when she broke up with Carl. She didn't even cry at her own wedding.

"Mattie, tell me what's going on."

I eyed the pedestrians on the street. No one looked at me. I kept moving. Sirens. Close.

"He didn't come home last night. I thought he was working late. But he never came home."

I looked at my watch. It was almost six o'clock. Three in LA. Five-hour flight. I was too far away. She was still crying. Shit.

"Mat, I'm coming out there. Have you called the cops?"

"Yes. They've been running through the house all morning. They keep asking me all these questions and I just don't know."

"The cops have been there already?"

I slowed my pace. I was moving too fast. Too obvious. Think.

I had spent my entire life studying cops. This was not standard procedure. Alarms blazed in my head.

Lightning flashed above me.

"When did you call them?" I asked.

"I called them this morning when I woke up, and he wasn't here. Luc, they want me to take a polygraph."

Polygraph. For what?

"Mattie, calm down. What did the cops tell you?"

"Nothing. They won't tell me anything. They just keep asking me questions. I'm so scared. What if something happened to him?"

She paused, and I could hear her talking to someone. I flicked the cigarette into the gutter and kept moving.

"I have to go, Luc. They don't want me talking to anyone."

And there it was. All my anger returned. No one got in the way of me talking to Mattie.

Thunder shook the buildings. Umbrellas opened and people ran for cover.

"Mattie, listen to me. Tell the cops to get the hell out of the house. Tell them you won't talk until I'm there with you."

"They said they have to look through his things."

"Tell them to come back with a fucking warrant!" I screamed.

People stared. Mattie cried. And then the sky opened and the rain fell.

"Tell them to get out. Now. If they refuse to leave, call your father. Stay in the house and wait by the phone. I'm on my way."

CHAPTER 2

▼

Tuesday, November 2, 2004
9:42 PM
Somewhere above New Mexico

The flight was too long. It was too damn cold. The seat was too small to fit me comfortably. And the turbulence prevented sleep. I hate planes. I hate flying.

To make things worse, they played some horrible Disney movie. I hate Disney movies. It's always about some kid who grows up poor wanting something he can't have. In the end, he always gets it. Just like real life. I wanted to throw my shoe at the screen.

At least the first-class cabin was almost empty. A fat man across the aisle. Crumpled suit. Rising politician or businessman. In front of me, some fake blonde who wore too much makeup. Hiding the massive wrinkles or trying to look like the latest pinup. Wannabe, over-the-hill movie star. That's LA.

I called the stewardess. She was young, maybe twenty-two. And gorgeous, with long black hair and exotic eyes. And she didn't have a ring on her finger. I couldn't resist.

"Why don't you come here and help me forget my problems?"

"I've had better offers," she said, with an accent I couldn't place. Maybe English. "You'll have to beg elsewhere."

"Oh, I don't beg."

I was pleased when she looked at me and smiled. I knew it wasn't just my sweet talk that charmed the ladies. I winked at her.

"With those looks, I doubt you would."

"I'm more than just a pretty face. I'm extremely talented, too."

"And I bet you're charming as hell," she said lowering her voice. "But something tells me the ride with you would be a scary one."

I grinned. "Some girls enjoy danger."

"And some *women* like to keep their feet on the ground."

"But you're a flight attendant," I smirked.

"Only for the money," she said. "The stereotype you're looking for went out the window years ago."

"Fair enough. How about I take you out to dinner and we'll see how restrained I can be."

"And you can show me how wild I can be?" she finished. "Sounds like an offer I can't refuse."

"I was hoping you'd say that."

"Other than a date, Mr. Actar, what can I get you?"

"Can I get a coffee, black? With a slice of lemon. And call me Luc."

"Lemon?" she eyed me, then shrugged. "You got it."

I watched her ass dance in her tight navy blue skirt as she walked toward the front of the plane. I imagined pulling that skirt up and—

"Excuse me," the large man across the aisle interrupted my thoughts. "I don't mean to be rude, but are you Luc Actar? The journalist?"

I was too focused on the stewardess to consider lying to or correcting the man. Ex-journalist. That was a lifetime ago. Ignoring the man, I returned my eyes back to the stewardess' ass as she bent down to look for my lemons.

The man pulled himself out of his seat and dropped his large ass in the seat next to mine. I didn't try to hide my annoyance. My thoughts had just turned from fucking a stewardess to carrying on a boring conversation about journalistic integrity and the public's right to know.

"Nice to meet you," he held out his hand. Reluctantly, I shook it. "I'm Bernie Maclay."

I finally turned toward the man. His brow glittered from perspiration. The worn black suit was wrinkled from constant use, not the flight. Reading glasses had been pulled up and perched on top of his head. "Sheriff Maclay?"

I had never met him, but I knew the name. He was elected LA County sheriff three years ago. Just after my big story broke. Just before I fled LA for good. Or so I thought.

He nodded and flashed a politician's smile. His eyes displayed the power that he was well-aware he had. Even I was tempted to bow to him.

"Nice to meet you. What were you doing in DC?" I asked, now interested in starting what could be a very beneficial relationship.

He huffed. "I was having dinner with some pompous senators. They make me beg for more money even though we're growing far beyond what we can afford. What about you? Still working for the *Post*?"

I shook my head. "Left over two years ago."

Well, forced out, anyways. The *Washington Post* likes to employ journalists who actually show up and submit articles every so often. It was a bad fit for me all around. That life seemed so long ago. I was surprised anyone had followed my career after leaving LA. Even I hadn't been interested in it.

"I'm now self-employed."

"Traveling to LA for business or pleasure?" he asked.

"A little of both, I'm afraid," I answered, not sure which I was more afraid of.

He nodded again. "Still trying to chase corruption in the police force?"

"You telling me there isn't corruption out there to catch?"

I tilted my head and watched his reaction. I expected the normal anger or at least a flat denial. He only laughed at me.

"I'm sure there is. But I try very hard to keep it out of my department. And we've been extremely successful in lowering the crime rate."

"I've heard you've done an excellent job."

I know I sounded like I was kissing ass, but the sheriff is always a good person to know. And I was not above asking for favors when necessary. He pulled out a business card and handed it to me. Exactly what I needed.

"If you need anything while you're in town, feel free to give me a ring. I try to be available for the press."

I smiled at the lie. I hated law enforcement just as much as he hated the press. We both knew it. But I kept the card anyway.

He got up and returned to his seat just as the stewardess returned with my coffee.

"I'm afraid we're out of lemon."

"That figures," I said, taking the black coffee.

She smiled again at me, but the moment disappeared.

I wasn't pleased to be reminded of my past. I took a sip of the hot coffee, wishing it were a shot of Jack Daniel's. Ignoring the itch to jump off the wagon, I lapped up the hot liquid. I didn't watch her walk away.

I looked out the window. The clouds did little to brighten the sky. LA wasn't too far. Three years. I didn't want to go back. I had left too much of myself there. But this was Mattie. Again, I was left with no choice. I drifted off to sleep, hoping the dreams wouldn't come but knowing they would.

CHAPTER 3

▼

1988
Torrance

Luc rolled another joint. He handed it to Joey without looking up from the drugs spread across the table. Taking the fresh joint, Joey laughed at the porn flick playing on the thirteen-inch television.

Both the television and the VCR were new toys Luc had just stolen from the home of a police captain. It made Luc smile every time he thought about it.

He had stopped counting his run-ins with the cops. The last time hadn't been pleasant. As soon as the police captain had him handcuffed and wiped Luc's spit from his face, he had severely beaten Luc. A beating he was not likely to forget anytime soon.

He swore it would be the last time an officer laid a hand on him and lived. Stealing from the asshole had made the bruises only minor inconveniences. But the anger had lasted longer than the bruises.

Ignoring the corny movie, Luc picked up the revolver and continued the tedious task of filing the numbers off the barrel. The gun belonged to the captain, too. He would always be proud of that.

At thirteen, his six-foot frame was becoming lean and trim from his daily workouts. He didn't eat enough to have fat on his body. But his workouts had turned his skinny arms hard. His legs were tight and powerful. He wasn't a scrawny little child anymore.

Joey was a year older than he. He was weaker than Luc, but then he hadn't lived on the streets.

Luc liked him nonetheless. Joey had shrugged off gang life, just as Luc had. They both knew it was the best way to survive on the streets, but it was also the easiest way to get killed. Luc would gladly take a bullet meant for him. But he sure as hell wasn't about to die for someone else.

So they became friends. Neither willing to take a bullet for the other, but still helping each other when good opportunities arose.

The drugs had fostered a good partnership for both of them. With Luc's contacts on the street and Joey's ability to sell just about anything, they were starting to turn a profit. Slowly, but then Mattie had always told him making money was hard work.

But the days were getting longer. And Luc was starting to wonder how long this daily routine would last.

He woke in the morning for a workout with Joey's weights, then an hour of boxing with Joey. Joey wasn't much competition, but it helped tone his body. Their afternoons consisted of getting high, stealing cars, or planning their next big heist.

Then Luc would spend the evenings with Mattie. And Joey would spend his evenings either selling bags of weed or fencing loot from a recent job.

It was a good life. And it was a hell of a lot easier than school. But Luc was still looking for another way out. A better plan had to be on the horizon.

Luc was fading from reality. It wasn't a surprise to him. In fact, it didn't even bother him when the counselors at school told him he would end up just like his father. He told them it wasn't true—he knew he would never survive that long.

Luc heard the knock on the door and dropped the gun between the cushions of the dilapidated couch. Joey ignored the knocking. Luc punched him in the arm and ordered him to answer the door.

Luc grabbed the joint from him and took a pull. Joey reluctantly got up and headed for the front door, his eyes still glued to the two women on the television. He knew Luc could kick his ass. And he wasn't in the mood to fight.

"It's your girlfriend," Joey yelled from the door. He walked back, and Luc got up from the couch.

"Turn that shit off, bitch," he yelled at Joey. "And she's not my girlfriend." Luc blew smoke at him.

"Whatever," Joey said as he fell back into the couch.

Luc debated whether to go to the door or beat the shit out him. Deciding he could always fight Joey later, he headed for the door.

Mattie was standing just outside. She refused to come in when Joey was there. Luc didn't mind. He didn't want her around the drugs and sex anyway. He closed the door behind him and left the moaning inside.

She was wearing tight jeans drawing attention to her long, lean legs and brand-new white tennis shoes. Her golden brown hair was pulled neatly into a ponytail revealing her soft, smooth skin. Her high cheekbones were brushed lightly with blush and her eyes highlighted with just a touch of gold.

Only eleven, she could easily pass for sixteen. He knew it could get her in trouble some day. Which was why, he told himself, he spent so much time watching over her.

She had the stubborn, firm look on her face. She crossed her arms over her chest and stared at Luc, drilling into him with her eyes. He knew he was in trouble for something.

"Why the hell weren't you in school again?" she demanded.

"You continue to talk that way, your mother won't let you see me anymore."

Mattie's mouth snapped shut. Luc smiled. He had used the threat before and was finding it very effective.

He closed his eyes as he sucked on the joint. It took away the chill in the air.

Mattie was so careful around her mother. She was expected to be sophisticated, womanly, and most of all obedient. If her mother knew she was using foul language, she would pull Mattie out of that public school she had begged to attend with Luc. She would rather die than let that happen. And he knew that well.

She continued to stare at him with her chin raised in defiance but saying nothing. He ran his hands through his hair and watched the fight in her eyes. When he saw it fade, he shrugged.

"I didn't feel like going."

He threw what was left of the joint off the balcony and watched it hit the dirt below. He didn't care about wasting the pot. He was already getting bored of the drugs. It never seemed to take the pain away.

"So you're just going to spend your days getting high?" She looked away from him and leaned on the railing.

"Hey, we both do what's expected of us."

Instead of looking at her, he focused on the empty street below. Soon the streets would be full of trouble. Those selling drugs or selling themselves.

"You're expected to go to school and get this great education, have a great career and marry some prestigious wealthy bastard that can take care of you the rest of your life. I'm expected to do this," he said pointing back to the apartment. To what had become his life.

"That's funny, because this isn't what I expected from you. I don't think my parents expect this of you. So who exactly expects this from you?"

He knew she was serious. She was angry that he had missed school again. Luc didn't think it was that big of a deal. It was just a waste of his time, anyway.

"Who expects this of me?" he asked. "How about my father? The kids at that damn school. Hell, even the teachers and counselors expect this of me."

"And you care about what those people think of you? What about you? What do you expect of yourself?"

"To survive," he said getting frustrated with the conversation. It was hard to fight with her when she had the strong-willed look in her eyes. "Why do you have to put the bar so fucking high for me?"

"I guess I'm just a little surprised with how low you put it for yourself. You can do more than just this."

"I'm too stupid for school," Luc said.

He could barely read, let alone write. He couldn't do the simplest of math problems. He had started too late. He was too far behind. And the teachers had given up trying years ago. He had given up, too. He knew what he was meant to do. And it wasn't in the classroom.

"So let me tutor you," she suggested.

"You're two years behind me." It was a lousy excuse. He knew she could do it. She was smart, and she could teach a pigeon to dance. She could definitely teach him his math homework.

"I can learn the stuff you are learning and teach it to you," she insisted. He could tell she wasn't going to give up on him. He wondered when she was going to turn into that submissive upper-class girl everyone expected her to be. When would she stop caring about the poor and the neglected?

"OK, fine," he agreed. It would give him a chance to keep a better eye on her anyway. "Will you lay off me about the smoking and drinking if I go to school?"

"Well, it's a start," she grinned.

"You know that no matter how smart or how successful I become, I'll still be the same? It only changes how people see me."

"That's fine. As long as you keep fighting, you can be whoever you want to be." She winked at him.

"Your daddy teach you that?" he asked smirking.

"Yes," she challenged, her chin shooting up again.

He couldn't remember one fight he had ever won with her. Not when she was in this mood.

"Well, it sounds better than what my old man fuckin' taught me," he muttered.

CHAPTER 4

▼

Wednesday, November 3, 2004
12:04 AM
Los Angeles International Airport

I tried to shake off the dream as I waited for a taxi outside terminal two. The intense smell of airplane fuel and bus exhaust overwhelmed me. The only light came from the streetlights and taillights.

LA is a place of opportunity. If you know where to look. As most young men growing up in the outskirts of LA, I learned quickly that my success could only come through criminal activity. Drugs, gangs, and crime aren't just for the inner-city poor anymore.

Most people think that major crime only exists within the boundaries of the city of Los Angeles. Like in other major cities, the Los Angeles Police Department has worked hard trying to eradicate the gangs, drugs, and violence prospering for years within its walls. But their success has only pushed the crime wave to the suburbs, just outside the city into LA County, where the LA Sheriffs are forced to deal with it.

Crime waves flow just like a river. Wherever the land is low and poor, crime washes through its streets. It's these low-lying cities in LA County that thrive on violence and fear. And the county deputies are tasked with fighting unknown evils spread among eighty cities and ten million people.

People across the country view LA as the hellhole of the country, hell on earth. Gangs. Drugs. Violence. Police brutality. Political corruption. It was a perfect place for someone like me. Born with nothing to lose and fighting for any way to survive, I thrived.

I had the help of some friends, like Spencer and Mattie, but most of my success came from my ability to adapt and find the opportunities. I didn't want to be homeless or hungry again. It was hell. I survived. I escaped.

I didn't have a chance to pick up more smokes, and the nicotine addiction was suddenly eating at me. A group of four teenagers smoked across the street. I dismissed the thought of asking them for a cigarette.

Their eyes scanned the sidewalk for possible targets. Although I would have loved the challenge, I was dismissed because of my height and build. Since I didn't have my knife, I only nodded to them. They turned away. They were smarter than they looked.

I spotted Sheriff Maclay approaching a Lincoln Town Car. He smiled and waved me over.

"Get in. I can have the driver drop you off."

I looked at Maclay as the driver took my bags.

"I'm pretty sure this would constitute a misuse of funds."

I felt it strange that my mind had switched from criminal to journalist with just a plane ride. LA was already back in my bloodstream. Another sheriff's scandal was all I needed.

He seemed amused. "You can check all you want. The car was paid out of my own pocket. No county funds. Get in."

The drive was short. I kept my eyes on the moving streets outside the window. The LA streets looked the same to me. Dark and cold.

Spencer and Mattie still lived in their Malibu home, only a short drive up the Pacific Coast Highway. Mattie bought the house when she turned twenty. I helped her move in. Spencer moved in right after the wedding a year later.

Movie directors, producers, and aging movie stars retired here for the security. Their fancy mansions hid behind large brick walls. Gates were patrolled by video cameras and collections of well-fed dogs. In their feeble attempt to protect their priceless crap from people just like me.

As we pulled in front of Mattie's house, I gave my thanks and said good-bye to Maclay. He mentioned having lunch sometime, but I knew it would never happen.

I stepped from the car and was punched with the inviting scent of the Pacific Ocean and the roar of the waves hitting the sand below. I was back.

My stomach knotted as I looked up at the large, two-story, white mansion. I could feel the cold air tightening around my throat and constricting my lungs.

The house looked like a castle compared to the other homes in the neighborhood. And that said a lot for Malibu. Located on a cul-de-sac, the estate had incredible whitewater views overlooking the famed Surfrider beach. The large display windows were frosted and they veiled the soft light from inside.

Mattie was standing on the porch, the light from the house glowing behind her. A white blanket wrapped around her shoulders and stuck out like wings. The white silk robe she wore flowed easily down to her bare feet. I couldn't tell from the shadows whether she was crying, but her slouched shoulders told me she was exhausted.

She didn't say anything as I approached. She didn't need to. I could see everything she was feeling on her face. And I wanted to take the pain away. Someone would pay for this.

I noticed the cordless phone was clutched in her hands as she opened the door for me. A soft scent of flowers replaced the ocean's perfume. I felt myself shiver as the warmth attacked me.

"Have you heard anything?" I asked.

She shook her head. "Spencer," she began, but was unable to finish. The tears threatened to spill. I didn't want to see it. I turned and walked into her home.

Mattie's dog, Charlie, led me up the stairs to the spare bedroom. I dropped my things on the bed. Mattie came in to pull Charlie aside, but he wouldn't budge from my side. I removed the blanket from her shoulders and pulled the phone from her grasp.

Mattie looked the same to me but more fragile and delicate then the child I remembered. Her face looked pale. Fresh tears glinted on her face.

Her golden brown hair was cut short and framed her tender face. She didn't have any makeup on. She didn't need it. Her dazzling brown eyes demanded enough attention. She looked like a Southern belle, a rich debutante.

I looked into her eyes and wondered how I had ever found the strength to leave. If anything was home, she was it.

I pulled her into my arms and held her for what seemed like hours. I could feel her relax against me but was glad to feel there was still some strength in her. She would need it.

"Go to bed. We can go over everything tomorrow morning."

"I can't sleep," she mumbled. I could feel her body collapsing in my grasp. She was tired and worn out.

"I got a sleeping pill. You'll thank me in the morning."

She only shook her head. "I don't take drugs."

"Then let me put it in your drink. I have no problem drugging my friends." I knew she wouldn't fight me. She hadn't won a fight with me since we were children. "I'll find him, Mattie. Trust me."

"Thank you for coming."

"Hey, a friend will help you move." The words came out naturally. As if I hadn't been gone for three years. As soon as they left my mouth, I regretted them.

New tears inched their way into her eyes. But the faint smile gave me hope.

I grabbed some pills from my bag and led her back to her bedroom. The walls were white, trimmed with warm silver. A four-poster bed stood in the middle of the room. It was draped with a white down comforter and several expensive-looking pillows.

She didn't say anything as she took the sleeping pill. I helped her in bed. Charlie settled in at her feet. I patted his head and he licked my hand. We had an understanding. Even after three years, he knew who was in charge.

I pulled a chair up close to the bed. I stroked her head until she finally fell asleep. I could have watched her sleep for hours. I had been gone too long.

I left the room, shutting the door behind me. I hesitated at the two French doors that led to her balcony. The sheer white fabric hid the darkness behind the doors. I felt the pain in my chest increase as I pushed myself toward them.

My chest constricted. I couldn't breathe.

The thought of walking through the doors terrified me. I reached out to make sure the doors were locked and felt a bolt of static surge through my body.

I quickly headed back down the stairs and away from the doors and the balcony beyond.

I paced the house to see if there was anything different, locking everything as I passed. The house looked the same. A few more pictures of Spencer and Mattie together, but for the most part the decorating and setup were the same.

The living room was open and airy. It was the size of my entire apartment in DC. It had been splashed with purple tones. The clean pine floor was accented with a brilliant purple area rug. The ivory walls displayed impressionist paintings of France and Italy. Antiques lined the wall and were highlighted with spotlights hidden in the ceiling.

I felt like I was in an elegant museum or exclusive resort. I was afraid to touch anything. It was the home of a woman with taste and money. It reminded me that I had often stolen from homes just like this. I didn't belong here.

Mattie loved this house. It was her house.

I turned the lights off and moved to the kitchen. Mattie never liked the kitchen. It was filled with state-of-the-art appliances, including a subzero refrigerator and stove probably used only by Spencer.

But Mattie's tastes were displayed here, too. A fresh bouquet on the counter filled the room with a pleasant scent. Dish towels in a vibrant red lay on the spotless gray marble countertop. The white Spanish tile floor had been mopped recently, probably a maid, and sparkled.

Unlike Mattie, I loved the kitchen. It was warm here. I opened the refrigerator and stared at the stacks of food. The gnawing pain of hunger had been seared into my memory as a child. It never went away. I could escape LA, but I knew I would never escape the memory of starvation. Even though I wasn't hungry, I reached in.

I made myself a turkey sandwich and sat down at the large dining table. Mattie had left a copy of the *Crime Reporter* on the table.

I flipped through it but didn't find a single article that interested me. There were stories on the budget crisis and the Policeman's Ball. There was an editorial on local protesters fighting for an addition to the LA County Jail. And a story on the hopelessness of the failing war on drugs.

During my final year at UCLA, I applied to all the local papers. I secretly hoped the *LA Times* would call and offer me an editorial position. I wanted to make a difference. I wanted people to hear what I had to say.

But they never called. Even though my grades were good, I didn't have the experience they wanted. I didn't have the background they wanted, which probably meant I didn't know the right people. There was only one paper that would take me.

The *Crime Reporter* was a thirty-two-page newspaper that few people had even heard of. We didn't have a sports page or a comics section. And we had very little advertising, which meant we were paid intermittently.

There were ten of us at that time, each working harder than we had ever worked in our entire lives. There were a few burned out reporters that had left some of the local newspapers and magazines, probably not by their choice. And there were some of us that were too young to be any good in the business.

At the *Reporter*, the stories that made it to the front page were filled with murder, misery, and despair. My type of newspaper all around. We thrived in Los Angeles only because crime scurried through the streets like rats.

I started as a copy aide, which essentially meant I was an assistant to the other reporters. It was a less than glamorous job, but I learned to pay attention to everyone around me. I hated it, but it paid me and kept me fed. Most of the time.

I spent my time delivering press releases, which I memorized religiously, and answering phones. The reporters tended to be arrogant assholes and treated me like shit. I spent much of my time finding ways to screw with them and their stories.

The rest of the time, I read what the reporters were writing. I listened to the story ideas and worked on creating my own angles.

I worked quickly and spent my free time researching and writing my own stories. I even spent my lunch and my evenings locating sources and conducting interviews. Even at that early stage, I was able to get two of my articles published.

By the time I graduated college, the *Reporter* had hired me as a full-time copy editor. It was often boring work, but it brought me further into the fold of the news business.

Eventually I was assigned a few stories. A year later, my big break came and everyone in LA knew my name. Then just a few months later, I transferred to the *Washington Post* and walked away from it all.

Leaving the uneaten sandwich, I turned the lights off and returned to my room. I didn't want to sleep. I knew the dreams would return. I had no desire to return to the hell I had left behind. To LA or to the dreams that haunted me. Yet here I was.

CHAPTER 5

▼

1990
Manhattan Beach

Mattie climbed the stairs of the tree house. Luc helped her on the last step. She struggled with the bag slung over her shoulder.

Luc watched her silently as she pulled items out of the bag. He downed the rest of his beer and tossed the bottle in the corner. He immediately wanted another. Needed another.

The sun was setting on the horizon and only a sliver remained to light the tree house. The sky glowed amber. The ocean was just turning from blue to gray.

"Here's your dinner. And I brought you the paper," she offered.

Luc looked at the sandwich she handed him. "Did you make this?"

"Shut up and eat it, Luc. It's all you're going to get."

"If you made it, I won't touch it." He could go without eating. He had once gone a month without eating anything but half a piece of stale bread he stole from a crippled vet. But the memory of that hunger still remained. He knew he would eat the sandwich.

"Miss Jennings made it. So eat it. She also made the lemonade."

Even though he was hungry, he was more interested in the paper. He put the sandwich down and picked up the newspaper. He quickly scanned the headlines, then settled on an editorial about police misconduct.

She pulled out some bandages from her bag. He cringed.

"Don't even think about it," he warned.

"If you want the cuts to heal properly, you need to take care of them. Let me see," she insisted.

"Forget it. I want scars. It makes me look tougher." He tried to hide his arms from her.

"You're already tough enough. You need to stop provoking him, Luc."

He smiled, then winked at her. "He doesn't need provoking when he's drunk."

He looked proudly at the bruises and scrapes on his arms. His right elbow had turned a brilliant shade of purple where his father had first grabbed him as he walked in the door. His ribs were bruised. Both shins were black and blue. He had just noticed a new bruise forming on the back of his right thigh. He couldn't remember how he had gotten that one. Nor could he remember what had caused the fight.

At least his father had learned never to hit him in the face. He had learned quickly that bruises on the face would bring unwanted attention from the social workers. Luc knew his good looks were worth protecting. He was fifteen and knew just how far his looks could get him.

"You could just hide in your room."

"Where's the fun in that?" he asked. "It's more of a challenge than beating on Joey. A fair fight, that's all I ask. Besides, I think he got the worst of this fight," he told her.

"I think I got the worst of it. You don't care about the hurt you cause him and he doesn't care about the hurt he causes you. The only one that gets hurt is me."

He saw the worry on her face. He hated to see the delicate, fragile Mattie. He had started seeing it more and more lately.

He suddenly felt bad for the fight.

"I'm sorry." He focused on the paper again, not wanting to look at the sadness on her face.

"How is it that these guys get to write whatever they want about the cops?" he asked.

"The First Amendment. They get to go wherever they want and do whatever they please."

He put the paper down. "What do you mean?"

"They have a press badge and a constitutional right to say and do whatever they want. It's like a key to go anywhere. And people listen to them. The cops can't stop them from printing their stories. They get to tell the truth, even if people don't want to hear it."

"Really? How do I get one of those press badges?" He was intrigued at the thought of messing with the police. They had attacked him and he needed to find a way to fight back.

She laughed. "You can't steal one, Luc. You have to earn it. You need a college degree and work for a paper that will give you one."

He sighed and pushed the paper away. He wanted to read it, but he was too embarrassed to let her see how long it took him to read it. Even with her help, he was still behind and college was not in his future.

"Are you going to school tomorrow?" She opened the bottle of alcohol. He knew she was trying to distract him from what she was about to do.

"No, I want another day to heal. I don't want the teachers asking questions."

"What about practice?"

He loved football. A chance to hit and punish the boys that thought they were so tough. And he wasn't kicked out of school or sent to juvie for making a good hit. He was cheered. He was congratulated. It was a perfect way to release his aggression.

And the best part was the girls that sat and watched the varsity team practice. He hated disappointing his fans. But he had work to do away from school.

"Just one more day."

"Coach is going to drop you from the team if you keep missing practice." She dabbed the alcohol to the scab on his arm. He winced, but she didn't notice.

"Nah, I'm his star. He loves me. He can handle another practice without me."

"A star player that doesn't go to practice and refuses to listen to his coaches."

"I don't like being yelled at."

He grabbed the sandwich and took a bite. He was hungrier than he realized. But he knew the pain in his stomach would never go away.

She put the alcohol back in the bag and sat down next to him. He finished his sandwich and stared out over the treetops toward the ocean.

Silence took over. Mattie drank the lemonade in the thermos. He heard a bird rustling in the tree. It was the only sound in the crisp autumn air.

Luc watched as Mattie closed her eyes. The last bits of sun sprinkled her face. The gentle breeze taunted the strands of hair that had abandoned her ponytail.

"How's school going?" he asked, staring at her.

"Fine," she answered too quickly. "It's just boring without you." Her eyes flicked open and turned to him.

"Well, that's a given. Don't be in such a rush to get to high school. Trust me. It sucks."

"It's got to be better than junior high."

"Are the kids teasing you again?" He continued to watch her.

"If they were, I'd kick their ass." Mattie smirked.

"Watch the language," Luc scolded. "Does your mother know you talk like that?"

Mattie looked away, the hostility in her gone.

"You need to concentrate on your schoolwork."

"Fighting's more fun," she muttered.

"Pretty girls don't fight. You should let others take care of you," Luc said. Mattie shrugged and looked away again. Defeated, she began to sulk.

"Come watch my practice next week."

"No way. I refuse to sit with your groupies. All they care about is getting a boyfriend."

"I just want you to have some friends."

"You want me to get a boyfriend?"

She looked intrigued at the thought. Luc was not.

"For God's sake, no. That's the last thing you need. You need some female friends."

"You just want some young girls to flirt with."

He laughed. "I have plenty of those already, sweetheart."

"Don't call me that." She pouted again.

"Sorry." That sad pout always tore him in two. He turned to the setting sun. "You better get back inside before Mom and Dad realize I'm out here."

Darkness was easing in. She packed up her bag and headed for the stairs. "I'll see you after school tomorrow."

"Thanks, Mat." For everything.

"That's what friends are for." She smiled at him and continued to descend. "Remember a friend will help you move…" she whispered as she disappeared into the darkness below.

He pulled his sweatshirt on as the cold drifted in. He grabbed his cigarettes from his pockets and lit one. As the nicotine eased his mind, he looked out toward the ocean, where the seagulls took rapid dips for their evening meal. He watched the crowds of adolescents mingling around the pier even as curfew approached. He breathed in the fresh ocean air and closed his eyes.

As he heard Mattie walk into the house, he realized he was so close to heaven.

CHAPTER 6

▼

Wednesday, November 3, 2004
8:30 AM
Malibu, California

I opened my eyes slowly. My eyelids felt heavy. I reached for the pack of cigarettes that should have been on my nightstand. Then I realized I wasn't in my own bed, and there were no cigarettes waiting for me. I cursed and closed my eyes again.

The smell of frying bacon reminded me I wasn't in my tiny DC apartment. I kicked the covers off my sweaty body. I jumped from the bed and ran down the stairs to the kitchen.

"What the hell are you doing?" I asked.

Mattie jumped at the roughness of my voice.

"Sorry. I didn't mean to scare you."

"I'm cooking you breakfast. I refuse to let you starve while you're staying in my house."

She was wearing the same robe she wore the night before. This morning, it hung open to reveal red sweatpants and a Paris T-shirt. Her face was a little brighter and her eyes were full of life.

I smirked. "And you think I'm going to eat anything you cook for me? I haven't been gone that long."

She smacked my arm. I pretended it didn't hurt.

"I've gotten better. Even Spencer will eat my cooking." She pulled out a chair at the table. "Sit down." She looked me over. "Unless you want to put something on first."

I looked down at my boxers. Years ago, I wouldn't have cared that she saw me in my underwear. She had seen me in far less when she caught me screwing Carrie Lipkey under the bleachers in high school.

But that was a long time ago. A previous life.

She was staring out the window when I returned, dressed but still tired. I came up behind her and wrapped my arms around her. She wiped her face and hugged me back.

"Sit down. I'll get some coffee."

"I'll get it." I grabbed two mugs and poured the coffee.

"There's lemon in the fridge," she waved as she poured the eggs on two plates.

And for the first time in probably three years, I smiled. I quickly sliced the lemon and squeezed a small amount in my coffee. The bittersweet taste jolted me awake more than the coffee.

I sat down and waited for her to join me at the table. "Tell me everything, Mat. Don't leave anything out."

She didn't look at the food on her plate. She just stared into her coffee mug, the steam surrounding her face. Charlie sat stoically beside her, watching her.

She paused to think. I waited.

"What's today? Wednesday?" I nodded, she continued. "On Monday, Spencer left for work. He said he would be working late, but that was it. I haven't heard from him since."

I took a bite of the eggs and then spit them out.

"For God's sake! Spencer eats this shit? He must really love you." I got up to dump the eggs down the sink. "I'll make something edible."

I saw her eyes turn down and her bottom lip quiver. She still had that same pout. It made a man feel aroused and guilty at the same time. I turned away.

Grabbing the carton of eggs, I turned to the stove. It was easier than looking at her.

"Did you go to work?" I asked.

She shook her head. "I'm currently unemployed. The district's been hurting for money. The school laid off several teachers last month. I wasn't tenured so I was in the first group let go."

"Damn school district is run by politicians instead of educators," I muttered, smacking an egg on the pan.

They all care more about money than helping children. I knew firsthand. They had tried to kick me out of school three times. The only reason they hadn't succeeded was Mattie. Her father came to the rescue and made sure they kept me in school. Not that I didn't deserve to be kicked out for the problems I caused. But they never tried to help me. They only tried to sweep me out with the trash.

California spends more money on opening prisons than opening schools. More money on feeding inmates than children. Protesters curse at the overcrowded jails but ignore the overcrowded schools and the underpaid teachers. And then the government wonders why we have more criminals than educators, why the prison population raises with the dropout rate.

It was that type of bullshit that had led me to investigative journalism. It was also what led Mattie to teaching.

Mattie had always wanted to help those who couldn't help themselves. She wanted to help give every child the chance to succeed and break from the system that was designed for their failure. She had helped me.

She had done well academically. She tutored several students, including me. When she graduated high school, she took learning even more seriously. She spent every waking moment with her nose in a book.

I had seen less of her then. I needed her help but refused to ask again. She had gotten me that far. Of course I found other ways to pass my classes. I always knew how to get the special attention from my professors. And I found I was pretty talented with computer hacking.

Mattie never needed any help when it came to learning. She was smart. I knew she was a great teacher. I was disappointed that she wasn't teaching. Angry.

Even more so because she hadn't confided in me. I wondered when things had gotten strained between us.

"God, I could use a cigarette."

"Smoke outside," Mattie said pointing toward the door.

"It appears I have given up smoking."

"Really?" she asked, looking up from her coffee mug.

I shrugged looking back at the burning eggs. "Sometimes you're kinda forced to."

"Did Kelly make you quit?"

She spat the name as if she hated her own tongue. I had to laugh. She never liked any of my girlfriends. But then again, I never liked any of them, either.

"Kelly dumped me two years ago. After the *Post* tossed me on my ass."

"Oh," she said, dropping her voice. "I didn't know."

I looked back at her, but her eyes were focused on the ground. I guess she wasn't the only one holding back information.

"You were home all day?" I asked, forcing my mind back on the real problem.

"I went out grocery shopping around noon. I didn't expect Spencer for dinner so I ate alone, about six. I walked Charlie at seven. I expected Spencer to be home by nine. But at eleven, when he wasn't home yet, I tried him at the office. When there was no answer, I tried him on his cell phone. But there was no answer there, either. I assumed he was on his way home or just working late again." She fidgeted with the cross that hung from her neck.

I scraped the eggs on her plate and told her to eat. She just stared at the plate.

"What exactly did Spencer say before he left in the morning?"

She didn't get to answer. Charlie bolted to the hallway and erupted in barking. A knock on the door made Mattie's face tighten. She jumped up and went for the door. I grabbed Charlie so he wouldn't attack. Two detectives from the Los Angeles County Sheriff's Department walked in.

"Good morning, Mrs. Hardwin. We need to follow up. Your delay is only costing us valuable time."

She looked back at me, and I nodded.

Even though I was tempted to release him, I took Charlie to the backyard. He continued to bark at the intruders. I shouted at him and he sat down and grew quiet. This was my turn.

I marched back to the living room. Mattie was already handing coffee to the detectives. I wouldn't have been so accommodating. Both men watched me suspiciously.

I held out my hand. "I'm Luc. I'm a friend of Mattie and Spencer."

The younger detective shook my hand and told me his name was Hatcher. He looked too young to be a detective. His closely cropped hair, straight back, and narrow eyes reminded me of the first cop that had hit me. I already didn't like Hatcher.

The other detective ignored me completely. He reminded me of Brutus from the Popeye cartoons. Big and strong and just stupid enough to relax around me.

Hatcher turned to Mattie. "I think it best if we speak to you alone."

"I don't," I said before Mattie could respond.

She sat down in the rocking chair in the corner and the two detectives sat on the couch. I stood guard in the corner, ready to attack but holding the chain.

Mattie seemed to know these guys, so I guessed they were the same detectives that were in the house yesterday. It only made me hate them more.

The older detective opened a notebook and stared at the page. It took longer than it should have. I guessed there was probably nothing on the pad. He was stalling. I wanted to know why.

"Can you move this along?" I asked, releasing the chain just a bit. "As you said, the delay is costing you valuable time." He gave me a look that was meant to scare me. It didn't. I folded my arms over my chest and looked down at the two men.

"Mrs. Hardwin, have you heard from your husband since Monday?" This from Brutus.

"No, not since Monday morning when he left for work."

"Do you know what he was working on at the office?"

She looked confused. "I don't know. I told you yesterday. You'll have to ask the firm. He doesn't talk about his work with me."

"Not at all?" he asked.

"Rarely. He obviously can't talk about anything that is lawyer-client privilege."

"So you don't know who his clients are?"

"No. The firm can probably get you a list."

"They're not being overly friendly. You know lawyers," he said. He laughed as if this were a joke. Mattie continued to stare at him.

"Is there any reason that you can think of that he might want to skip town?"

"No."

The older detective scribbled in his notepad. Hatcher, who had kept his eyes on me while his partner fired away at Mattie, finally turned to Mattie. He picked up the questioning.

"What about your relationship? Was everything going OK?"

"Yes. We are very happy. He would tell me if he was going somewhere." She answered the question too quickly. I watched as she fidgeted with her necklace.

"Did you two fight recently?" he asked. Hatcher closed his notebook and looked at Mattie.

She looked down at her feet. I knew the answer to the question. Unfortunately so did the cops.

"Ma'am, you need to tell us everything."

Mattie looked up at me and I could see the pain in her eyes. The tears spilled out before I could reach her.

"Give us a second," I told the cops and I pulled her into the kitchen.

"I can't do this, Luc," she said, shaking her head. "It's not my fault he left."

She collapsed in my arms and I held her as she sobbed. I hated when women cried. I never knew what to do.

"Mattie, I know this is hard. But you need to tell them everything you can remember. If you had a fight, they need to know about it. It might help explain where his head was."

She nodded and wiped her eyes, but the tears kept falling.

"I didn't drive him away, Luc. He wasn't angry enough to leave me."

"I know, Mattie. But right now we need the cops to help us."

I walked her back in the living room. The detectives were now standing, ready for an argument.

"Mrs. Hardwin, you need to tell us what you two were fighting about."

I ignored them and helped her back to the chair. I stood behind it as she settled in. She took a deep breath but kept her eyes on the ground.

"It was a recurring argument. I wanted to start a family. He wasn't ready."

"Was he angry with you?" Hatcher quickly wrote something down.

"No, he was just frustrated to have to go through the argument again."

The detectives settled back into the couch. It appeared the older detective had run out of questions and was bored with the line of questioning.

"What about the life insurance policy?" Hatcher again.

She looked up at him. "What about it?"

I looked at him, too. I knew where the questioning was heading and I didn't like it. They were already treating Mattie as a suspect. But I didn't stop the questioning. I needed to hear what they had on her.

"You recently added to his policy. But you left your policy the same. Any reason for that?"

"He must have changed the policy. I don't know."

Brutus grunted but said nothing.

"What about other women? Do you know if he was sleeping around?"

I wasn't surprised with the question. It was expected that they would dig into Spencer's background. What surprised me was Mattie's answer.

"Yes," she hesitated and looked at the ground again. "Last year he was with a paralegal at his firm. It ended a month after it started. It was nothing. It meant nothing and—"

"What the fuck?" I barked. "You didn't tell me he was cheating on you!"

She didn't look up at me. I watched the tears fall down her face. She didn't bother to wipe them away.

I knew the cops were watching me closely. I didn't care. If they were lucky enough to find Spencer Hardwin alive, I was going to kill him myself.

"Sir, I think your presence here is infringing on our investigation. I think it best if you let Mrs. Hardwin answer our questions. Why don't you wait outside?"

"I don't want to wait outside. I want to know what you think happened."

I turned my attention and anger back on the officers. Since Spencer wasn't here to take the brunt of my anger, I had to direct it somewhere.

"We're looking at all options at this point."

"Including kidnapping?" I growled.

"We have yet to hear from any alleged kidnappers. At this time we're assuming he left on his own free will."

"Then why are you harassing his wife? She wasn't the last person to see him. Go interview those at his fucking firm. Put an APB out on his car."

"We don't need your help working this case. What we need is for you to stop interrupting. We're just trying to rule out any foul play on Mrs. Hardwin's part."

"Fine." I knew they were right. But I didn't have to like it.

I needed to know more about Spencer's disappearance. I put my hands in the pockets of my jeans so it would be harder to strike out at anyone.

"Go ahead, but watch the questions."

"Are you her lover or her lawyer?" Hatcher sneered at me.

"Neither. Do you think she needs a lawyer, Hatcher?" I barked back.

I was more than frustrated with these guys already. I knew they weren't seriously trying to provoke me, but I was upset and needed someone to hit.

"No, sir." Brutus answered. He obviously didn't like conflict or the thought of lawyers. He opened his jacket enough for me to see the butt of his gun. He was calm as he watched me size up Hatcher.

"It seems like you guys are already naming Mattie as a suspect. Is that correct?"

"No, sir. We think Mrs. Hardwin is lying to us. We're just trying to dig at the truth."

"Well, I don't like the way you started digging this hole. I think this interview is over."

"You don't have the authority to end this interview," Hatcher insisted.

I pulled my hands out of my pockets and took two quick steps toward the detective. Hatcher quickly stood and faced me. He was tall but I still had to look down at him. I tried to release the tension in my fists and bared my teeth.

I was just waiting for another cop to put his hands on me. It had been more than fifteen years. I was just a kid then. This time the fight would be fair.

"Get the fuck out of here," I growled, "before I do something I won't regret. It's been a long time since I've hit a cop but I didn't forget how to do it."

"Sir, I don't like to be threatened," Hatcher said as his hand shifted to his gun.

I knew I could take him before he even pulled his gun. I was skilled with guns and knew cops always hesitated just enough. And I was unbeatable with my fists. And I had no problem decking a cop or taking his weapon.

A flicker of fear crossed the young man's face. The older detective finally stood and moved between Hatcher and me. He placed his hand on my shoulder to hold me back. I had a distinct impression he was trying to hide a smile.

"We'll leave when this interview is over, or we'll drag Mrs. Hardwin down to the station. I'm sure her posh Malibu neighbors will enjoy the scene. The choice is hers."

My gaze moved to the hand on my shoulder. Quickly realizing his mistake, the detective dropped his hand.

"I don't like you. And I just lost all my patience," I whispered just loud enough for both detectives to hear me. "Unless you have a warrant, I suggest you finish this interview another time. Get out or I will have this place swarming with so many damn lawyers, your head will spin. Then I'll sue you both for harassment and that little illegal search yesterday. And I won't stop at your badges. I'll want your asses."

Detective Hatcher gave up first. He huffed and headed for the door without another word. The other detective followed slowly. He turned back as he stepped onto the porch.

"You're making a big mistake, buddy."

"No bigger than yours," I said slamming the door behind them. I turned to Mattie. She was hiding her face in her hands. She was crying again.

"Mattie, how come you didn't tell me?" I asked, trying to soften my harsh voice.

She jumped from the chair and ran up the stairs. I heard the bedroom door slam.

I wanted to hit something. Since there was no one around, I went to my bedroom and grabbed my cell phone. I knew the perfect person who I could take my anger out on. And I still had his card in my pocket.

CHAPTER 7

---▼---

I remember being jealous of Spencer in college. He had a close family. Loving parents and an older brother that picked on him. They always had large family gatherings, especially on the holidays. They ate together. They prayed together. They laughed together. They actually enjoyed each other.

I hated my father. And since he spent most of my childhood ignoring me, I would suspect the feeling was mutual. I guess enormous wealth helps with relationship building. I know it helps with the happiness part.

Now Spencer had a beautiful wife, a mansion in Malibu, and a prestigious law practice. I knew firsthand that if a man were forced to leave the perfect life, he would head for what felt right. To Spencer, that would be family.

It took less than an hour to track down Spencer's parents. They were vacationing in their Florida bungalow, while their Hollywood Hills estate was being renovated. They were shocked to hear of Spencer's disappearance. Apparently, the cops hadn't told them. Neither had Mattie.

His mother seemed concerned and promised to let me know if she heard from him. I comforted her the best I could and hoped she would have some idea where Spencer would have gone. They gave me nothing. She hung up without saying good-bye.

His brother had moved to Toronto a month earlier and hadn't heard from Spencer since. Unconcerned about his disappearance, he told me to tell Spencer he owed him fifty bucks from the UCLA game. I promised to pass the message along.

I closed my cell phone and pulled out a small notebook. I wrote "$50" on the blank sheet and tapped the pencil. Realizing I had nothing to add, I closed it and put it away. My first lead was dead within forty-two minutes.

My next option was something I didn't want to think about, but it was the most logical. If he didn't come home, it was very likely there had been an accident of some sort on his way home.

I called several of the local hospitals. I also called the coroner's office to request a search of its morgue. I wasn't sure what I was hoping to find. No Spencer Hardwin. No John Does fitting his description. I was relieved I had to continue my search.

Spencer owned a black Lexus LS430. It was a sweet car. And one I would have likely picked up if I had found one accessible.

I dialed an auto shop in Long Beach that I knew would help me. Joey's uncle had opened the shop when I was in high school. I had worked there one summer. I didn't know how to flush a carburetor, but I learned how to steal cars from some of the best. A few years later, I helped him out when the cops started looking too closely at him. I gave him a clean front and helped him expand across the Southland. And now he worked for me. We had kept in touch over the past few years. He sent my share of the proceeds and I sent him business.

I never called him directly, so I had to look up the number. A woman I didn't know answered.

"Thank you for calling LB Motors. We can fix anything, just bring it in. How can I help you?"

"Can I speak with Mac?"

"Who's this?" She didn't sound happy to help me.

"What does it matter?" I snapped back. "Put Mac on the phone."

"You have the wrong number," the woman said.

I heard the click before I could respond. I dialed again. This time I didn't wait for the bitch to say her spiel.

"I need to talk to Mac. If you don't put him on the phone in thirty seconds, I will see to it that I close up your chop shop and kick you out on the street myself."

"If you're a cop, get a fucking warrant. I don't have time for bullshit."

She was yelling now. And if I had actually been listening to her, I might have missed the click of another line being picked up.

"Mac, I am very disappointed in your selection of guard dogs. I don't like to be kept waiting."

"Dana, hang up the phone. I got it."

I waited for the muttered obscenities to end.

"How's it going, Mac?" I asked.

"Luc, what the hell are you doing calling me here? What happened to your contact?"

"I'm not in DC. I'm back."

"Shit. I thought you said you ain't never comin' back, boss."

"Things change. And I need your help."

"Yeah? Let me know where you're at and I'll get a garage open for you. Bring what you got by."

"Actually, I'm shopping, not selling. I'm looking for a black Lexus LS430. 2004."

He laughed. "Not here, you ain't. There's a Lexus dealership in Cerritos. The Auto Square. Right off the 605 Freeway. They have a great selection of new 2004 and 2005 vehicles." He sounded like a commercial.

"I'm looking for a slightly used one that may have crossed your path within the past two days."

"My men don't touch the luxury models, Luc. With my luck, they'll bring in a car with that damn LoJack system and my whole operation, and your investment, I might add, collapses. My guys deal in the easy models—Camrys, Accords, and the cheap shit. Now, I know how you prefer the price tag to be high for you to even take a second look."

"I prefer speed over luxury, Mac."

"Yeah, well, if you got something to drop off, you let me know. Otherwise, I can't help you."

"Keep your eyes out for it, Mac. And just a warning, if you see it, back off. This one is hot and about to get hotter."

"Thanks for the warning. You might want to try the towing companies," he suggested.

"I'll check there next. By the way, now that I'm back in LA, I'll be watching my investments more closely."

Mac laughed a hearty laugh. "I'll fire her today. Anything else you need, boss?"

I thanked him and promised to stop by the shop to see his setup. It was the least I could do since I had paid for it.

I tried several local towing companies. If Spencer had left it somewhere for the past two days, no one had reported it. After another hour, I came up empty.

"The cops are back. And they brought reinforcements," Mattie called from the kitchen. I hadn't heard her come out of her room. I jogged to the kitchen window and smiled.

There were four cops now. The two detectives that had stopped by earlier, stood by the car. They didn't look happy.

"Stay here." I went to the front door and opened it before the other two could knock.

"Hi, Johnny," I said. "It's been a long time."

"Three years ain't nearly long enough," John Carliss hissed.

We stared at each other. No words were needed. The obvious hatred and silent threats passed between us without either of us trying. Years of practice will do that.

"Who's your girlfriend?" I asked.

He sighed, then turned to the man standing next to him. He wore an expensive gray suit. Recently pressed. Much classier than the two earlier assholes. I guessed homicide or vice. Those detectives were easy to pick out. They're usually cocky as hell and easy to piss off. His chin was up, and he looked ready for a fight. I almost liked him. He would be fun to tear down.

"This is Detective Ward. He works homicide. Don't panic. He's one of the best detectives we got. He'll be working your case."

"Good, come on in. You can leave those two idiots to watch the car," I said ushering them inside. "So Johnny, why did they send you out here?"

"It's Lieutenant Carliss, Luc. And I asked to come."

I smirked. "You shouldn't let those titles go to your head, Johnny. You might actually start thinking people care."

"What's the problem, Luc?" Carliss sighed. He looked tired. I wondered if it was because of me.

"Those assholes back there don't know how to run an investigation. I don't like their attitudes, and they're ugly. So I threw them out. Their own mothers would have done the same."

"Why didn't you call me? I could have fixed this quietly. Did you have to go all the way up the chain and call Sheriff Maclay?"

"I didn't have your number handy, you know with us not being friends and all. And I just happened to have Maclay's card. I met him yesterday on my way back into town. Nice guy. Hard lines. Probably a bitch to work for."

"Yeah. Well, he chewed them out after you threatened to go to the press. We would really like to keep the press out of this case."

"Too late, Johnny. I have the *Times* and the *Crime Reporter* running the story tomorrow and two network TV stations running it tonight on the six o'clock news. Still working on the others. But they'll turn."

"Shit, Luc. Why don't you let us do our job? Those detectives out there are good cops. They know what they're doing."

"Relax, Johnny. The story is on Spencer Hardwin's disappearance. Although the ineptitude of your department would have been a much juicier story, I decided it could wait until we found Spencer."

I smiled as he realized his mistake. He only sighed again. It was too easy to wear him down. I looked to Ward.

"Detectives Hatcher and Medina are still on the case, but because you caused a fuss, you get Detective Ward handling the interview. Will you let him interview Mrs. Hardwin?"

"How nice. A fucking task force. I don't want to hinder the investigation. That wasn't my purpose. Do you know who the wife is?"

He shook his head, confused.

"It's Mattie."

"Shit. I should've figured."

He stared at me without saying anything else. I knew what he was thinking. It wasn't pleasant. We had a history that neither of us wanted to talk about. Deciding it wasn't the best place to relive the past, he turned to face Detective Ward.

"One thing you should know about Mr. Actar. He doesn't like rules, doesn't like authority. Don't make any deals with him because he'll only be challenged to break them. There is no law he hasn't already broken or would jump at the chance of breaking again. Oh yeah, and he'll probably be your number one suspect."

I smiled at him. "Now Johnny, you're making me sound like some deranged murderer."

He didn't smile back. "Attempted is close enough for me."

I laughed but kept my mouth shut. It was just too easy to antagonize him. And I had a feeling if I opened up my mouth again, I would end up with cuffs around my wrists.

Carliss turned to Ward and mumbled, "Good luck."

He turned back to me, daring me to speak. But I really didn't want to spend the night in a jail cell. Not unless I knew he would be sitting next to me.

"Finish your visit with Mattie and then get the hell out of Los Angeles." Then he grinned, the weariness almost disappeared. "And tell Mattie I said hello."

"You know I won't," I said. I watched him walk out the door, and then turned to Ward. I offered a big smile.

"So you like to speed when there are no cops around?" Detective Ward stepped in to look around the house.

"Where's the fun in that, Ward?" I directed him into the living room. "There's no challenge if the cop isn't already behind me."

He wasn't amused. "So you have lots of tickets? I'll have to check your record."

"Not a one." I smiled at him. I knew he would check anyway.

He sat on the couch across from me. His eyes scanned the room then narrowed on me. He knew I didn't fit in this environment. At least he was observant.

"Mr. Actar, I need to question Mrs. Hardwin on the disappearance of her husband. I know you hate rules, but you'll have to follow mine or this will get increasingly difficult for both of us. I've been up against much worse, and I don't crumble as easily as those young detectives outside."

Yeah, he was a hard-liner. Black and white. And by the book. But, if he pulled out the book and started reading from it, I would have to beat him with it. And I would enjoy it.

"Call me, Luc," I said, dismissing his speech. "First off, you should know that the woman you are going to question is my best friend. I've known her since she was six years old. Her parents practically raised me so I think of her as family. But I am also very close to Spencer. Spence was my college roommate. I introduced them. I wouldn't be here today if it wasn't for the two of them."

I paused as Ward pulled out an old notebook and began to write. I had the strange sensation that we were very much alike. I guessed his notes were probably more important than mine right now.

"I'm going to be honest with you. It looks like their relationship was a little rocky this past year," I continued. "But then again, it's hard to find a relationship that is smooth. One other thing you should know—Mattie's father is William Connor of Connor & Associates."

Ward stopped writing, and I watched as the information settled in. I knew he recognized the name. He looked up slowly.

"Connor & Associates was responsible for the large-scale investigation into the sheriff's department four years ago. And his attorneys took the lead in the lawsuit that crippled the department. He still doesn't trust the department and wouldn't flinch at opening that wound again. Especially if he knew his daughter was harassed."

"Luc Actar," he paused, thinking of the name. "You were the journalist that broke the story. I remember that. That was three years ago. The department's barely recovering from the blows you threw."

"I'm not here for another story. And I hate lawyers just as much as I hate cops. But there are others out there that would love the story or the lawsuits. Police corruption only breeds legal corruption. I'm only asking to be included in the information. I'll share what I know if you share what you know. And we keep the bloodsucking lawyers out of it."

"Fair enough," he said, closing his notepad.

"I got some questions for you," I said, "before I bring Mattie out." Ward nodded. "I want to know why those deputies jumped on this so quickly."

"What do you mean?"

"Those idiots outside have no idea who Mattie's father is, nor did they have a clue who I was. I want to know why this case took precedence."

He looked confused and shook his head. His eyes focused on his notepad.

"You're complaining that you got such a *great* response? Man, the department just can't win with you civilians."

"Mattie called the cops yesterday morning. By noon her house was swarming with detectives searching the house." I looked toward the kitchen to make sure she couldn't overhear me. "I want to know what your guys know. What were they looking for?"

"I don't know why the rush to search the house. I was told Detective Hatcher and Detective Medina were handling the case. I was only brought in this morning. I will consult with them and find out what happened."

"Spencer wasn't even gone twenty-four hours. Someone knows something. I want to know, too."

"When I find out, I'll let you know. Can I talk to Mattie?"

He changed the subject too quickly and I wondered if he really did know more. I guessed that the information sharing wouldn't be as open as I had hoped. I knew I shouldn't complain since I had no plans on sharing my information with him. At least the bullshit would run both ways.

"Where is your questioning going?" I asked.

"I'll need to ask some questions about his work. And a little about their relationship. You said it wasn't perfect. The detectives seem to think it was very far from that."

I shook my head. "Why? What have they got?" I knew he didn't have to tell me, but he also knew I didn't have to bring Mattie out.

"They told me on the way over here that Mr. Hardwin has been talking to someone about getting a divorce."

Cursing, I stood up to pace. I understood why the cops were taking the route they had. Mattie was a suspect.

If he had asked for a divorce when she was pushing for a family, there was a major miscommunication. With the insurance policy and Mattie out of a job, it stunk of foul play.

I debated whether I should get Mattie a lawyer. I quickly discarded the idea. It would only slow the investigation down by forcing Ward to concentrate on Mattie. I needed him to know what Mattie knew so he could move on with the investigation and discount Mattie.

"I'll get her."

Detective Ward stood, too. "I'd prefer to go with you."

I looked at him. Maybe he was a good cop. At least he wasn't stupid enough to let me warn or prepare Mattie for the questions. I nodded my understanding and let him follow me into the kitchen.

Mattie looked up from the table as we walked in. She looked upset. When she saw me, the tears started falling again. Sadness replaced anger. And it caused my gut to ache for her.

"Mattie, this is Detective Ward. He's going to ask you a few questions. I'm going to step outside for a few minutes. I think it will make it easier for you to answer his questions without me. Please be honest with him. Tell him everything."

"Luc, I don't want you to go," she pleaded as she moved into my arms. She shivered.

"It's OK, Mat. He promises to be gentle." I looked back at Ward, hoping he understood what I was offering and what I could easily take away.

He gave a slight nod and sat down at the table.

"Mrs. Hardwin, I just want to get a feeling about Spencer. We need to find him."

She nodded and wiped the tears from her face. I grabbed my jacket and headed out the door to find Charlie. I didn't want to hear the questions he was going to ask her. And I had a feeling I didn't want to hear her answers.

CHAPTER 8

▼

Wednesday, November 3, 2004
12:25 PM
Malibu, California

Connections are important when you need something. And I had a lot of connections in LA. Surprisingly, not all of them were in the criminal field.

I spent the morning faxing photos to several old friends at the local newspapers and television studios. I begged and pleaded with most of them. Some hung up on me. Others only agreed if I stopped harassing them. But I got what I needed. Prime coverage of a story about a missing LA lawyer.

I decided it was time to call Bill Connor and let him know what was going on before he saw his son-in-law on the news.

Mattie had disappeared into her bedroom again. I had hoped she would take a nap. I could hear her crying behind the door, but she refused to open it for me. I didn't know what to do about her anyway.

I hadn't spoken to Bill in weeks. We had always found ways to keep in touch. He was like a father to me. More so than my own father. He had adopted me early on when he had seen how much I meant to his only daughter. It didn't matter that I was two years older. It didn't matter that I came from the wrong side of the tracks. Bill was one of the few people that always saw the good in people. And at that time, there was very little good in me. His wife could agree with that.

"Hi, Dad," I said when he picked up the phone.

Bill and I had a strange relationship. It wasn't exactly a father-son relationship. He never lectured, yelled, or even threatened to discipline me. Even when I needed it. He understood I wasn't looking for a father.

And he knew about most of the stupid things I did. Even the time I landed in jail for assaulting a cop's son. And yet he never held it against me. I respected him for that. He respected me because he knew I would do anything to protect his daughter.

I called him dad and he called me son when Mattie was around. It was just natural. But when I called to talk business, I called him Bill.

"Luc, how are you?" He sounded concerned. "Where are you?" He had noticed I called him dad.

"I'm fine. I'm actually in LA."

"Really? Have you seen Mattie?"

"Actually, that's where I'm staying. She was kind enough to let me take the spare bedroom."

"Well, of course she was. She's a good girl. She knows how to take care of family. Are you in town for business?"

"Actually, your daughter called me. And when she asks, I come running." I smiled at how true the statement was.

"What's going on, Son?" I could hear the worry in his voice. I hated to be the one to tell him the news. But it would be even harder for Mattie.

"I don't want you to panic just yet, but it looks like Spencer is missing. He didn't come home Monday night and Mattie got a little worried. I'm sure it's no big deal, but I wanted to let you know."

It was the best I could do to downplay the situation when I had spent the last few hours trying to inflate it to the press.

"Missing? Where the hell would he go?"

"I don't know. I'm working with the sheriff's department and the press. If he doesn't walk through the door in the next couple of hours, I'm sure someone will drag him home."

"I don't like this. How's Mattie taking this? I think I should drive down."

"That would be a good idea, Dad. I can't sit here all day without doing anything. But I don't want to leave her alone."

"I'm sure you've been doing a lot already. You would do anything for her. I'll be down there in an hour. Sit tight." He hung up the phone.

I passed by Mattie's room and found the door open and the room empty. I walked quickly past the French doors and down the stairs, without looking out to the balcony. Mattie was sitting on the couch looking at the blank screen of the television. Her face was dry but still red from crying.

"You knew what he was going to ask, didn't you?" she asked, rubbing her red eyes.

I nodded and sat down next to her. "Why didn't you tell me what was going on?"

"You were across the country. You've been so busy."

"That's no excuse. You know all you had to do was pick up the phone. Has there been anytime where I haven't dropped everything for you?"

"I didn't know how to tell you. I guess I didn't even want to think about it." She looked at me. "I know he loves me, Luc. And I love him. It's just not enough."

"It should be," I said. I pulled her into my arms. The friendship that we had so long ago had never left, just cobwebs on the past three years.

"I called Dad."

"Oh no! Now he's going to come down here and make a fuss over me." She pulled away so she could look me in the eyes.

"That's a good thing. You need it. You're a stubborn woman, and I can't bully you without having some backup."

"I'm not stubborn."

"Not as much as you used to be, but I still see it every now and then." I kissed her head. "Besides I need to run some errands. I need to get out there and look for him."

She straightened. "I want to come with you."

"There's that stubbornness. I need you to wait by the phone. I want you here in case he comes home or calls."

She slipped back into the couch.

"Do you think he's coming back?"

"Of course he is, Mat. But I need your help. I need you to talk to me."

She nodded and stared at her palms. The tears reappeared in her eyes.

"I know, Luc. What do you want to know?"

"I need to know the woman's name. The one he had the affair with last year."

It took awhile before she answered. I sat quietly, waiting for her to open up to me.

"Mary Fictner. She married shortly after. I don't think she changed her name though." She contemplated. "She was a paralegal at Spencer's firm then left when she passed the bar. I don't know where she went." She turned to me. "It wasn't serious, Luc. It lasted only a month, and he felt so guilty he told me all about it."

I nodded. I wondered if it was the truth or just what she wanted to believe. I couldn't tell.

"Did he tell you how it started?"

"A firm function, a dinner for a client at a hotel. Spouses weren't invited. He said he drank too much and the two of them ended up sleeping together. He said they were together a month and then he ended it because he knew it wasn't what he wanted."

I knew I would make him pay for cheating on Mattie. And I would make him pay even more for telling her about it. It was one thing to sleep around. I would kill him for that. But it was another to make her heart break by finding out. He would hurt for that. He was one of my only friends. And he had saved my life once. But this was Mattie.

"What about the divorce talk? Did he mention anything to you?"

"Not recently. He threatened it a couple of times, but that was before we started going to that stupid marriage counselor."

"What about the argument this weekend? What exactly was said?" I asked.

"I told him my parents were asking about us starting a family. He said he didn't think it was the right time. He said our lives were a mess right now and he didn't see it anytime in the future. He told me to forget all about it. I got angry and refused to talk to him. He slept on the couch."

"Why did he say your lives were a mess right now?"

"I assumed he was talking about me being out of work and him working longer hours. And the fact that he wanted to continue counseling and I thought it was useless."

The counseling bothered me.

"Did Spencer ever go to counseling by himself?"

"I don't think so."

I asked for the counselor's information. She got up and retrieved a card from her purse.

"Do you mind if I ask him questions about your meetings?" I asked.

She shrugged. "I don't mind, but I don't think he will tell you."

"If you tell him it's OK, he'll talk to me."

She nodded and picked up the phone. She dialed his number and talked briefly to the doctor.

"I told him you were going to stop by this evening. He leaves at seven. He promised to meet with you for a few minutes. He couldn't promise anything."

"Thanks, Mattie." I took the card from her and grabbed my cell phone. "I need to make a few more calls, before I go. Let me know when Dad gets here."

"And you don't want me to overhear?" she asked.

I smiled at her. "We're going to bring Spencer home," I said changing the subject.

Orin McKay was in his fifties but looked to be in his sixties, with white crisp hair and a rough, although he called it rugged, face. He claimed to have been a journalist all his life. And he claimed to have been born and raised in Dublin, although his accent was clearly from Boston.

He also had a bad habit of quoting strange Irish proverbs. Although to me, it sounded less like a proverb than it did bullshit he made up on the spot.

Orin had been with the *Crime Reporter* for more than ten years. He was extremely talented and eloquent. But he was also underused when I worked there.

The managing editor had pigeonholed him into the obituary writer position. But, he had a gift. Orin wanted to be an investigator, not an obit writer all his life.

My first months at the *Reporter* were spent trying to make a name for myself and more often than not falling flat on my face trying. Orin had saved me during some rough times. He would take me aside at the end of the day with his fatherly advice on life.

I hated it and would have avoided it completely if he hadn't finished the talks with a round of gossip about the other reporters. I came to hate the others as much as he did. And I had ammunition to knock the reporters out of my way. Orin and I became an unbeatable team.

He helped me with my writing and I helped him with his investigation skills. I taught him my three ways to get information. Lie, cheat, and steal. It worked every time.

I quit shortly after my big story broke. Orin held on and was finally able to break free from the obit daily. He was a rising star at the *Reporter*. And I knew he would be able to help me.

Proving me right, it took him only an hour to track down Mary Fictner. She was listed as working for Cowen & Cowen out in Santa Barbara, but she left two months earlier. They didn't have a current work number, but Orin had found a home address in Santa Barbara.

"Perfect. Thanks, Orin."

"If this turns into something, I want a heads-up."

"Of course. Thanks again for running the Spencer story tomorrow."

"No problem. I even got approval for picture space. You're lucky it's a slow week. Although you owe me since the talking heads get the story first."

"Just name your price."

I heard the laugh and wondered what I had just agreed to.

Mattie's father arrived shortly after I hung up with Orin. He looked much older than I remembered as I watched him hold onto his daughter. The graying hair had started to thin on top. The glasses he used to wear only when reading appeared to have become permanent.

He looked like a father should have looked and it made me wonder what my father looked like after all these years. If he were still alive.

I saw the worry and concern fade from his face as he turned to me. He looked confident as his deep blue eyes drilled into me. I shook his hand, but neither of us could find the words to say to each other. It was often like that with him. I nodded and explained I needed to go.

Mattie insisted I borrow her car instead of spending money on a rental. I gave her another sleeping pill and begged her to sleep. I said good-bye to Bill. For old time's sake, I grabbed my tape recorder and went looking for a story.

CHAPTER 9

▼

Wednesday, November 3, 2004
6:45 PM
Malibu, California

I missed Los Angeles. I had no idea how much I would miss it when I moved to DC. The stunning orange and pink sunsets over the crisp blue ocean. The beautiful women strolling the streets in bikinis and halter tops. Even in November. This was heaven.

The sky was clear and blue. The air just a bit crisp, the way it gets when a storm has cleared out. Or when a storm is approaching. I looked for clouds, but the wind was keeping them at bay.

But that wasn't what drew my attention. It was the expensive cars parked along Pacific Coast Highway that had me taking second glances. Southern California. The only place with more cars than people. A car thief's wet dream.

The one thing I didn't miss was the LA traffic. I inched Mattie's Mercedes forward, cursing everyone in my way. It was slit-your-wrist traffic. Staring at the red brake lights, I wished I had a gun.

As I crawled up Pacific Coast Highway, I followed a black BMW 325i. Lowered, with aftermarket rims. The license plate frame read, "Good girls need spankings, too." She was driving way too slow and with the traffic, and I couldn't get around her. She stopped at every yellow light and waved to pedestrians she knew. Cruising. When she pulled into the Starbucks, I cruised through a red light.

I thought about Spencer and wondered why he hadn't confided in me. Why hadn't he told me there were problems in the marriage? I had considered us friends since we had first met in college. Although he took a little longer to adjust to me.

I wasn't looking forward to the college classes or the long hours of studying. I definitely wasn't looking forward to the football practices. When I accepted a scholarship to the University of California, Los Angeles, I couldn't wait to move out of that dumpy two-bedroom apartment.

I was looking forward to the dorm room. The long nights of partying, drinking, and hell-raising were all part of the college experience.

But I was shocked when I met Spencer Hardwin. Already a junior at UCLA, he was focused on learning. He couldn't care less that his new roommate wanted to spend his time getting high and getting laid.

Spencer moved into the dorms after his parents sold their Bel Air home. His parents moved to their home in the Hamptons. And Spencer moved on campus to be close to his studies.

I hoped to have a roommate like myself—full of hormones and brass. I got the complete opposite. Instead of getting upset about this, I decided to take it upon myself to corrupt the young man.

Spencer Hardwin was upstanding, honest, and dependable. He came from a wealthy family of lawyers. He didn't drink or smoke. He spent as much time primping in front of the mirror making sure his suit fit just right as he spent studying. He had a great sense of humor and loved to be around people. He was my exact opposite.

He never complained when I dragged him out to frat parties or bars. He watched me drink and smoke and only shook his head when I offered anything to him.

When I kidnapped him to join a few of the football players at a local strip club, he only watched us and laughed. Some of the players taunted him and questioned his masculinity. He never challenged nor shrank away. He just continued to drink his diet cola and watch the door.

I knew after a month that there was no way I could get him to cross the line. He had decided sometime ago that he wanted to be a lawyer and nothing was going to get in the way of that. Even a wild roommate. I didn't like it, but I respected it.

I found his resolve inspiring but refused to give in. I continued to party and I often dragged him out just so he wouldn't be shut up alone in our room. He never criticized me for my behavior. And I protected him from all the evil we ran into.

But it was Spencer that had saved me. He had literally picked me up when I was at my lowest point and brought me home. Two weeks earlier I had stormed out of the dorm room without a word to him. He figured I would be back, but after two weeks, he began to worry.

When he found me, I was too high to even recognize him. Thinking he was a bum, I tried to kill him. But my strength was gone. My will shot. He dragged me out of the abandoned building I had slept in for the past week.

I never asked how he had known where to find me, but I had my suspicions.

When he got me to the dorm room, he threw me in the shower, turned on the cold water, and went to bed. I sat in the shower as the water flowed over me. I watched the dirt and blood swirl down the drain and cried.

The next morning I returned to find everything back to normal. I didn't apologize for my behavior that night. I didn't offer an explanation for my disappearance or the state I had been in when he found me. And Spencer never asked.

I guess that is what real friends do. They accept you the way you are. Spencer accepted me as I was. So I accepted him.

I drove to Dr. Waldhanz's office in Santa Monica. I parked the car in a small parking lot in front of the three-story medical building. It was sandwiched between a bank and grocery store. I guess therapy needs to be convenient.

Across the street, two young men smoked and talked outside a small pub. They didn't look at me. They were interested in finishing their cigarettes so they could rush back to their beers. The poor man's therapy. I bet the bartender's therapy cost a whole lot less than what Spencer paid his shrink.

As I walked to the front door, I glanced at the cars in the lot—Escalade, Hummer, Mercedes, Audi, Jaguar, BMW. I wondered why you never see a motorcycle or an El Camino parked outside a psychiatrist's office.

The entryway was bright. A wall waterfall greeted the guests. It reminded me I had to pee. The beige and mint green walls reminded me of a hospital or prison. Or my old high school. I immediately felt uncomfortable.

A blonde receptionist, who reminded me of my fifth-grade math teacher, sat behind a large desk with a phone to her ear. She waved me in and pointed to set of chairs but otherwise ignored me.

Classical music drifted in from some unseen speaker. It took me a minute before I realized it was Christmas music. It wasn't even Thanksgiving. I guess if you find the holidays joyous, you want them to last as long as possible. I often spent the holidays alone. I refused to let Mattie do the same.

Instead of sitting, I searched the lobby hoping to find coffee. With no luck, I reluctantly sat and waited for the blonde to get off the phone. I fidgeted in the uncomfortable chair for half an hour as she discussed the cost of her Botox shots and giggled about Brad Pitt.

By the time she hung up, Dr. Waldhanz was ready to see me. I was ushered into a large office. The large windows were draped with white miniblinds that allowed only a bit of the night to peak in.

I had never seen a shrink's office before, even though I knew I probably needed one more than Mattie and Spencer. I was surprised to actually see a couch, just like in the movies. I told Dr Waldhanz this as I settled into it. It was much more comfortable than the chair in the lobby.

"I do marriage counseling, Mr. Actar. I don't want my clients sitting in two separate chairs."

"Psychological warfare," I joked. He only stared back at me. It's true that therapists have a lousy sense of humor.

"I'm afraid I can't help you very much. I am bound pretty tightly by the doctor-patient privilege."

He finally sat behind his desk, his fingers steepled, and his glasses low on his nose.

"Mattie said it was OK for me to know what was discussed."

"But Spencer didn't. I understand he is missing, but I am sure it has nothing to with our sessions. Without his approval, the rules remain."

"I don't need specifics, doctor. I just want to know if he ever came here without Mattie."

"No."

From his tone, I knew he was holding back information. I wondered if the information was important. If I had my notebook, I would have jotted down a note. Something very unpleasant about Dr. Waldhanz, maybe. I remembered my tape recorder but decided it would only push me out the door faster.

"What about Mattie. Did you see her alone?"

"From time to time," he said. He sure was exciting. I wondered if he was married.

"Why is that? Were the problems mostly hers?"

He smiled. It was a fake smile he was used to offering new patients.

"There are no problems in a marriage. Just hurdles. We don't put blame on anyone."

I smiled back. Mine was fake, too.

I could tell this guy didn't like me. I could beat the information out of him. But I didn't want to start off on the wrong foot.

"Was there any sign that he might be looking for a way out of the marriage?"

"I can't answer that."

"I understand he had an affair with a coworker last year," I pressed on.

"I can't discuss that," he responded shortly.

"Did he ever mention cases he was working on?"

"No. He understood the importance of confidentiality." He sneered at me as he said it. I had hoped to get more information before pushing him too far.

I sighed. I was starting to hate therapists as much as I hated lawyers.

"OK. Well thanks for seeing me, Dr. Waldhanz." I stood and shook his hand. "It was nice to meet you. If I have any referrals, I'll send them your way." It was a joke, but he didn't smile.

"It was nice to finally meet you, Luc. I hope you find Spencer," he said. "Please ask Mattie to call me when she has the time."

I stopped in the doorway and turned back to him.

"Finally?" I watched him take a quick step back. He looked confused. "You said *finally* meet me. What did you mean by that?"

"Your name came up a couple of time in session, that's all." He turned his back to tell me the conversation was over, but I refused to let the door close.

"Why? Why did my name come up? What did I have to do with their sessions?"

I grabbed his arm and turned him back around. I was pleased to see a flash of fear cross his eyes before he composed himself. He had heard more about me than my name.

"I'm sorry. I can't discuss that. Good evening, Mr. Actar." He leaned forward and closed the door in my face.

Dr. Waldhanz had offered me nothing. I was tempted to knock the damn door down and beat his face in. But time was short. I made a mental note to return and finish the interview my way.

I hoped my next lead would give me something I could work with. Mary Fictner lived in a small townhouse in Santa Barbara. The houses all looked the same. White stucco, tile roofs. BMWs in the driveways.

Mary opened the door on the first knock. She was a tall woman. Her red hair was styled high on her head, giving her the appearance of an older rich debutante. She was pretty but definitely not worth cheating on Mattie.

I introduced myself as a friend of Spencer. She smiled at me as she wiped her hands on a dishtowel. Polite and passive.

"Spencer? I just saw the news a little while ago. He's missing?"

She wore a sleeveless dress that dropped all the way to her ankles. She had beautifully smooth shoulders that looked artificially tanned. Her arms and fingers were decorated with gold bracelets and flashy rings. They looked real. She looked like a Stepford wife.

I couldn't picture her as a lawyer.

"Mrs. Fictner, I'm trying to find him. I just have a few questions for you, if you don't mind."

She opened the door more and waved me in. It was too easy. She'd be an easy mark.

"What did you say your name was?" she asked.

"Luc Actar. We were roommates in college. But we've kept in touch over the years."

"Yes, yes. UCLA. He mentioned you." I wondered why everyone seemed to be talking about me.

She motioned me to the living room. I noticed a short skinny man sitting on the couch watching a basketball game. The Lakers were losing. He pushed his glasses up the bridge of his nose and threw me a grin that told me he was bored with me already.

"This is my husband, Ken."

I tried not to cringe as I shook his hand. I really didn't know what I could ask in his presence. I would have to be delicate.

Mary must have seen my reaction. She winked at me. Smiled even brighter. I wondered if the politeness was a ruse. Something perfected in the courtroom to catch you off guard. On impulse, I put my guard up and watched her closely.

"Ken knows about Spencer and me. It happened before we were married. We were engaged at the time." She looked at her husband. He nodded but said nothing. His attention drifted back to the television, and he scratched his armpit. Charming guy.

"Have you heard from Spencer recently?" I asked. I had my tape recorder in my pocket but decided not to use it. I wished I had brought my notebook. I wanted to write down, "waste of time."

"No. In fact, we haven't kept in touch at all. I left the firm last year. I haven't heard from him since." Her face stated she was being completely honest.

"I understand the relationship was short?" I said, hoping to gain points from both of them.

"Yes, very short. We were together only once. Just once."

Her demeanor had suddenly changed, and I had a strange feeling she wasn't telling the truth, so I pressed further.

"Can you tell me what happened?" My eyes drifted back to the rings. She was fidgeting now.

"I was helping Spencer with a case." She glanced at her husband, who was focused on the basketball game.

"Turn that down." She returned her focus to me. I wondered why she wanted her husband to hear this. Maybe I was interrupting something.

"It was late, and we were working alone in his office. We didn't realize how late. I wasn't in a rush to get home. One thing led to another."

She paused. For effect, I wondered? "We both knew it was a mistake. But Ken and I were fighting. And Spencer was feeling as if his wife didn't love him." She looked nervous as she remembered.

Revenge? Something didn't fit.

"And both of you decided to come clean?" I probed further.

"Yes. We thought it best to come clean. I love Ken. I was just angry with him. And Spencer loves Mattie. He just wanted to get her attention. She had become depressed."

I nodded. I couldn't think of anything else to ask so I thanked them both for their time. I felt a little better as I was leaving and I was glad I had come. My confidence took me by surprise and made me wonder if it was what she had wanted me to feel.

Before the door closed behind me, I turned back and asked Mary, "What were you and Ken fighting about?"

She leaned out and whispered to me, "He wasn't in a rush to marry me. I needed to encourage him." Her eyes sparkled, and her brow furrowed as if remembering a great secret.

"There was no relationship, was there?" I tested.

Her eyes snapped toward me. They no longer looked pleasant. "What do you mean?"

"Either this whole thing has been a lie or you are covering for something else. My guess is you two made up the whole thing. Your stories don't match up. My question is why?"

"We didn't make up anything," she shot back. Her arms folded across her chest and her chin shot up. The lawyer was coming out.

"OK, then tell me what you're hiding. Have you seen Spencer? Was there more than one occasion?" I stepped closer to let her know I wasn't in the mood for lies.

"No." She walked out on the porch with me and closed the door behind her. She looked up at me, fear in her eyes. It surprised me. "What do you want?"

"I want the truth. I need the truth so I can find Spencer. So I can make Mattie happy and get the hell out of LA. I don't care about your husband or the kinky games you two play with each other."

She glanced back at the closed door and sighed. "Fine. We were friends. But nothing happened."

"You lied? Why?"

"I don't know why Spencer did. I made up the story so Ken would finally get on the ball and marry me. He's one of those guys that doesn't know what he's got until someone threatens to take it away."

I wondered if he knew what he had ended up with.

CHAPTER 10

▼

1993
Manhattan Beach

"Pull over, Luc!" Mattie screamed at him.

Luc smiled as he swung the Mercedes-Benz to the curb and slammed on the brakes. Her face had turned a brilliant shade of red just bordering on absolute rage.

"What's wrong? I didn't hit anyone." He batted his guilty eyes at her. He put the car in park and looked at her.

"This is my car, Luc. If you want me to teach you to drive, you have to listen to what I say."

"I was listening. You said something about insurance. And something about resale value, right?"

"Get out." She waited for him to get out of the car before sliding into the driver's seat. "You have to follow the rules if you want to drive my car."

"I don't like rules," Luc said as he walked around and got in the passenger seat she had just vacated. "I'm sorry," he said when he got in.

She smiled at him to let him know it was OK. The anger was gone. She could never stay mad at him for long. She carefully pulled back out onto the street.

"When are you going to get your license?" she asked. She was calmer now. She liked to be in control.

He didn't need the driving lessons. He had been stealing cars for the past three years. He knew how to drive better and faster than Mario Andretti. It was a talent he was proud of and one that had made him a lot of money. A license didn't change that.

"Why do I need a license? I have my sugar mama here to drive me anywhere I want."

She laughed at him. Her laughter was sweet and innocent, and it made him smile as he watched the joy dance in her eyes. She was always happy when she was around him.

He shrugged. "I don't know. I guess when I can afford a car to take the test in. Is your dad handing out any more cars?"

"Well you're practically family. I can ask if he can help you out."

"I was kidding, Mat. I don't want his help." His voice grew harsh and distant. He opened and closed his fists. He wouldn't ask her father for help. He liked the old man and he knew the guy liked him to a point. Since her father did a great job of never bringing up money around him, he would make damn sure he never begged for any.

He watched as a black BMW passed them. It was brand new. No license plate. He wondered what the resale value was.

"I didn't mean it like that, Luc. I just figured you could use a car. Although you'll probably only use it to score in the backseat."

"Yeah, probably. It's got to be more comfortable than the bleachers."

She laughed again. He watched her turn up the music on the radio. She mouthed the words to the song. It was an Eagles song. She sang along with Don Henley about a woman's lying eyes.

At one time, she would have belted the words out. Now she was too shy to hear her own voice. But her love of singing was still there.

He thought the habit was cute as he watched her lips dance. Maybe he could steal a guitar. It might be fun to learn. Mattie would probably dig it.

Flipping the air conditioner on, he looked at the speedometer and noticed she was speeding. She was still smiling. She had that daring stubborn look on her face.

"Mat, slow down."

She laughed, and he smiled despite himself.

"I'm only going five miles over the speed limit."

"That's enough to get you a ticket. You don't want that on your record."

But she didn't slow down. "You can drive reckless without a license, but I can't go a few miles over the speed limit."

He felt the car speed up. His voice grew sterner. "Mat, how many times do I have to tell you? We're different. The rules don't apply to me."

"Maybe I don't want to follow the rules, either."

"If your mother knew you were speeding, she would take this car away from you. And you know I would be the one she would blame."

He felt the car slow and watched the speedometer slip down under the speed limit. She didn't say anything. She backed off, but she wouldn't look at him.

The silence that remained made Luc uncomfortable. He was using the threat too often. He knew it but he also saw how effective it had become. She was no longer acting like the stubborn child that got everything she demanded. Her mother would be proud. He had to take some credit for that himself. Even if he secretly missed the excitement in her eyes.

"Do you have to work tonight?" she asked. "I thought I could stop by and see you."

He turned to look back out the window. She waited for him to answer.

"I don't work at the shop anymore," he finally said.

He had lost three jobs in two months. Although he knew he needed the money, he just wasn't fit to work with people. He hated being nice to people. He hated being phony. It was stupid to think he could keep a job. But the social workers insisted he learn some discipline somewhere.

She sighed, but her eyes remained on the road. "Did you fail the drug test?"

"No. I didn't like my manager."

He noticed the worry cross her face and cringed. He knew she was going to ask. And he knew he would tell her.

"What did you do to him?"

"He pissed me off. So I hit him." He shrugged. "He got me arrested. Juvie is making me see some drug counselor and I have some social worker coming to talk to my dad tomorrow."

He may not have needed the job, but he did need the money. He had given up stealing. It often took too long to unload the items and still get a decent price.

He was still making good money selling dope. He made even more by not paying his supplier. But the overhead was expensive. More so, the drugs bored him.

"I'm gonna see Joey's uncle tomorrow. He's opening an auto body shop in Long Beach. He said he'll show me the ropes and if I can keep up, he'll even pay me."

She shook her head. "You're going to be stealing cars for him."

"It's what I'm good at," he muttered.

"So what's going on with Jenny? I've been hearing rumors you two are done for good."

"She's seeing that new kid, Robbie." He didn't care about Robbie. He wasn't even jealous of him. He had never been the jealous type. There were too many girls out there to be picky over one.

"I would have dumped you for Robbie, too. He's cute."

"Thanks, Mat. I appreciate you always standing beside me," he joked. He hoped she wasn't serious. He couldn't shake the thought of Mattie and Robbie together. He felt his hate for Robbie growing.

"Why did she break up with you?" she asked.

"She said she only went out with me because I was a bad boy. Now that I'm going to college, she doesn't see the thrill anymore."

"You're going to college?" she asked surprised.

He had yet to tell her. But night after night, he had watched the replay of the Rodney King beating. The police beat a man just because they could. They handed out their form of justice just as they had for years on those they proclaimed to be guilty. Just as they had done to him. It was time someone stopped it. He would fight back. Not just for himself, but for all of them.

He shrugged, but let the smile creep onto his face.

"And this is my fault, right?" she asked, trying not to smile back.

"No way. I ain't going to college for you, sweetheart. If the school is going to hand me a free education, I ain't too stupid to pick up on it."

"And I'll use it to change the system that tried to keep me down. I won't be that weak poor little kid ever again. I'll never stop fighting, Mat."

He watched as she pulled into her driveway.

"I saw you talking to John Carliss yesterday. What did he want?" he asked.

"He wants to go out with me."

"What?" An overwhelming anger engulfed him. "No way, Mattie. I'll talk to him." They both knew there would be little talking.

"You are impossible." She laughed, but it didn't help his mood. Putting the car in park, she glanced over at him. "You know this older brother thing is getting old."

"I don't mind you talking to boys. But John is too old for you and—"

"He's the same age as you," she interrupted.

"That's too old. I know what guys like that think about."

"Good, because I'm thinking the same thing."

He put his hand over his ears. "Shit, I don't want to hear that." He wasn't sure which was worse. John or Robbie.

"You need to stop worrying about me. You're going to be gone next year, and I don't want to sit at home knitting with my mother. I want to have fun."

"I'll always worry about you," he said putting his hands down. He felt the pain in his stomach rising. He could only protect her for so long. How the hell was he supposed to protect her once he was in college?

"You're right. You deserve to have a life. Why don't you go to the prom with me?" He didn't know why he asked. It just came out. But the second it did, he realized what a great idea it really was.

"What?"

"Jenny's taking Robbie to the prom. I don't want to sit at home knowing he won."

"Does it have to be a game?" she asked.

"Of course. Come with me. We can sit there and make fun of everyone. We can spike the punch and watch everyone get stupid. It'll be fun."

"You're going to take a sophomore to the senior prom? Won't that ruin your reputation?"

"First, I'll be taking the most beautiful sophomore. Second, it will help your reputation more than hurt mine. Besides, I would like to have a closer look at this Robbie kid. And third, you suck at knitting."

"OK, I'll go, but only if you promise that we can go bowling afterward." She grabbed her backpack from the backseat.

"Deal." He got out of the car. "Thanks for the lesson, sweetheart."

CHAPTER 11

—————————— ▼ ——————————

Thursday, November 4, 2004
7:40 AM
Malibu, California

"I want to offer a reward," Mattie announced.

I considered her request as I started the coffee. "How much?"

"Whatever it takes. This is taking too long."

I couldn't agree with her more. The nights were getting harder to sleep. The days were getting harder to breathe.

But Mattie wouldn't be spending a dime of her money. I had acquired enough to cover whatever she would need. It would just take a little work to clean up the trail.

"I'll discuss it with Ward."

I watched her drop into the kitchen chair. She looked tired. Her eyes were red. I squeezed a little lemon in her coffee. She could use the jolt.

"What did you learn from Dr. Waldhanz?" she asked.

"Nothing helpful. Although he did mention something I found interesting," I said, handing the mug to her.

She looked at me, hopeful. "What?"

"He mentioned that my name had come up in your sessions."

She shrugged. "Of course. You're a big part of my life, Luc. How could I talk about myself and not talk about you?"

I nodded. It was stupid to think it was more than that.

"Why did you sometimes see him alone?"

"Spencer seemed to think I was the one with the problem. He didn't have a problem. He had an affair and admitted it to me. Me, well, I was the problem in the relationship because I was unhappy."

"Are you unhappy?" I asked surprised.

She got up from the table to pace. "How can I be unhappy? Haven't I done everything everyone has expected of me? I did well in high school, just like everyone wanted. I was educated at a great college, graduated with honors. Had a great teaching career and sculpted young minds. I married a wealthy lawyer with a large prestigious family, and I live in a great big house on the shores of Malibu. How could I be unhappy?"

"You didn't want all that?" I asked. I wanted to go to her, to hold her. But I couldn't find the strength to get up. She had been so happy when we were kids. When had that changed?

"I wanted it. I wanted it because everyone wanted it for me. It made everyone else happy. Now I don't want it. I don't want any of it. So now Spencer is gone and everyone's going to think I drove him away." She rubbed her eyes to keep the tears from falling.

"I don't think that."

"Of course you do." she snapped back. "That's why you wanted me to tell the detective everything about our problems. We may have had some problems, but he didn't disappear because of that, Luc. I know it. I just wish you believed me and not the cops."

She was right and I knew it. I was thinking about Spencer's disappearance as just another missing person case. But I knew Spencer. And I knew he wouldn't leave Mattie because things got rough.

Spencer had to be involved in something that he couldn't handle. I remembered Hatcher and Medina. They had started their questioning with Spencer's clients. Then slipped in his personal life.

"You're right, Mat. I'm sorry. I've been listening to the detectives and following where they led me. I need to focus on his business. I need to go to his office."

"Detective Ward said the law firm wasn't helping," she said.

I looked at her. "Ward asked about the firm, too?"

She nodded. "He asked me what cases he was working. He asked me if I had heard Spencer mention any names." She tried to remember. "He had a list of names, but I don't remember them. I told him again that Spencer didn't talk about work."

Damn it. Ward had sidetracked me. And the second I was out of the room, he had moved in. He knew I would be too busy worrying about Mattie's relationship when I really needed to focus on Spencer's clients.

I walked into the study. Mattie followed me.

"Does he keep anything in here?"

"No, he keeps his clients' files at the office. He always said things weren't secure here."

The study was organized and neat. I looked through the filing cabinet first. Spencer had his tax returns filed according to date for the past ten years. I laughed at how opposite we were. I kept my receipts in a shoebox under my bed, if I remembered to keep them at all.

Spencer also kept files for each of his business trips. The trips ranged from San Francisco to Chicago. I briefly looked through the files and itineraries he filed. But there were no trips for the past month.

I closed the cabinet and looked through the desk. Mattie watched as I flipped through Spencer's notebooks looking for anything that might be a lead. I found nothing. I was frustrated, but I knew I needed to see the files in his office.

Before I could organize my next plan of action, Charlie started barking. Detective Ward smiled as I opened the door. I was tempted to let the dog at him. Unfortunately, Mattie ushered Charlie out to the backyard.

Ward was holding a folder, but his focus was on Mattie as she walked from the room. His eyes watched her a little too intently. My anger continued to grow.

"What's up?" I snapped.

"We still have no news. I just have a few questions," Ward said following me into the living room. He glanced back to the sliding glass door and watched Mattie release the dog in the yard.

"I think she's tired of all the questions, Ward." I nipped at him. I was hoping he would bite back, but he remained controlled.

"I was actually talking about you," he said, finally turning to me. He smiled at my response. He had expected the anger.

"I wasn't here when he disappeared. And I don't know where he is. Why don't you go out and prove to me that you're a real detective."

Mattie walked into the room and looked at both of us. I didn't realize I had raised my voice.

"Don't worry, Detective. He may bark a lot, but he doesn't bite."

I knew she was referring to me, not Charlie. I kept my eyes on Ward.

"You've never had the privilege of seeing me bite, Mattie."

Detective Ward laughed and made himself comfortable on the couch. "He's not as tough as he claims, huh?" he asked Mattie.

He smiled at her and ignored my stares. He was trying to suck up to Mattie. I noticed Ward kept his eyes locked on her. I didn't like it. She smiled back at him. Ward had more charm than I realized.

"Oh, he's tough." She pulled my arm and directed it toward Ward. "See those scars? When our teachers used to tell him to put out his cigarettes, he would try to shock them by putting them out on his arm." She shrugged and released my arm. "But then, he's scared to get a tattoo."

Detective Ward finally tore his eyes from her and looked at me. He waited for me to disagree. I only shrugged.

"I don't like needles. I had a bad experience with heroin as a kid." I sat down across from him.

Ward placed the folder on the table in front of me. "So, tough boy, how many times have you been arrested?"

I looked at the thin folder and tried not to laugh. "That's all you guys got on me? I guess you had problems accessing my juvie record. I've been arrested twice as an adult. No big deal."

"Would you like to explain?" Ward asked without looking at the folder.

"What does this have to do with Spencer's disappearance?" Mattie asked suddenly concerned.

"We're doing a thorough investigation," Ward said. He was still glaring at me. The charm was gone. It was business now. He was stupid to think he could match my anger.

"It's OK, Mattie. They just need to clear me. I know the routine. I've done it before." I looked quickly at Mattie, my face softening. "Sweetheart, can you get Ward some coffee?"

Mattie jumped up. "Oh, of course. I'm sorry. I'll be right back."

I waited for her to leave before I turned back to Ward, letting him see my anger.

"The first arrest was for assault and battery."

"With a loaded .357," he shot back.

"I wanted to get his attention."

"You fired it four times."

"I was aiming for his tires. I'm a good shot."

"And the fight?"

"I put the gun down before the fight. It was fair."

"When was this?" he asked.

"After I graduated high school. The charges were dropped."

"Why?"

"You would have to ask Johnny that question."

"Lieutenant Carliss?"

I smiled. Ward hadn't done his own research or he would have dug further. I settled back and watched Ward think it over.

"That's who I was fighting with."

I spent my first night in the dorm rooms getting drunk and looking for trouble. I was alone. And I was angry. Back then I had no leash. I found myself back in Torrance looking for John Carliss. I had a score to settle. When I found him at the mall, I shot the tires out on his truck and pointed the gun at his head.

"Johnny and I were arrested. He promised to drop the charges on me if I dropped the charges on him. His father was still a cop at the time. I believe he helped with the red tape."

In all reality, John had been my best sparring partner. He was quick on his feet and had a great body blow. It was a tough fight. But I had more experience, and I finally landed a right hook to his nose that had crumpled him. I knew he would never forgive me for the nose. Or for embarrassing him by landing him in jail.

But the embarrassment was higher on my end. Instead of calling my father, John's father had called Mattie. And I had to beg Johnny to keep her away from me. The sight of me on my knees made him smile and almost made up for the broken nose.

I had to make a lot of promises I wasn't ready to commit to. I had to finish college. Or his father would find a way to bury my ass in a dark cell somewhere. Away from Mattie. In some odd way, he probably saved my life.

"But you had a firearm. And you fired it in a public place. Your charges were much more serious."

"I guess he did me a favor then." I looked back at the kitchen door. I heard Mattie getting the coffee mugs from the cabinet.

"Mattie doesn't know you were arrested?" he asked, catching my gaze.

"She knows. But we haven't spoken about it since." I looked back at him. "I would really like to keep it that way."

Mattie walked back in and handed a steaming mug to Detective Ward. He flashed a smile at her. I waited for him to continue.

"What about the second arrest?" Ward asked, moving on.

"I was arrested by a campus cop for breaking into a professor's office."

"Why?"

"Why did I get caught?" I laughed.

"No, why did you break into the office?"

"I had started a little side business while I was in college. I helped those less fortunate get the grades they needed to graduate. I find pleasure in helping the underprivileged."

"You changed grades?" he asked, surprised. I guess I don't look like the computer hacking type. "How?"

"Trade secret."

Ward, let it go. "How much money did you make?"

"You gonna charge me with a crime, officer?"

"Just curious."

I shrugged. "Probably close to five thousand, tax free. Used it to buy a motorcycle. Wrapped it around a tree a month later. Had to buy another one. I still hate that tree."

I smiled but didn't look at Mattie. I was pretty sure she was still angry with me for driving drunk.

"The charges were dropped again?"

"The cops had no proof that I had done anything other than trespass. The professor decided not to press charges. They let me go."

"It also helps when you're sleeping with the professor," Mattie muttered.

"He didn't need to know that part, Mattie," I said, winking at her.

Ward watched the exchange and kept his eyes on Mattie as she played with a loose string on the chair.

"Was Spencer involved in this scheme?" Ward asked, moving on.

I laughed. "No way. Spencer would never get involved in illegal activity. He had no idea I was involved. He probably would have reported me to the dean. Friend or not."

"How did a punk like you get into college anyway?"

"Football scholarship."

"No kidding?" Ward said, finally smiling at me. "I played at Cal. Offensive guard. I liked to protect the quarterback. What position?" I found his interest just a bit confusing.

"Defensive end. I liked to attack the quarterback."

Ward grunted, thought about that for a while. Then he turned his eyes toward the folder again.

"You don't have any records after college. Did you decide to stop causing trouble or did you find God?"

"I got smarter."

"When was the last time you talked to Spencer?"

Ward pulled his notebook out. I thought about the notes on my notebook and wished we could trade. His notes were probably much more exciting.

"Probably a month ago. We discussed UCLA's chances for the Rose Bowl."

"Did he ever mention any cases to you?"

"No. Is there a case that interests you?" I asked.

"Just curious. What else did you two normally talk about?"

"We were friends. We reminisced. We laughed. We wept. We bonded."

"Sounds like you three are very close."

When I didn't respond, Ward grabbed the file that sat on the table. I realized too late that it wasn't my police records in the file. Ward had set it up perfectly. All I could do was wait for the blow to come. Whatever it was.

"I pulled your phone records from DC. In the past two years, you haven't made a single call to this house. Is there a reason for that, considering the three of you are so close?"

Ward stared at me, waiting for my answer. But I didn't turn from Ward's glare. I could feel Mattie staring, too. I wondered if she had noticed it before or if she was just realizing it now. I couldn't look at her.

I shrugged easily. "My long distance plan sucks."

Ward let the silence drag on a little long then finally nodded. I think my heart stopped as I waited.

"I see." He flipped through the rest of the file. I felt the tension in my shoulders and forced myself to relax.

"Why did you leave LA?"

"It would have been a hell of a commute to the *Post* every day."

"You only stayed at the *Washington Post* for a little over a year. Why did you leave?"

"They asked me nicely."

"You were fired?"

"I prefer the phrase 'released from my obligations.'" I was getting tired of the questions. And the need for nicotine was making my skin crawl.

"And now?"

"I freelance where needed. Thinking of writing a book about police misconduct. Care to help?"

Ward ignored me. "And when exactly did you get into Los Angeles?"

A much easier question. I allowed myself to breathe.

"I'm sure you have my flight information already. I landed in LA Tuesday night, close to midnight."

Ward nodded and continued to peruse his notes. Just when I was expecting him to pounce on me again, he closed the folder and looked back up at me.

"Is there anything else you can think of that might help us find Spencer?"

"Yeah, I suggest you look outside of this house."

CHAPTER 12

▼

Thursday, November 4, 2004
10:12 PM
Malibu, California

I waited until ten before leaving the house. Mattie insisted I take her with me, but I persuaded her to stay put. Breaking into Spencer's law firm wasn't going to be easy and Mattie's presence would have made it much more difficult.

I slipped her another sleeping pill so she would rest and promised I would give her a full briefing in the morning. Then I headed to Robinson & Robinson, Counselors at Law.

I drove quickly to Spencer's office but slowed the car as I cruised past the empty parking lot. I made a U-turn at the next light and circled back to make sure there was no security around the building.

I pulled off on a side street and parked behind a red Honda Civic. I waited in the car for a few minutes to make sure the car couldn't be spotted from the building. Convinced I had not been noticed by anyone, I got out and walked toward the office building.

I watched the building for another hour. I wasn't just making sure the place was empty. I cased the setup of the building for all possible entrances and exits, hiding spots, and vulnerable areas.

The street in front of the building was empty. With no residences nearby, I knew there would be no witnesses. And I knew I could get in quickly. My only concern was the cops. Since Spencer was missing, I figured there would be a cruiser rolling by every so often to make sure nothing looked out of the ordinary. I needed to make sure I didn't attract their attention.

When I was positive there was no movement inside the building and had run all possible escape routes through my head, I put my gloves on and moved in.

I found the sign of AGS Security on the side window and smiled. AGS was still the best system on the market. They advertised a quick response to all alerts.

Joey and I had spent a summer breaking into homes. It was always surprising to find homes with the doors left unlocked. Or sophisticated alarm systems turned off. Or safes left wide open. I guess the rich figured they had some sort of protection from the criminals outside their gates. I wondered where they got their strange sense of security.

Mostly, we stole money and prescription drugs, but I soon moved up to stealing anything we could sell on the streets that wouldn't cause unnecessary attention from the police. After a few months, I found crawling through open windows too easy, and I wanted something more challenging.

I decided to move to office buildings, where the alarm systems required much more planning and the loot was much more valuable. AGS had been a favorite of mine.

I located the telephone box next to the gas and electric meters. I jammed the door open with a rock. Cut the telephone wires.

With the phone lines cut, there was no way to alert anyone at AGS. There would be no quick response tonight.

After a quick check of the street, I moved to the front door. It took me less than three minutes to pick the lock. I scanned the walls. No security cameras. No motion detectors. Beautiful. I moved in.

I could hear the beeps on the alarm panel. A red light flashed like a beacon. They would know in the morning that the office had been broken into. Tonight, I had plenty of time.

Elevators were on the right, but I despised elevators. They were nothing but traps.

I moved toward the staircase. I walked the three flights of stairs. Turned left toward Spencer's office. The door was locked. Another minute to pick the lock.

I lit up the room with the flashlight. Searched the walls and ceiling. Satisfied there was nothing to give me away, I walked in.

The inside of the office looked the same as when I had first seen it three years earlier. A trio of framed dark jungle abstracts on the wall. Dark green berber carpet, like limp grass. The large window overlooked the empty parking lot. The real wilderness.

The top of the mahogany desk was bare except for a telephone and a laptop. It had recently been wiped of dust and smelled of lemon cleaner. A shiny black filing cabinet sat in the corner of the room. A wedding picture of Spencer and Mattie rested in front of a small laserjet printer.

I chose the filing cabinet first. But found it locked. I moved to the desk. I searched the drawers first. The top drawer contained office supplies. Pens. Pencils. A blank pad of paper. Post-it notes.

He was too damned organized. I found a set of keys that looked like they belonged to the filing cabinet. I put the keys on the desk. I kept digging.

In the bottom drawer I found a day planner. I quickly glanced through it. Monday, the day he disappeared, was blank. The last notes were from the previous Thursday. He had an appointment with the managing partner, Tim Robinson. Scribbled below: "Meeting with Angel." I put the planner in my pocket for later reference.

I moved back to the filing cabinets. I smiled as the keys unlocked the cabinet. I wasn't sure what I needed to look for so I started searching for any files with the name of Angel. I didn't find anything. So I pulled out all the files that looked like they were still active and placed them on the desk.

I made a quick check of the parking lot and the street below. Seeing no movement, I settled into Spencer's chair and did a thorough reading of each of his active cases. It made for very boring reading and not being a lawyer, I was confused with a lot of the paperwork. Nothing set off alarms to me.

Spencer had been working a number of cases. Apparently simultaneously. I spent the next hour reading the notes of anything dated within the past year.

Most of the cases were corporate cases. Cases that would be settled between two lawyers. Spencer hadn't seen the inside of a courtroom in several years.

I wondered which of these cases could have caused Spencer's disappearance. It was like looking for a needle in a haystack. Then I wondered if I was just wasting my time. Maybe what I was looking for wasn't even a needle.

Time. I glanced at my watch. I needed to finish. I moved to the laptop. Booted it up. It made several bleeps and displayed a security clearance. I looked at the screen for a few minutes and realized I had no idea what Spencer would use as a password.

It took me another minute to log in as the system administrator and locate Spencer's password. Another minute to log in as Spencer and open his e-mail. I glanced through a few of his recent e-mails. They were just as boring as the files. Only one of any interest.

Tim Robinson had sent Spencer an e-mail reminder about a meeting on Tuesday. Spencer had replied to the e-mail on Monday afternoon with a quick note: "I'll call you." Unfortunately, by Tuesday morning, Spencer was gone.

I thought about taking the laptop with me but dismissed the idea. The theft might be noticed and taken much more seriously than a simple breaking and entering. I had no desire to add to my arrest record. And spending time in jail would only slow my search for Spencer.

I was frustrated with my lack of success. But then again, what had I really expected? If I had found a joint or a parking ticket, I would have known I was in the wrong office. This was Spencer's office. The worst thing he could ever do was accidentally take some of his office supplies home.

I checked the parking lot again. Still no movement. I put the office back the way I found it and wondered what notes I would take on this visit.

Heading toward the stairs, I realized how easily it would have been for Spencer to leave his office without anyone noticing him. The stairwell was next to his office and he couldn't be seen from the receptionist's desk.

At the bottom of the staircase, I noticed two doors. The one that led to the lobby was the door I had come through earlier. But there was another door, labeled "Parking Lot." Spencer would have found it rather easy to disappear.

Another thought crossed my mind. If it was that easy to sneak out, it was just as easy to sneak in. I checked the door leading out to the parking lot. With the right key, anyone could have made it up the stairs and into Spencer's office.

There were scratch marks on the doorknob. Marks that a pick would make. From an inexperienced thief. I wasn't the only one who had come searching for clues. Looking for a needle in a haystack. Someone had beaten me here. That someone had the needle I was looking for.

CHAPTER 13

▼

1993
Manhattan Beach

Luc knocked on the door and smiled when Bill Connor answered the door. He walked in from the bitter cold.

"Hi, Dad. Is your daughter ready for her first date?" He laughed because he knew how funny it sounded. Her father laughed, too.

Luc was wearing a stolen tuxedo. The only one he could find. It didn't fit just right, but at least he looked good. But he always looked good.

"Come on in, Son. Mom is fussing with pictures."

Mattie's mother rushed over to him and gave him a big hug. "You look so handsome."

"Thanks Mrs. Connor. But no pictures."

He watched as Mattie walked into the room. The black strapless dress looked elegant on her. She looked classy, beautiful. She looked like a million dollars. He tried to hide his shock but found he couldn't find words.

"She looks so beautiful," her mother gushed. He pulled his eyes from Mattie and looked at her mother. He didn't want to stare.

"Well, of course she does. She takes after you," Luc said.

"Dad, she's going to need something to cover her up. I can't keep back all those boys from hitting on her."

"Do your best, Son."

Mattie gave them both a nasty look. "Do you hear this, Mom? Because of these two men, I'll be single forever."

"That's not a bad thing, dear," her father said. "So Luc, Mattie tells me you got a few offers from colleges. Have you selected anything yet?"

"Well, I got offers from Stanford and UCLA to play football. Full-ride scholarships. I'm leaning toward UCLA."

"Why's that?"

"Closer to home," he answered before realizing he had no idea where home was.

He nodded but added nothing. It was just like Mr. Connor to never judge.

Luc smiled and called out to Mattie. "Come on Mat, we don't want to be late. And I promised a game of bowling afterward."

"You got a limo?" Mattie asked as he opened the door for her.

"Of course. I couldn't exactly take you on my skateboard."

"I could have drove, Luc. I know you're saving up for a car. How did you pay for this?"

"Credit card," he said. He would tell her later that the card was stolen. He didn't want to start the night off with a fight. Besides, it was either the limo or a stolen car. And he wouldn't risk driving her in a hot car. Especially after what the LAPD had done to Rodney King.

"Sweetheart, you deserve to go in style. Besides, I decided I'm gonna buy a motorcycle. It's cheaper. Not to mention a chick magnet."

She laughed. "And how are you supposed to make out on the back of a motorcycle?"

"I won't need to. Soon I will have my very own dorm room to take them to," he said proudly. He sat down next to her in the backseat of the limo.

"What happened to you last night?" she asked as the driver pulled out into the street. "I thought you were coming over to study for your algebra final."

"I had something to take care of." He was thankful for the darkness and hoped it helped mask the change in his mood. He turned from her and looked out the window.

"I heard about Joey. I tried to find you. Are you OK?" She grabbed his hand and held it. He didn't pull away. He needed the comfort as much as she wanted to give it.

"I'm fine. The funeral is Tuesday."

"I'll go with you." It was stated as a simple fact, not a question.

"You don't have to. You didn't even like him."

"That doesn't matter. Funerals are for the living. I want to be there for you. Besides, it doesn't matter what he did in his life or what people thought about him. Only God can judge him."

He looked at her now and saw the understanding in her eyes. She would be there for him. Not just to comfort him but to hold him strong.

He would need it. He had grown close to Joey. He couldn't picture his life without Joey there beside him. He was his friend, his partner in crime. He had protected him like an older brother. And now he had lost him. It hurt him more than he had expected. He didn't understand where the pain had come from.

"Where did you go last night? I looked everywhere for you."

"I needed to do something for Joey. Something he didn't get a chance to do."

"What did you do, Luc?"

"Don't judge me, Mattie," he barked at her.

"I'm not. I'm asking a simple question," she shot back. He was surprised she didn't shrink at his raised voice.

"You didn't see his face. You weren't there. I saw the bastard shoot him." He didn't tell her the bullets were meant for him. Or that he had wished they had been on target.

She sat quietly in the seat next to him. She still hadn't released his hand.

He looked at Mattie and softened his voice. "I don't have that faith in God that you do. I wanted to make sure he paid for it while he was still alive."

She turned her eyes away from him. He hated that she could make him feel so guilty just by averting her eyes.

"Relax, Mattie. I didn't hurt him. I just burned his house down."

He struggled to keep the smile off his face. Watching the house engulfed in large red flames had almost made up for the pain and anger he had felt when he cradled Joey in his arms.

"Do you know for sure no one was hurt?" she asked. It was barely a whisper. Ever the angel.

"No one was in the house, Mattie." Just a whole lot of dope.

"They're going to know it was you."

"I'm sure he will." He had made sure Chavez knew exactly who had done it.

"What if they hurt you?" she asked. She struggled not to cry. He had never seen her cry before. He was shocked that he would be the one to do it.

"I'm sorry, Mattie. They're not going to hurt me. I can protect myself."

"Are you carrying a gun?" she asked.

She turned to him. The sadness and pain were gone. The tears replaced with anger. She pulled her hand from his and reached for his jacket, searching.

"No—" he said too sharply. He stopped her hands.

"You don't believe me?" he yelled at her. He stared into her frightened eyes.

"I believe you." She dropped her hands on her lap, folding them slowly.

"Mattie, I would never do anything to put you in danger. You know that. If I thought it wasn't safe for you to be here with me right now, you wouldn't be. I already lost one friend. I'm not about to lose the only one I have left. If someone even thinks of hurting you, they're dead. Believe that."

"I'm not worried about me. I'm worried about you."

"Don't. No one will ever hurt me again. I know how to protect myself now. Can we forget about Joey and my fucked-up life for tonight? I want to show you a good time. I want to pretend to be a good person tonight."

"You would get bored being good."

"For tonight, I would like to see what it would be like. I'd like to see how it would feel to be good enough to stand next to you."

He smiled when she took his hand again.

CHAPTER 14

▼

Friday, November 5, 2004
10:22 AM
Malibu, California

As the scalding hot water ran over me, I pushed Mattie from my thoughts and tried to think like a journalist. I wasn't an investigator, and I was far from being a detective. But my training as a journalist always pointed me in the right direction. I needed to follow the money.

If Spencer had been kidnapped, we would have heard about a ransom. If he were dead, I was sure the sheriff's department or the media would have uncovered a body.

I had to assume Spencer left on his own free will. But where would he go? And why?

I dressed quickly. I checked my cell phone. No messages. I threw the phone on the bed and ran down the stairs.

Mattie was in the kitchen. She was no longer wearing the robe. She was dressed in jeans and a UCLA sweatshirt. Her cheeks looked alive. Her eyes hopeful.

"Any luck last night?" she asked.

I shook my head. She looked calmer than yesterday, but I felt bad for letting her down.

"Do you know anyone by the name of Angel?"

She thought for a minute. "No, but I think that was a name Detective Ward asked me about. I'm not sure though."

"I have another route I can check. I need to look at your finances."

"Sure," she shrugged. "Have a look."

"I may need you to make some calls. Can you handle that?"

She nodded, and I explained what I was looking for. If Spencer had left on his own, he would be spending money somewhere. His car would only take him so far without refilling for gas. He would need food and a roof over his head. I hoped that I could find him by following the money trail.

Mattie and I spent all morning and half the afternoon scouring over their bank and credit card records. We camped out in the study; with papers spread out on the floor, we took turns looking through their financial records.

I was surprised to learn that Spencer handled the bank accounts, the bills, and the money. Mattie had always been good with money, even better with math. But she handed it all over to Spencer when they married. I questioned her about it, but she only shrugged.

"It's just one of those things people expected me to hand over. So I did."

I started with the checking account. Spencer had kept meticulous records of all bank statements for the past year along with a collection of posted checks that had been returned.

It took me an hour to get through the statements, even with Mattie's help. I think she was relieved to see the calculations were correct.

It appeared Mattie and Spencer both used their joint checking account for just about everything. They had two car payments, a hefty mortgage, utilities, and a gardener. They used their debit cards for gas. Mattie also used the card when she did grocery shopping.

Spencer received deposits every other week from his law firm that more than covered their expenses. No other deposits.

No strange purchases appeared on the checking account after Monday. Spencer wasn't using the account.

But I did find a withdrawal on the Friday before Spencer disappeared. Mattie had no idea what it was for. I located the ATM near Spencer's office. The withdrawal of three hundred dollars had taken place at 11:45 that morning, probably during his lunch break. Was he taking a client to lunch? Or did he need immediate cash for another reason?

I highlighted the transaction and then pulled the last two months of statements. Nothing was out of place. No other odd withdrawals. If Spencer were being blackmailed, there would have been a pattern of withdrawals.

Mattie said everything else looked normal. But the withdrawal still bothered me. I knew that the sheriff's department had probably already found the transaction as well. What did they think it was for?

I made a note of the account then moved to the credit cards. There were no transactions on any of the cards after Spencer disappeared. He was not using the cards and that bothered me. I didn't want to think this was another bad sign. My only hope was that he was getting financial help from somewhere else.

I went back three months looking for any odd amounts or places that Spencer had used his card that he would have no reason visiting. But found nothing. He seemed a creature of habit. He paid the credit cards in full every month and visited the same places.

Mattie handed me his cell phone records. She admitted she had no idea what to look for. I perused the past month. He had made several calls to work and home, and I quickly crossed those off the list.

Three numbers were listed for the Monday that Spencer disappeared. Only one repeated. The first call had lasted five minutes. Spencer had then called back an hour later and talked for almost twenty minutes. I dialed the number and found it disconnected. I highlighted the calls so I would remember to ask Orin to trace the number.

The second number was to a local law office that claimed to handle civil cases. I inquired whether Spencer Hardwin was a client, but the receptionist told me she didn't have client records nor was she able to give out that type of information. Client privilege and all. I cursed her and hung up.

I dialed the third number and was connected to Connor & Associates. I hung up and looked at the statement. Spencer's call lasted five minutes. I wondered why he would have called Mattie's father. I wrote myself a note to ask Bill about it.

The phone rang at a quarter to five, taking me away from all the paper and alleviating the stress on my eyes.

"Luc, where the hell are you?" It was Orin.

"I'm at Mattie's. Why? What's going on?" I asked.

"Turn to channel 2," Orin instructed. I jumped up and ran to the television. I flipped it on and did as he said. Mattie watched me but my focus was drawn to the newscaster.

A red banner on the bottom of the screen told viewers there was breaking news. Spencer Hardwin's Lexus had been found in the parking structure of LAX Airport. There was a helicopter broadcasting pictures of the airport, but the Lexus was hidden from view. Instead it focused on the numerous patrol cars and news vans scattered around the terminal entrance.

"Shit," I muttered. "When did this happen?"

"I just got the call a few minutes ago. I thought I would get the story before anyone else."

"Orin, I didn't know. The cops have been quiet all day." I watched Mattie as she crouched in front of the television to listen to the reporter. "I'll call you back when I hear something."

I hung up the phone and saw that Mattie was crying again. I didn't have time to comfort her. The phone rang and I snatched it up.

"Luc, this is Detective Ward." The voice was gruff, hurried.

"What the hell is going on? Why didn't you notify me?" I yelled.

"I just found out myself. The airport policeman who found the car was anxious and looking to get his face on television. He called the media before calling us."

"What have they found?"

"I'm on my way over there now. My understanding is there is no sign of foul play in the car. The car was parked normally in a temporary lot. They have cameras at the entrance so we'll do a full check. I'll stop by when I'm done. I can give you an update on what we have. Then we can discuss your little adventure last night as well."

"Of course. I'll be here all night." I wasn't about to admit to breaking and entering, but I wasn't going to deny it, either.

Mattie and I spent the next hour watching the news. The reporters knew very little and were all waiting for a statement from the sheriff's department about the status of the case. I was glad to see that the story was getting good airplay. But I also worried about what the turn of events meant.

Did Spencer leave LA? Did he leave voluntarily? Was his car stolen and driven there for another purpose? And if he did leave, where the hell would he go?

The three-hundred-dollar withdrawal was not looking good. He could have purchased a one-way plane ticket to just about anywhere in the United States for three hundred dollars. Did he know on Friday he would be flying?

I was beginning to feel that maybe I didn't really know Spencer at all. The man I knew would never have left Mattie like this. And I was starting to think that whatever Spencer was involved in, he was definitely in over his head.

I clutched my cell phone, waiting for word. But it was the doorbell that finally pulled me away from the television at eight that night. It was Detective Ward. He was alone, which I was thankful for. But he looked bothered, and that worried me.

The three of us sat at the kitchen table. He offered nothing more than what we had learned from the news reports.

The car had been found but there were no new leads. The video camera at the parking structure showed only one person in the car when it entered the parking structure. But at the angle of the screen, they couldn't determine whether Spencer was the driver. Ward had checked the cameras throughout the airport. No other camera had caught Spencer Hardwin.

I asked about the passenger manifests. The cops didn't find a Spencer Hardwin departing on any flight in the past three days. Unless Spencer was using another name, we had to assume that Spencer had not flown anywhere. I wondered if Spencer wanted us to think he had. Or if the car was brought there by someone else.

Mattie said she wasn't feeling well. I convinced her to try to sleep and gave her another sleeping pill. She looked worn out, and I judged the news hadn't done much for her hope.

After I tucked her in, I returned to the kitchen and found Detective Ward staring out the kitchen window.

"What are you not telling me?" I asked.

"Let's discuss your little B and E job last night." He turned back to me. "Did you find anything?"

"That depends. Is the firm pressing charges against whoever broke in?"

"They have no idea who broke into their offices last night. Nor did they find anything disturbed or missing. The offices remained locked. They are scratching it up to kids screwing around. So you're safe. Tell me what you found."

"Nothing."

"You're lying."

"I'm afraid I'm not. But that alone tells me something. Someone made a trip to his office before me."

"What do you mean?"

"Did your deputies search his office?" I asked.

"No, Robinson didn't give us access to anyone in the firm. He wouldn't even allow us to look inside the office."

"Well, there's a file missing. Either Spencer took it with him, or someone was there after he disappeared."

"What file?" he asked.

"You know what file," I lied. I was hoping I could bluff my way into learning what he already knew. "The file on Angel."

"Shit," he muttered. I smiled as I realized I just scored. "Sit down."

"I'm going to the media with the Angel story if I don't get some answers," I kept the charade going, hoping he would not call my bluff. I sat down and watched his reaction.

"Fine. I'll tell you what I know, you promise not to go to the media." He sat down across from me. "Spencer was under surveillance when he disappeared."

"Why?" I tried not to sound too surprised at this news. I wanted Ward to think I knew as much as he did. I really needed to see his notepad now.

"Last Thursday, before Spencer disappeared, Detectives Medina and Hatcher got a call from Angel Martinez stating that his lawyer was paying him to lie about his case. They didn't really care, but before they could interview him, Angel disappeared.

"The detectives questioned Angel's mother, and she told them Spencer was handling his case. They questioned Spencer on Friday afternoon, but Spencer denied everything. He said he couldn't reveal information on a current case or his clients. So they started following him to see if they scared him."

"Spencer's a suspect in a missing person case? Angel could have disappeared for a number of reasons. What makes you think his lawyer would be behind it? Besides, who says Angel didn't just shack up with his girlfriend?"

"Late Tuesday evening," Ward continued, "I was called to a homicide. A young Hispanic man shot between the eyes. Close range, execution style. He was identified as Angel Martinez. He had been hiding out at his friend's house since Friday.

"His friend confirmed that Angel was scared of his lawyer, who had told him to lie about his upcoming case. Spencer is a material witness at this time."

I took a deep breath and let the information soak in. I had plenty of questions about Angel's case but knew Ward wasn't going to give me anything.

"You weren't brought in to handle the case because of me. You were brought in because of the homicide." I was thinking out loud, wondering what all this information meant.

He nodded. "Detectives Hatcher and Medina are working Spencer's disappearance. I'm working Angel's homicide."

"If he was under surveillance, how did they lose him?"

"I wasn't on the case until Angel was found Tuesday evening. Hatcher and Medina followed Spencer to work on Monday. He never left. They sat there all night waiting for him to leave. The figured they had missed him leave. But when Mrs. Hardwin called the next morning to say he hadn't come home, it was routed to Detective Hatcher.

"They went into the firm and demanded to see Spencer's office but were refused entrance without a search warrant. The receptionist said Spencer wasn't there and could not explain his car in the parking lot. When they walked back to the parking lot, Spencer's car was gone. They panicked and decided they needed to search the house. They were looking for any type of information that could link Spencer and Angel."

"It was an illegal search."

"I know this. And they have been reprimanded for this. But their priority at the time was finding and protecting Angel Martinez. And in a matter of hours, it turned into two missing persons. We haven't been able to determine Spencer's whereabouts after Monday evening. Angel's time of death was established around three o'clock Tuesday afternoon."

Out of habit, I tried to recall my alibi. I had just interrupted a punk kid from stealing a brand-new Porsche, prompting my batting practice. I was not a suspect in Angel's death. But Spencer was.

"Your guys totally screwed up. I should get my lawyers in here and pull their badges." I stood up and paced the floor. I reached for a cigarette before realizing I had none.

Spencer was in deeper than I had thought. He was a suspect in a murder. And now he was missing. He was either guilty or scared. Or he had followed the same route Angel had and was lying dead somewhere.

"I understand you're upset. And I am being honest with you, hoping you don't go to the press with this. We're all after the same thing. We all want to see Spencer come home safely."

"Bullshit. You just want to close a murder case. And I'm not promising I won't leak this to the press if I have to."

"You leak anything, our information passing stops. Simple as that. There isn't an arrest warrant issued at this time. He is only wanted for questioning. If you go to the press with the illegal search, we go with Angel Martinez. I have enough for an arrest warrant. Angel's mother identified Spencer's picture."

I nodded reluctantly. "Do you have the file on Angel?"

"No. But we would love to take a look at it."

"I would, too." I would have to make a visit to Tim Robinson. If he didn't have the file, he would at least know more than me.

"Is Mattie under surveillance?" I asked.

He nodded. "We have the house under surveillance. We need to know if he tries to contact her."

"What about me?"

He shook his head. "He probably doesn't even know you're in town."

I knew he was wrong but didn't correct him. Spencer would know I would be there for Mattie.

"Is the phone bugged? Is the house?"

"No, we don't have enough for that," he said looking at his empty coffee cup. His answer wasn't convincing. I wondered if he was lying or just didn't know.

I needed to know more about Angel and the case Spencer was working on. I explained to Ward that I wanted to talk to Angel's mother and friend. He promised to set something up the following day.

"Can I ask you a question? Just to clear things up so I can move on," he asked. "What?"

"What's the deal between you and Mattie? I mean, you claim she's your best friend, but a week after she gets married, you hitch a ride to DC. You give up your career, your friends, your life here to get away from her."

"I didn't give up anything. The *Crime Reporter* was only a stepping-stone. I was done here. The timing was irrelevant." I didn't like discussing my past.

"You never call her or visit her. You didn't even know their marriage was having problems. And yet you fly across the country the second Spencer is out of the picture."

I stared at him and restrained my temper. I placed my palms down on the table so I couldn't make a fist. I forced my breathing to slow.

"Don't cross that line, Ward," I hissed through clenched teeth.

"Did you two date before she hooked up with Spencer?" Ward asked, unconcerned with the threat.

"No. Absolutely not. We're friends. Nothing more."

Ward shrugged and leaned back in his chair.

"Not that I can blame you. She is pretty damn hot."

I pushed the table into his gut. I was happy to hear the grunt of breath exiting his lungs. "I warned you."

Ward tried to laugh it off as he got up from the table.

"That's exactly my point," he said catching his breath. "You act like a jealous boyfriend with her."

"Or a big brother," I added. "Don't try to see things that aren't there, Ward. Nothing sinister is going on here. She's the only family I have. She means the world to me and I don't want to see her hurt or taken advantage of."

"Yet you never visited in the past three years. Never called her?" he questioned. He shrugged, moving toward the door. "You're probably right. I was just interested. Besides, it's none of my business."

"She had Spencer to take care of her. I protected her through the first part of her life. It's her husband's job to protect her through the rest."

"It's a bit amusing how you work so hard to protect her and take care of her. From what I've seen she's a pretty strong woman. But for some reason she keeps that strength hidden when you're around. Just something to think about." Ward turned and walked out the door without another word.

I stood at the window watching him walk toward his black sedan. After he drove off, I dialed Orin's cell phone.

"Tell me you have a lead," he said.

"Maybe. I need you to dig up all the information you can find on an Angel Martinez. Lived in LA County."

"Address?"

"Don't have one," I responded.

"Date of birth or Social Security number?"

"No."

"Do you realize how many Angel Martinezes there could be in LA? Do you have anything useful?"

"I do have one piece of information that may narrow it down. He was shot to death on Tuesday afternoon."

"Really?" I could hear the excitement in his voice. "Still at the coroner?"

"Not sure."

"I'll find out and let you know."

He hung up before I could respond.

I was completely exhausted. I opened Spencer's date book and looked for Monday's notes. I found the meeting with Tim Robinson circled. Maybe he had kept that meeting after all. I wondered if he would remember me. I made a mental note to visit him soon as I searched the rest of the book.

CHAPTER 15

▼

1993
Torrance

The black strapless gown clung to her body like it was made for only her. Her dress and simple black heels weren't flashy or overstated and showed off her natural beauty. She had only a touch of makeup that sparkled on her young face, and her hair was wrapped up, allowing only a few strands to delicately tap her face.

Several guys asked Mattie to dance, and after scaring off the fifth guy, Luc pulled her to the dance floor himself.

She was beautiful. He knew that. And she was sexy, especially in the strapless prom dress. He would have to be blind not to see it.

But this was Mattie. She had that touch of class that far exceeded the depths of this crowd. She deserved more than the stares these boys were giving her. Even the other girls were leagues below her.

She was a sophomore and never had a boyfriend. He knew that was his fault. He would have to let her go. He spun her around the dance floor then dipped her.

She laughed at him. "OK, who taught you to dance?"

"I asked your mom to give me a few steps. I didn't want to embarrass you on the dance floor." He stared into her bright eyes. She seemed so happy.

"You could never embarrass me."

"Well you've had lessons and everything." The song turned slow and he pulled her close. He had to admit he felt strange having her in his arms like this. "Is this the first time we've danced?" he asked.

"No, we danced at my cousin's wedding."

"OK, I was eleven, Mat. That doesn't count."

"Sure it does. I think you've gotten much better."

"Thanks."

Her smile lit up her face. It seemed the night was a weird dream. He was overwhelmed with the thought of being with her. He even forgot that he wasn't supposed to be enjoying something so formal.

He leaned in and kissed her. Luc told himself later that it was the Jack Daniel's that he had drunk earlier. Or just normal male hormones that made him do it. But he would never admit it was a mistake.

He put his right hand behind her neck because he would have died if she had pulled away. He had planned on just a light innocent kiss. A touching of lips and a simple brush of his tongue on her lips so he could taste her innocence.

He had expected a soft, gentle response. An inexperienced kiss full of shock and hesitancy. A pure sweetness that would snuff any desire he felt for her.

But the second he tasted her, he knew he wanted more. He felt her mouth ease open and he explored further. He realized his mistake too late.

Her tongue touched his, teasing him and driving him over the edge. At that moment, he had no idea how he thought kissing her would ever be simple. He felt the wall he had built up start to crumble. He was losing control.

Then he remembered the pain that had come from losing Joey. The fear had him pulling back, emotionally and physically. He didn't open his eyes because he wasn't ready for her anger.

"What—" she started.

"Don't say anything. Just kiss me again," he said as he forced his mouth back on hers. He knew it was a mistake to take this further. His gut told him the pain this would cause would be like nothing he had ever felt before. But before he could break away, she was kissing him back. The soft sweetness was there but it was hidden by a warm pulsating desperation that made his head spin.

There was heat here. Much more than he could handle. He knew he would have a hard time going back to the bitter cold that often engulfed him.

He lost all sense of where he was. He forgot about the prom. He forgot about the people standing all around him. He couldn't hear the music. All he could feel was his body weaken. He found he liked the feeling. Then he remembered whom he was kissing and he pulled away.

"I'm sorry," he said quickly as he looked into her eyes. He saw confusion in her eyes, and that hurt him. Then he saw the familiar sign of anger wash over the confusion.

He wasn't scared of her making a scene on the dance floor. He knew her too well for that. But as she grabbed his arm and pulled him off the dance floor, he was slightly scared of what she was going to do to him. She led him to a corner and was about to start screaming at him when he held his hands up.

"Don't be mad. I wasn't disrespecting you, Mattie. Let me explain," he began.

"What the hell was that?" she asked, ignoring his pleas.

He quickly discarded the thought of criticizing her language. He wanted to survive the night.

"I was thinking about what you said earlier."

"What did I say earlier?"

"About not having any boyfriends. I feel bad because it's my fault. I've done a great job keeping guys away from you. But I didn't realize how that might hurt you."

"So you thought kissing me was the answer? Tell me the truth. Is this supposed to help your shattered image or did you just want to make it clear to everyone here that I'm off-limits?"

"No. Nothing like that. Here is what I was thinking. You see, I'm going to graduate next month, and you're going to be here at this school for another two years. I want to make sure you're going to have fun and go out with guys."

"I don't understand what that has to do with that kiss."

"Well," he smiled. "I plan on telling all the guys what a great kisser you are, but that you dumped me because I didn't respect you. This way they will respect you," he explained.

"That is the stupidest thing I've ever heard."

"But it'll work. I know high school boys." He smiled at the brilliant idea. All the guys wanted her. But now they would know they had to respect her.

He didn't want to add that he also wanted to make sure her first kiss was with someone who really cared about her.

"OK, that explains the first kiss. But why the second?" she asked.

He realized he didn't know the answer to the question. "I, uh, I guess, I don't know." He looked into her eyes. "I was planning on telling everyone that you were the best kisser I've ever had. I didn't realize it would be true."

"You liked the kiss?" The grimace turned to a grin.

"Hell yeah." He found it strangely comfortable to talk to her about it. The wall was safely in place. "You're better than Jenny. For someone as inexperienced as you are, I was a bit taken aback."

He felt better. He was always able to talk to her about anything. Why would this be any different?

"Who said I was inexperienced?"

He looked at her, suddenly very serious. "Who kissed you?" He tried to ignore the sickening feeling in his stomach.

"John kissed me last week."

"What? I'm going to kick his ass. How come he didn't tell me?"

He pushed the jealous thoughts from his head and replaced them with the anger he knew would get him in trouble. He didn't care. Little Johnny would pay for this misstep.

"Not all guys kiss and tell, Luc. And what happened to letting me live my own life?"

"Fine. But I have to approve of anyone kissing on you. Especially with a kiss like that. You could bring a guy to his knees."

"You think so? That means a lot considering you've kissed half the girls at this school," she laughed.

He laughed, too. He was still angry with John, but that problem would be solved when the time was right.

"I think it's more than that."

He saw Jenny walk in with Robbie and backed farther into the corner. "Jenny's here."

Mattie looked around and spotted her. She turned back to Luc. "Tell me when she's spotted you."

"Why?" he asked, watching the girl across the room. She was beautiful. But compared to Mattie, she was nothing more than a trashy whore.

"Because, we're here to make her jealous, remember?"

He looked back at Mattie. "She's looking at us now."

He suddenly didn't care what Jenny thought of him now. But he didn't have time to think about it. Mattie leaned over and kissed him.

Luc understood, wrapped his arms around her and kissed her back. He pushed her gently back against the wall and kissed her deeply. He tried not to laugh at the thought that he was making out with his best friend. Or the fact that he was enjoying it so much.

Mattie pulled away and looked around. "She's still watching." She smiled. "Grab my ass."

Luc pulled away from her but didn't release her. "No way, Mat. I won't disrespect you like that. Not even for Jenny."

She laughed at him. "How righteous of you. And just when I decided I want to be really bad. Kiss me, she's still watching."

Luc obeyed. He felt her hands comb through his hair, and he pulled closer to her. His head began to spin. He forgot all about Jenny and Robbie and continued to kiss Mattie. He forced himself to remember she was not like the other girls he kissed. This would not be going any further.

She finally pulled away, but she didn't look at him. She looked past him.

"I think she's a little pissed off at you now," Mattie said.

"Who?" he asked, breathless. He was desperately trying to control his arousal as he looked at her.

It upset him just a little that she looked in complete control of her emotions. His head was spinning; his body was Jell-O. And yet, she looked strong, determined, in control. He remembered how he had always found that part of Mattie intoxicating.

She looked back at him. "She's refusing to look this way now." She laughed, pleased with herself.

"Let's get out of here." He didn't want to think of Jenny anymore. And he was a little disappointed in himself for treating Mattie as an object. And for enjoying it so damn much. "We got some bowling to get to."

"I need to change first."

"No way, sweetheart." He snatched her hand and led her toward the limo. "I want to see you bowl in a dress." He pulled out a flask of whiskey. "And you get to see me bowl drunk."

She tried to grab the flask from him but he raised it over his head. "How about me?" she asked.

"Nope. You're not old enough to drink."

"Neither are you. That doesn't stop you."

"That's because the rules don't apply to me. You, on the other hand, are too pretty and rich to be getting drunk and disorderly." He opened the door for her.

"I thought it was my night to be really bad," she teased.

"And I thought it was my night to be really good. I guess neither of us can pretend to be something we're not."

CHAPTER 16

▼

Saturday, November 6, 2004
Noon
Lynwood, California

The drive to Lynwood was uncomfortable. Ward picked me up in his department issued sedan and although I was allowed to sit in the front, I still felt like a criminal. I didn't want to talk to him. And I knew he didn't want to talk to me. He had promised to take me only because he knew I would go without him.

Mattie agreed to stay by the phone in case there was word from anyone. I wasn't worried about leaving her alone as I knew there were several officers watching the house.

Orin had called earlier to tell me the coroner had released Angel's body. The funeral was scheduled for Monday. Orin had the information he needed to do a thorough search. I also gave him the number I had seen on Spencer's phone bill and asked him to trace it. He promised to get back to me as soon as he had something.

Pacific Coast Highway transitioned to the 105 Freeway, and the scenery changed from beach communities to inner city. From the rich to the struggling families that never seemed to get ahead. The silence dragged on.

When Ward exited the 105 in Lynwood, I looked out at the small broken-down homes and the mass of apartment buildings far beyond repair. The homes were sandwiched together, their windows and doors covered with iron bars. In LA, the owners preferred to create their own prisons. It's better than someone else imprisoning them.

Ward did his best to avoid the potholes that the city ignored. The streets were lined with trash—broken beer bottles, cigarette butts, broken needles, and dirty diapers. Weeds poked through the cracks in the sidewalks. Graffiti lined the brick walls surrounding the homes.

As we waited for a light to change, I watched a homeless man wearing three shirts and flip-flops beg for money outside a liquor store. Most of the patrons ignored him. They knew he would only spend it on the liquor inside. A young boy stared at him, mouth wide open, before his mother tugged him past.

This definitely wasn't Malibu. There were no BMWs or Mercedes here. No gated communities with surveillance or hired security to protect the homeowners. Datsuns and old Buicks lined these streets. Gangs protected these homeowners.

People didn't live in places like this. They just tried to survive. This was the LA I had lived in, the LA I survived.

The Martinez home was a single-story house with a small yard only a block from a liquor store and a gas station where crack was being sold by the high school dropouts. At least fifty years old, the house had endured a century of torture. The light brown paint was chipping around the edges. The windows hid behind black bars that were meant to keep the criminals out. One window was broken and had been covered by cardboard. Anything to keep the cold and danger out.

The lawn was just a consortium of dirt, weeds, and trash. A tire rested at the far end of the yard. I wondered if it had been dumped there or if someone had brought it home for a reason.

Detective Ward pointed up the walk to the iron gate that hid the aging, warped door. It reminded me of the tiny apartment in Torrance where I spent much of my youth.

"Ana Martinez."

I watched his gaze move to a blue Toyota Camry parked across the street. The car looked new. And with this neighborhood, I wondered if it was stolen. I watched Ward punch in the plate on his dash computer. He was thinking the same thing I was.

"Let it go, Ward."

Ward kept his eyes on the screen. "It's the law, Luc."

"Everything has to be black and white to you guys. That's the problem. The world is not black and white."

"Maybe it should be."

He grunted as the computer beeped then stepped out of the car. I followed.

He glanced at a group of children playing down the street. To the untrained eye, they were innocent enough. Just kids playing on a Saturday afternoon. Both Ward and I knew different. They were spotters sent to watch the cop that had just pulled up. They didn't need a black-and-white patrol car to peg Ward as a cop.

The youngest of the four kids, maybe ten years old, kept his eyes on me. He had already dismissed Ward. I knew immediately he was the smartest of the group. Sometimes you just have to have that gut feeling. He would be the one to survive. I winked at him as I got out of the car. He flipped me off. I smiled and hoped he would survive.

Ward promised to let me interview Angel's mother alone. He insisted he needed to watch the car anyway. It was probably a good idea. I watched the kids as I walked up the two stairs and knocked on the gate.

Ana Martinez was wearing black jeans and a black T-shirt. Her dark hair was pulled back from her face but still hung past her shoulders. She couldn't have been more than thirty-five. She didn't have any makeup on. Her eyes were red, reminding me of Mattie.

She was still in mourning over her only son. I felt sorry for the woman, not only for her loss, but also for the fact that she had to relive it every time someone came with more questions.

She allowed me to enter and we settled in her living room. In one corner, a small stone fireplace blew heat to warm the room, making me wonder if it was the only heat source in the house. The house seemed colder than outside.

The room's center of focus was a fifteen-inch color television with bunny ears that sat in another corner. The faded gray couch faced the television and an oversized brown recliner faced the fireplace. The carpet was worn and appeared to have been white once.

I spotted several framed pictures of Angel Martinez. I looked at the young man and recognized the look in his eyes. He was poor and it had hardened him. The look of suffering oozed from his eyes. I understood it. Angel and I were much alike. I wondered how I had survived and he had fallen.

I picked up a recent picture of Angel. He had his arms around a beautiful young woman, probably a girlfriend. It looked like a prom. Remembering my senior prom, I put the picture down.

Ana Martinez took the recliner, and I took a seat on the couch. She clung to the rosary that was wrapped around her knuckles.

I pulled out a tape recorder and she eyed it suspiciously.

"I'm a journalist, Ms. Martinez. I work independently from the police and sheriff's department. I am just trying to determine what happened to Angel. Do you mind if I tape our conversation?"

"I don't know," she said. She looked out the window. I followed her gaze.

"I promise that this is for my use only. The detective outside and no one in the department will have access to what you say to me."

She finally nodded and I turned on the tape.

"First, I want to tell you I am very sorry for your loss. I know it must be hard."

She stared at me. "He was a drug dealer, Mr. Actar. No one cares about those types," she challenged. She had just a slight Mexican accent. I wondered if she had been born here or across the border. Either way, I knew her life had been hard from the start.

The information about Angel didn't surprise me. I had expected as much. Growing up poor brought you face to face with drugs, gangs, and violence. Whether you wanted it or not, it was a part of your life.

"Losing a life at such a young age is a terrible thing, Ms. Martinez. It doesn't matter what he did during his life. I had a friend who was shot to death at just seventeen years of age. I didn't care that he sold drugs and guns. I only cared that he was my friend. To this day, I don't care what people say about him. He was my friend."

She nodded. I could see the understanding in her eyes. We had more in common than she would like to admit.

Ana closed her eyes to prevent the tears from coming.

"He is a good kid," she whispered.

I waited as she composed herself, feeling awful for putting her through this. She wiped at her face as a tear escaped. I looked down at the tape recorder. I wanted to leave. I hated when women cried.

"I understand Angel was working with a lawyer."

"Si. Spencer Hardwin, the guy that's now missing. He's been on the news. I know the cops are behind it all."

"What do you mean?" I asked.

"I know the cops killed my boy. They probably killed his lawyer, too. They just wanted to shut them up."

"You think the cops killed your son?"

"Si. He was going to sue them. When they found out about the case, he had to go into hiding."

"What was the case?" I asked.

She eyed me. "My son, he was arrested a couple of months ago. He was beaten, uh, bruised. They arrested him for selling drugs he didn't have. He was selling pot. But my son, he was not into anything else. They say he had cocaine. I know it was not true. So he called a lawyer."

Ward had failed to mention Angel's lawsuit was against the sheriff's department. I wondered why.

"Ward, the detective on the case told me that your son called the cops and told them Spencer was telling him to lie about the case. He said he was scared of his lawyer and asked the cops for help."

"That's *mierda*. If you met Mr. Hardwin, you would know that. He was nice. He was, how do you say, a gentleman and treated me with respect. He wouldn't lie. The cops are the liars."

I couldn't argue with that. Spencer never had been a good liar. And I had seen firsthand what cops were capable of.

After about an hour, I walked out of the house and found Detective Ward leaning against his sedan. The kids were gone, but Ward kept his eyes where the kids had been. I wondered if he was protecting the car or using it to boost his self-esteem.

"You failed to mention the case Spencer was working with Angel on was against the sheriff's department."

He shrugged. "Thought you knew. I'm told it was a bullshit case. Angel admitted that when he called asking for our help."

"I don't believe it. His mother seems to think the deputies are responsible for his death."

"She just needs someone to blame. The sheriff's department is always an easy scapegoat." He got in the car. "Get in."

"You actually believe that Angel was scared of Spencer?"

"I have no reason not to."

I laughed. "I just saw a picture of Angel. He's at least six-two and over two hundred pounds. Spencer was a thin, rich, white boy with no experience on the streets. No way was Angel scared of Spencer."

Ward pulled out. "A gun always changes the odds, Luc."

I knew it wasn't true. Angel wouldn't have been scared of a gun, especially held by an inexperienced lawyer. I knew Angel would have laughed in Spencer's face. I knew this because I would have done the same thing. Neither of us would have bet that Spencer had the balls to pull the trigger.

"I'll take you over to see his friend. Lito is pretty confident Spencer had something to do with Angel's murder. And he was the last one to speak to Angel. Since you won't believe a cop, maybe you'll believe a street criminal like yourself."

As the 105 Freeway took us away from Angel, I looked out at the concrete surrounding me. We crossed the 710 Freeway, and I noticed a sign for the LA River.

The river was almost invisible since it was encased in concrete and hidden under numerous freeways. That's one way of keeping nature out of the big city.

I wondered if the concrete walls were meant to protect the river from the filth living beside it or to protect the citizens from the chance that the river might succeed one day in taking the city back.

Through all the concrete, buildings, and freeways it was hard to believe that nature existed in a place like this. But it did. It was still survival of the fittest. The weak would fall to the teeth of the wolf.

Ward took the 605 and exited at Whittier. I was surprised to see the difference between where Angel had lived and where his friend was living. I scanned the neighborhood. Definitely a great place for a drug dealer to hide out. How the hell had his killer found him here?

"This is where Angel spent his last three days hiding. His friend Lito was visiting his mother when Angel was shot. I talked to him last night and he promised to talk to you, off the record, of course."

"For a street criminal, Lito was doing much better for himself," I muttered.

"Don't kid yourself, Luc. Crime is everywhere. Just last month, a man was beaten to death only a couple of blocks from here. Town is still on edge."

Ward pointed down a street. "Not far from here. He was murdered by a couple of the neighbors after molesting a little girl."

I shook my head, thinking of the poor little girl.

"Sometimes murder isn't a crime, Ward."

He glanced at me and smirked.

"That's what they'll say about Angel." He pulled up in front of a two-story house and parked.

"I'm just saying, different town, same story," Ward continued. "Money corrupts the soul just like poverty. Just because you can't see the crime, doesn't mean it's a safe place. You want drugs or sex around here, you pick up the phone and order it. That's LA, always trying to make it easier for the common man."

He sighed but didn't get out of the car. He wanted to hear himself talk, so I let him.

I looked up at the house. Fresh yellow paint. Pink and purple flowers bloomed along the stone walkway to the white door. It was well taken care of and probably worth three times what Ms. Martinez's landlord paid for her house.

"We'll never win the war on drugs as long as there is a market," Ward said.

"As long as there is a market, there's a chance for some of us to make enough money to get out of it all," I countered. "Crime does pay for some of us." I opened the door. I wasn't in the mood for an argument. And he seemed a little too interested in my responses.

Ward stepped out of the car and locked the door.

"There are other ways to get out."

I noticed movement in the window of a neighbor's house. I looked quickly enough to see a woman hide behind the curtain. Nosy neighbors were always good for a community. I wondered how much this lady knew about her neighbor and his guests.

"Not without money, there ain't. Some of us don't have the luxury of choices in life."

Ward started to protest, but I stopped him.

"Have you ever been so poor that you had to choose between eating and having shoes to go to school in? I was a step below that. I had to steal the food so I could eat. So why not steal the shoes, too?

"When you're desperate, it doesn't matter how you get food on the table or diapers on your baby. You just learn to survive. And look for your escape."

Ward knocked on the door then turned to look at me.

"Is that what you did? Escape? Or run away?"

Instead of answering, I glanced back at the neighbors.

"Let me ask you something, Luc. I know you lived on the streets when you were a kid."

"Wouldn't call that living," I muttered, hoping to end the conversation. Ward continued anyway.

"Fair enough. But child services found you and provided a home. The school system provided you a free education. You graduated and even went on to college. You survived because the system worked. You succeeded. Yet you don't give them any credit."

I laughed.

"I didn't survive because of the system. I survived despite them. The system failed me every step of the way. It took child services eight years to pull me from the streets and dump me in a school that wanted to throw me out the second it realized I needed to be taught something. The school systems are set up to fail the children that need it the most. They were quick to try to sweep me under the rug or pass me off so I could become someone else's problem."

Ward nodded and I realized he was really listening. I wondered why he was so interested in my life.

"So why do you only focus your energy on attacking law enforcement?"

"The others ignored me or pushed me aside. My social worker, my teachers, my counselors. I can deal with being ignored. I've had years of practice. But the cops attacked me. So I attacked back."

I looked at the door as he knocked again. "Doesn't look like he wanted to hang around for us."

Ward didn't wait for a response. He grabbed his cell phone from his belt and dialed.

I heard a ringing inside. Ward heard it, too. I saw the concern on his face. He peered into the dark windows.

Ward turned to me as he hung up the phone. "That was his cell phone. He doesn't leave without it."

He headed toward the side gate. I followed. He opened the gate and walked into the backyard. I noticed he had his gun at his side. I didn't notice him take it out of his holster. I wasn't sure if I should be worried or not. But it didn't stop me from following.

I saw the remains of crime scene tape still wrapped around a tall lemon tree. It flapped in the wind. Dried blood was splattered on the brick wall framing the yard. I guessed Angel had died somewhere around the tree. A fly buzzed past my ear.

It was too quiet and I wished I had a gun, too. I scanned the yard to see if I could determine where Angel's body had been found when I heard Detective Ward curse in front of me. I looked up at him.

"Get the hell back," he ordered.

I looked past him and saw a lump lying on the ground by the back door. Fresh blood and what appeared to be brain matter sprayed the sliding glass door. The body was crumpled on the ground with a pool of blood surrounding it like a deserted island. I looked into the blank eyes and tried not to be sick.

Nice to meet you, Lito.

Ward leaned down quickly to take a pulse. Finding none, he turned back to me. His eyes were round as bullets. Ignoring me now, he pulled his cell phone from his belt and stepped carefully back. Composed now, he spouted orders through the phone.

"Go back to the car," he yelled at me before turning his attention back to the dead body in front of him.

My week just kept getting worse. I'm sure Ward was thinking the same thing.

CHAPTER 17

▼

Saturday, November 6, 2004
5:00 PM
Malibu, California

Another dead end. Two dead bodies, and Spencer was still missing. Spencer was definitely in over his head. It was time to call in the reinforcements.

If Spencer were into something illegal or dangerous, I knew the detectives would take too long to find him. I needed a better source of information, someone who knew the streets. I needed someone that worked beyond the rules, like myself.

It took only a quick call before I located Big Jim. He wasn't referred to as Big Jim because he was almost four hundred pounds, even though he was. In college, I had dubbed him Big Jim so I could differentiate between him and our quarterback, Jim Suthers.

Big Jim was our starting center in college. He was big and surprisingly quick on the field. And he had grown up in the heart of LA, jumping from one gang to the next.

His criminal mind was intriguing to me, and we built an interesting friendship. He even went into business with me my last two years at the university. He helped recruit several of the ball players after I had been released from the team. But then again he owed that to me, since he was the one that had taken me out.

Jim and I had gone out partying and ended up at the Playboy mansion. I had no idea how we were allowed to enter, but we were both too stoned to appreciate it. I had picked up on a sexy brunette and had just convinced her to escort me to a private pool when Jim came rushing up behind me.

He tackled me, shattering my knee in one swift movement. I was in the hospital for two weeks and walked with a cane for almost six months. The numerous surgeries left me as good as new except for some nasty scars. But then I always liked scars.

Jim explained later that the girl looked like his sister. When I hooked up with his sister a year later, I knew it had been the drugs talking. By then it didn't matter. It was easy to forgive him. I had no desire to play football anymore. It had been only a stepping stone to my ultimate goal.

Even though he was practically born into the Crips, he had hoped that football would take him away from the lifestyle. But the gang life never left him. Even though I had been able to keep him in the football program by changing his grades, that was as far as I could help him. And he soon realized he was a better banger than a football player.

When he dropped out, Jim decided to work for himself. He became a hired gun for many of the local Crip gangs. A few years later, the police tagged him. They couldn't get a murder rap to stick but he went away for drug possession. We both knew the time wouldn't be long. With the prisons in California over capacity, drug felons were often kicked out early.

While he was away, I found his sister, Genie, working the streets for money. Knowing she wouldn't want Jim to know, I sent her some money to make a new start. I had heard she became a businesswoman. I didn't know if Jim ever found out about it.

I knew if anyone could get me information from the streets, he could. He was my expert in crime. And I hoped he was out of prison and still alive.

When I reached Genie, she told me Jim often hung around one of her dance clubs, Paradise, located off the 10 Freeway in West Covina. He pretended to be a bouncer and she pretended to pay him.

"Hey, Luc. How you been?" Jim asked when I finally got him on the phone. He didn't wait for a response. "Hey, I heard Spencer's missin'."

"Yeah, that's why I'm calling you, Big Jim. I need your help."

"Yeah? What can I do?" he asked, interested. "You need someone taken care of and don't want to get your pretty little writer hands dirty?"

"Hey, Big Jim, I'm on a cell phone and I'm not sure who's listening."

He hesitated. "You drawin' attention to yourself?"

"I don't think so, but you never know. I can't assume the line's clean."

"OK, so how can I help you?"

"I just need some information. I'm trying to find some information on a dealer. Name's Angel Martinez."

"Never heard of him."

"Doesn't surprise me. I think he was small-time. He lives out in Lynwood. Got shot in the head a couple of days ago and I need to know why."

"Deals go bad all the time," he suggested.

"Maybe. But Spence was working with him on a case and I need to know for sure. I need to make sure it had nothing to do with his disappearance."

"OK. I can ask around."

"Got another name for you, too. Lito Figueroa. A friend of Angel's. He was just found dead a couple of hours ago at his home in Whittier."

"Dead bodies following you everywhere. Same style?"

"Yeah. Execution, up close and personal." I remembered the amount of blood. "I don't know if he was a dealer or not. My guess is he was as dirty as Angel. Any information on either of them would be helpful."

"Give me your number. I'll call you when I get something."

I gave him my cell phone number. I didn't want to give him Mattie's number. I didn't want Mattie or Spencer connected to Big Jim.

"One question for you, Luc. If Spencer was in this much shit, why didn't he call you? He had to know you would fix it."

I thought about the question. "Probably because I was out of town. Too far to fix it quickly."

"That's not a good excuse. You would have called me to fix it."

"Maybe that's what Spencer figured. You know he likes doing things by the book."

"Yeah, maybe. But you gotta figure a guy like Spence is gonna confide in someone. If he didn't say anything to his wife and didn't bother to give you a call…"

"You're right." I said, thinking aloud. "He would have told someone. And that someone could have been the wrong person."

I tried to quickly run down all of Spencer's friends and associates. Another lawyer would be just what Spencer was looking for in a confidant. I needed to know more about the lawyers he worked with. I would have to make one more trip to his law office.

"Hey, you want to stop by and see the girls tonight? I got a few you might like," Jim offered.

"I forgot to tell you I gave up women," I told him.

"Bullshit. Unless you got your dick cut off, there is no way you'd give up women. What happen? You finally find love?"

"You ever wonder why you don't need to be hit in the head with a hammer to know it's gonna hurt?"

I hung up the phone as Jim considered this.

I checked on Mattie before retiring to my bedroom. I listened to the interview with Angel's mother and noticed the sadness in her voice was much worse than what I had seen on her face. I wished I hadn't taped the conversation. I didn't know how it was going to help me find Spencer.

I was starting to worry that Spencer was no longer alive. If he was involved with Angel and Lito, there was a good chance he was already dead. The odds were stacked against him. But if he were dead, I still needed to know why.

If he were alive, I knew I needed to find him, and not only for Mattie. I now needed to know if he was the same man I had met in college. I needed to know what went wrong and how badly he had screwed up his life.

CHAPTER 18

▼

1995
Redondo Beach

Luc watched Carmen pull her car into the restaurant parking lot. He was anxious. He was high. And he was just a little pissed.

"So how long has she been seeing this guy?" Carmen asked, breaking the silence that had filled the car on the thirty-minute drive.

"I guess about a month," he answered, tossing the spent joint out the window. He didn't want to talk to Carmen about Mattie. She wouldn't understand their relationship.

Carmen parked next to a Volvo wagon and got out. Luc followed. He spotted Mattie's car parked in the corner. Out of habit, he peeked inside.

He walked into the restaurant and found Mattie sitting at the bar. She was talking to a guy Luc guessed was Carl Palfy.

Luc startled everyone by grabbing Mattie's wrist and pulling her from the bar stool.

"You're too young to drink, Mattie." He was angry and didn't want to look at the punk who was now standing next to him.

"Let her go, man." Carl tried to sound tough, but Luc ignored him. He knew he could knock the scrawny punk down with one hit. He was much stronger now that his football practice included major weight training.

Mattie smiled and kissed Luc on the cheek. "Nice to see you too, Luc. I've missed you." She ignored his hand on her wrist and introduced Carl.

"Carl, this is my best friend, Luc Actar." She looked at Carmen. "You must be Carmen."

Luc released her hand. Mattie and Carmen shook hands. Luc watched them size each other up.

Mattie was wearing a conservative flowery dress that went down to her ankles, a hint of makeup and a simple gold chain, a cross dangling from it. A gift from her father.

Mattie was so formal, so sophisticated. It surprised Luc that she had changed so much. He found it odd that her determined chin was replaced with a fragile, delicate face. The strong-willed child no longer existed. She had grown up just as he had hoped she would—into that sophisticated, composed air that came with wealth and class.

It made him feel like shit.

Carmen was wearing a black leather miniskirt and a low-cut blouse that matched her dark green eyes. She had a lot to show and no modesty. She was twelve years older than Mattie, but she was slender and curved in all the right places. Her vibrant mane of black hair hung over her shoulders.

Luc suddenly felt embarrassed for bringing her. He wasn't sure now why he had.

"Our table's already ready," Mattie said. The foursome headed to the table. Luc held Mattie back a little.

"Can I talk to you before we sit down?" Luc asked.

"You're mad, aren't you?" she whispered. Her grin unnerved him. "Sit down and try to be polite."

"I'm always polite," he said.

Luc and Carmen sat across from Mattie and Carl. He ordered whiskey and ignored the look from Mattie. Instead, he looked at Carl over his menu as the others agreed on appetizers.

He knew he didn't like the look of Carl. He looked like white trash. He hadn't even dressed up for their double date. And he had let her get a drink at the bar. Mattie was only eighteen. What was this guy thinking?

"So, Mattie, I understand you're graduating this year. Have you picked a college?" Carmen asked.

"I was accepted at Whittier and Harvey Mudd. But I just accepted an offer from UCLA."

Luc turned his gaze to Mattie. "Really?"

"Isn't that cute? You'll be following Luc. Maybe I'll have you in one of my classes." Carmen picked up her menu.

Luc detected a hint of annoyance from Carmen. He ignored her and turned his attention back to Mattie. "You didn't tell me you were thinking of UCLA."

"You haven't kept in touch, Luc."

Her prim response stung. He didn't know how to respond. He knew she was right. Since he started college, he had spoken less and less to her. He had told himself it was for the best, for both of them. He now felt lousy for it.

And it was his fault that she had been dating this bum for a month now. He was supposed to protect her from these creeps. He had let his own life interfere with protecting her. He wanted her to be happy, but this guy wasn't qualified.

Mattie turned to Carmen. "So what do you teach, Carmen?"

"I teach English and creative writing."

"Did Luc tell you I want to be a teacher?" Mattie asked.

"I think he might have mentioned it," Carmen said.

Luc knew what that meant. He had mentioned it, but Carmen hadn't cared. He was angry at her indifference.

The waiter came over and took their orders. Luc and Mattie ordered the chicken. Carmen ordered a salad. Carl wanted to look tough and ordered a steak. Luc was beginning to really hate him.

Mattie stood up. "I'm going to make a quick trip to the powder room. I'll be back."

Luc watched as Carl slapped her on the butt. "Hurry back, love."

"Hey, show some respect, man." Luc said as he stood. "I want to talk to you, Mattie."

Mattie walked quickly from the table but Luc followed.

"Why are you with him, Mattie?" Luc asked, catching up to her.

"Why not? He's sexy." Mattie said, "And he makes me happy."

"He's trash. He just slapped you on the ass in a fancy restaurant. And he looks like he just woke up. He didn't even put on a clean shirt. He looks like he lives on the fucking street."

"Oh, for goodness' sake, Luc. So what if he comes from the wrong side of town. You did, too. I don't judge people like you do."

"I'm not judging him. I just think you deserve better. You deserve to be treated with respect and dignity."

"Why, because I'm rich and I can afford a nice boyfriend?"

"No, because you're a good person. You don't need to settle for someone like that. You're beautiful, sophisticated, and classy and you can get anyone you want."

"Not anyone." She sighed and pushed the door to the women's bathroom. Luc followed her in. It didn't surprise her. "Look, just try to be nice to him. I like him."

"Fine, I'll try not to hit him. But if he slaps your ass once more, I can't promise he'll live. Just tell me you're not serious about this clown." He looked around, glad that the restroom was empty.

"You mean am I sleeping with him? You should have called me earlier, Luc." She threw him a mischievous grin that made him cringe. She watched his reaction.

"Shit, Mattie. You slept with him? You've got to be fuckin' kidding! You should have waited until you were in love."

"Like you were?" she shot back. "Your first was Connie Winters. At least I didn't scrape the bottom of the barrel. That girl had no brains whatsoever."

He laughed, despite his anger. "I didn't exactly want to get my hands on her brains."

"Whatever." She dismissed his laughter. "And now you're screwing your English teacher? I think you should look at yourself before you judge me."

"That's different, Mat. You deserve better."

"And you don't?" she shot back. "You wanted me to be that sophisticated, classy girl. Fine, that's what I'll be. You don't even have to threaten me anymore. You want me to be a successful teacher. You got it. Whatever you want, Luc. But whom I date and whom I sleep with is still my choice.

"Now," she sighed, "I have to go to the bathroom, so get out of here. Besides, I wouldn't want to leave Carmen alone with Carl for too long."

He knew she wasn't worried about Carl. It was Carmen she was worried about. He pushed the door open and stormed out.

He walked back to the table in time to catch Carmen flirting with Carl. He had expected as much. She was a flirt. She was wild and liked younger men. That was how they had hooked up.

But he didn't care. He wasn't the jealous type. What angered him was that Carl was flirting back. He slapped his hands on the table and looked at Carl.

"Back off, Carl." Luc saw the boy flinch just enough. He also saw Carmen smile. She loved the thought of making him jealous. She hadn't yet realized that Luc didn't care. If he had been the jealous type, he would have whacked her arrogant husband a long time ago.

Luc was quiet through dinner. He listened as Carmen and Mattie talked about school. Carl would insert his opinion at odd times and Luc found it hard not to roll his eyes.

Luc stared at his empty glass as he twirled the melting ice. He needed another hit of something. The alcohol wasn't cutting it.

Carmen continued to talk, but Luc lost interest. He felt his control slipping as she talked and Mattie listened. He wanted the night to be over.

When the waiter dropped the bill on the table, Luc pulled his wallet out to pay.

"I'll get the bill," he said, smiling at Mattie. He showed off the extra bills in his wallet.

Mattie threw him a confused look. "Where did you get that?"

"Don't ask questions you don't want to hear the answers to."

He grabbed for the bill, but Mattie slapped his hands.

"I got it, Luc." She grabbed the bill before Luc could react.

"No way, sweetheart. My treat." Luc tried to pull the bill back from her but she wouldn't release it. He smiled as he forgot about the other two people sitting at the table. He wanted to see her get upset with him. He needed to see that stubborn girl he grew up with.

"Let my sugar mama pay for it," Carl interrupted as he kissed Mattie on the lips. "She's loaded."

Luc wanted to hit him. He did his best to ignore him and kept his hands on the table. He would keep his control to keep Mattie happy.

Carl looked at him, a glint in his eye. "I let my bitch pay for everything," he joked. He thought the joke was hilarious. Luc rose.

"That's it. Sorry, Mat." He turned to Carl, his eyes red-hot.

"Luc," Mattie pleaded.

His head snapped back to Mattie. "How much do you honestly think I can handle of this?"

Mattie looked down. She knew it was coming. And she also knew there was no way to stop it.

Luc watched the pout form on her lips and felt the anger in him rise as the control slipped further away. He turned back to Carl. "Outside. Now."

"What's the problem?" Carl asked standing up, too. He got to his feet but was much less steady.

Mattie quickly stood to hold Luc back. "Let it go, Luc. We're leaving anyway."

Luc didn't care that everyone in the restaurant was staring. They meant nothing to him. The restaurant meant nothing. But he wouldn't throw any blows until they were outside, so he allowed Carmen to pull him out the door.

Mattie paid the bill and quickly led Carl outside. Luc was waiting for him. She retreated with Carl. He was all too happy to have two women separating him from Luc. Luc could see the fear in the man's eyes.

"I'll call you later, Luc," Mattie yelled as Carmen pushed him toward the car.

"What an asshole," Luc said when he watched Mattie pull out of the parking lot. He never made idle threats and he knew in due time he would finish what the girls wouldn't let him start.

Imagining what he would do, Luc got in the car.

"What bothered you more—his manners or the fact that he's fucking your best friend?" Carmen pulled out onto the street.

"Don't say it like that." Luc didn't want to talk about it. Not with Carmen. Instead he watched the street move slowly by. Taillights lit the dark pavement. It was quiet. He wondered if a storm was coming in.

Carmen got the hint and changed the subject. "You're very sexy when you're angry."

"I'm sexy all the time," Luc muttered.

He watched as she pulled the car behind a minimart. She turned off the car and looked at him. He knew where this was heading. He wasn't sure why he was hesitating.

"I want you, Luc. Right now," she said.

"Here? In the car?" he grinned at her. He wanted this. He needed this.

"Yes, right here. Don't tell me you've never done it in a car before." She hiked up her skirt. He saw she wasn't wearing any panties. He wondered if she had planned this. "Fuck me, Luc."

Still hesitating, he shook his head. Something was missing. But he sure as hell didn't know what it was.

"I'm not exactly in the mood, Carmen. My thoughts are on Mattie and that punk kid."

"He's not a kid, he's twenty. Same as you. And I am sure I can get your mind off of Mattie." She moved over him and straddled him on the seat.

He watched as she unzipped his pants. He looked around to make sure they couldn't be seen from the street. He was already hard when she reached in his pants.

"I see your mind is already off Mattie," she laughed as she guided him inside her. She was wet. He wasn't surprised. She was probably planning it all through dinner.

It was fast and hard, just like Carmen wanted, but his thoughts never left Mattie.

CHAPTER 19

▼

Spencer was dead. Spencer had been gone too long, and I was sure there was nothing I could do to find him alive. I was too late.

I crawled out of bed. Even through my depression, I knew I couldn't give up looking for him. If he were dead, I would find his killer. Someone would pay for what happened to him. Someone would pay for putting Mattie through the torture of not knowing. And someone would pay for dragging me back to this hell.

I needed to know who was responsible. Someone knew something. I knew I needed to find the person Spencer had confided in.

Bill called and said he would stop by that evening. He was busy with a case but wanted an update. I told him I still knew nothing. I didn't mention Angel. I had no idea where it fit in, anyway.

Orin called next. He traced the disconnected number on Spencer's cell phone. It was traced back to Angel Martinez. It had been disconnected upon his death. I still felt a step behind.

He updated me on what he found on Angel. Angel was eighteen years old, born in LA. Orin had turned up Angel's arrest records. It appeared that Angel was a somewhat successful drug dealer and had been arrested twice as a minor and once recently as an adult. Orin was trying to locate his friends. He promised to have more information soon.

I told him about Lito Figueroa and his untimely death. I also told him that Angel was hiding at Lito's when he was killed.

"What's the link to Spencer?" he asked.

"What makes you think there is a link?"

"You wouldn't be looking into a drug dealer's murder if it wasn't connected."

"It appears that Spencer might have been defending Angel in an upcoming case against the sheriff's department."

Orin was quiet as he processed the information. Like a good journalist, he promised to find corroborating evidence. He could smell a good story here. He promised to look into Angel's case and report back to me. I made him promise to be careful. There were too many dead bodies already.

Tim Robinson was the managing partner at Robinson & Robinson, Counselors at Law. His father had retired years ago, but Tim refused to change the name of the firm, hoping that his son would one day join him.

Tim was in his midsixties and still practiced law daily. He not only ran the firm, but he also ran the lawyers and the paralegals. He knew everything that happened in his firm, from marriages and births to scandals and secrets. I thought he was the best person to start with.

Spencer had gone to work for him right out of law school. I think his father was a friend or business partner with Robinson at one time. Spencer had done well there, working his way up to a big office and hoping one day to be named partner.

The parking lot of Robinson & Robinson was full when I pulled in just after noon. I parked in a handicap spot and locked the car.

Not wanting to bother the receptionist, I found the door to the stairwell, picked the lock and made my way up the three flights of stairs. Robinson's office was just down the hall from Spencer's office. I was happy to see the light on in his office.

Tim had just hung up his phone when I walked in. He looked up at me and smiled.

"I'm sorry, do you have an appointment?" he asked. Ever the pleasant attorney. I knew it wouldn't take long to break him.

"I don't need one," I said, approaching his desk.

He looked just a bit rattled, then he recovered.

"I don't have time this afternoon, but I am sure my secretary can schedule you in later this week."

As he reached for the phone, I reached for the pair of scissors on his desk. Before he could call his secretary or security, I cut the phone cord.

The movement startled him. He looked up at me with the phone still clutched in his hand.

I smiled at him and sat down in the comfortable leather chair across from the desk.

"Nice chair. I bet it's expensive." When he didn't respond, I continued, "I just have a few questions. I promise not to take too much of your time. I doubt you remember me. I'm Luc Actar."

I saw the glimmer of recognition cross his face as he put the phone down.

"Ah, you do remember. See, I didn't really think you were that old and senile."

"How could I forget? You made a scene at Spencer's wedding. You brought that trash-talking whore to a classy upscale event."

"Actually she was a lawyer, but I can understand the confusion."

"What do you want?" he asked, leaning back in his chair.

"I'm looking for some information. I'm not sure if you're aware, but Spencer's missing."

"I am fully aware of the situation."

"Yet, you refuse to help the detectives find him. I find that very interesting. We should discuss that."

"This is a law firm, not a school cafeteria. There are certain things I am unable to discuss. We have clients that expect our discretion, even in times like these."

"Aren't you a little concerned that one of your lawyers—one of your friends—is missing?"

"Actually, I'm not. He needed some time to clear his head. You're the one making this bigger than it is."

"What do you mean?" I asked. I grabbed a bag of nuts off his desk. I hadn't had lunch yet.

"He was having some personal issues and needed to get away. Your media blitz is unwarranted. I'm sure he will be back soon." He watched me open the bag of nuts.

"You're talking about problems at home? With Mattie?"

"I'm sure it's no secret to you that there were problems in the marriage."

"Did he discuss divorce with you?"

"I'm not his attorney, Mr. Actar." He sneered at me.

"Yet, you know your firm inside and out. And you know your lawyers. Are you sure his disappearance had nothing to do with Angel Martinez?"

His eyes narrowed. "I can't discuss an active case."

"Oh, I can guarantee you that Angel is no longer active. He's dead."

"Dead?" The news hit Tim harder than I had expected. He probably didn't make it a habit to learn about the dangers of the drug business.

"Yeah, dead. It wasn't a sleeping pill shot between his eyes."

Robinson said nothing as he thought about this. He stared at his empty hands. He looked lost. Worried. But then it was gone. Composed, he looked back up at me.

I popped a couple nuts into my mouth and stared back. He would be tougher to crack than I thought.

Convinced the meeting was over, I grabbed a pen and Post-it note from his desk and wrote down my cell phone number.

"If you want to talk about it, call me." I got up to leave. "I'm taking the nuts with me, though."

"Wait. I can't discuss the case, but I can give you some background information."

I turned back and waited for him to continue. I was surprised he wanted to help. Maybe I wasn't such a terrible intimidator after all.

"A few months ago, a partner retired. The remaining partners decided to promote from within. I presented Spencer for the job. He is without a doubt the best attorney on staff. He works hard and brings in the most revenue. I thought he was a shoo-in. But the other partners outvoted me. They said he wasn't diverse enough."

"What's that mean?"

"Spencer concentrates on contract negotiations and disputes, mostly for the entertainment industry—studios, production companies, Screen Actors Guild. He knows contract laws and workplace laws like the back of his hand. But he knows little about criminal law, family law, or even civil law. The firm asked him to widen his range of cases. We were all pleased to see him pick up the Martinez case."

"Who suggested the case to him?"

Robinson shook his head. "I don't know. I think Angel found him."

"What about your meeting on Tuesday morning? Did you hear from him?"

"He called me at home. It was early. He said he needed to straighten some things out."

"Did you ask him what he was talking about?"

"No, we were interrupted. He told me he had to go. His lawyer was on the other line."

"What lawyer?" I asked.

He shook his head, defeated. "I don't know."

"If you think of anything else, call me." I got up and realized he was probably the only lawyer other than Bill that could look me in the eyes. Maybe that's why Spencer liked working for him. "Thanks for the nuts."

When Bill arrived at five o'clock, I offered to pick up dinner. The nuts just hadn't filled me up. I took my cell phone and promised not to be long. Mattie didn't protest. The days were beginning to drain her. She spent most of her time alone in her room. I could do very little to lift her spirits. And I was running out of sleeping pills.

I pulled up to the local Chinese restaurant. The parking lot was being resurfaced and was taped off. I found a parking spot across the street, jaywalked across the empty street and jogged into the tiny restaurant.

In DC, I had been unable to find a good Chinese takeout. LA has the best Chinese and Mexican restaurants by far. There was no wait, and since everything smelled good, I ordered way too much. I threw five dollars in the tip jar and headed back to the car, pleased with my bounty.

It was already dark and the air was starting to cool as if anticipating a storm. The moon lit the empty parking lot. Crossing the street, I noticed how quiet it was. It made me nervous as I scanned the other parked cars. There was no one around. I shrugged off my paranoia and unlocked the car.

Then I noticed a note on the passenger seat. I scanned the street again before putting the food down. I didn't see any movement anywhere.

The doors had been locked, and the alarm had been set. I had only been gone a few minutes. And apparently I was doing a lousy job of watching my back.

Having experience stealing cars, I knew that it was impossible for someone to disable the car alarm, unlock the door, and place a note on the seat in the time I had been gone. And how the hell did he get the alarm back on and out of sight without me noticing?

Since I didn't bring gloves with me, I touched the note on the edge and eased the white paper open. The writing wasn't familiar, but I didn't expect it to be. The note was scribbled quickly.

> *Meet me in my office after ten tonight.*
> *Make sure you come alone.*
> *—Dr. Waldhanz*

I reread the note twice before putting it in my pocket. I glanced around once more and wondered if I was being watched. I started the car and drove back to the house. I wanted to drive straight to the doctor's office, but Bill and Mattie were expecting me. And I needed to contemplate my next move.

I decided not to mention the note to Mattie or Bill. I didn't need more people worrying.

My hunger had vanished, so I watched Mattie and her father devour the food. Bill never mentioned Spencer in front of her. And I knew it was his way of protecting her from the pain. My way was just a little different. I had to get out of there.

At ten o'clock, I put Mattie to bed. I told Bill I was going to stop at the sheriff's station and swap notes with Detective Ward. I told him to call if there were any problems. He promised to stay until midnight then head home.

Driving quickly, I checked my rearview mirror every chance I had. I wondered if I would even know whether I was being followed. I suddenly felt like Bob Woodward meeting Deep Throat. I felt silly but took several unnecessary turns anyway.

I parked at the bar across the street and sat in my car for another fifteen minutes checking the traffic. The street was crowded with people coming and going. I knew I wouldn't be able to spot a tail, even if I knew what to look for. I got out and walked slowly past the bar then crossed the street.

Most of the pedestrian traffic was headed into the grocery store next door. No one glanced at me as I headed past toward the office building.

Glancing around once more, I ducked in. The receptionist smiled at me and waived me in. I wondered what they paid her to work on the weekends.

"Good evening, Mr. Actar. They're waiting for you." She got up and locked the door behind me.

"Who are *they*?" I asked, stopping short of the door.

She realized her misstep and blushed. "I mean Dr. Waldhanz is waiting for you." She quickly picked up the phone to avoid any more questions from me.

I knocked on the door and heard someone shout, "Come in." I reached in my jacket pocket and was glad I never left home without my tape recorder. Wishing it was a gun, I pressed record.

I pushed the door open and took a quick glance around the room. Dr. Waldhanz was sitting on the couch. I didn't spend too much time concentrating on him. My eyes quickly focused on the man seated behind the desk. The one with the gun pointed at my chest.

CHAPTER 20

▼

Sunday, November 7, 2004
10:35 PM
Santa Monica

It wasn't the first time I had a gun aimed at me. But I was amused nonetheless.

"Did you come alone?" the man behind the desk asked me.

"What's the answer you want to hear?" I asked. I raised my hands in surrender. Just like they do in the movies. I tried not to smirk.

"The honest one," he said, staring at me. There was no humor in his tone.

Other than the gun, Spencer Hardwin looked like a lawyer sitting behind the desk. He normally wore contacts but tonight had opted for his wire-rimmed glasses. They made him look smart, even thoughtful. He wore a black suit with his tie slightly loosened. I would never have expected him to look so disheveled in his life. But at least he wasn't dead.

I realized he looked older. Just as Bill had looked older. I wondered if it was the profession of law that aged a person so quickly. In thirty years, would Spencer look like Bill?

"I'm alone," I answered, hoping it was true.

I wasn't worried about Spencer shooting me. He probably had never held a gun in his hands let alone shot one. And I had already noticed his finger wasn't on the trigger. I knew I would be able to pull it from him easily. And he would be too scared to challenge me.

Dr. Waldhanz rose from the couch. He whispered something to his receptionist then closed the door behind me. He smiled at me. I assumed he was trying to comfort me. I didn't feel any comfort from it.

"Are you wired?" Spencer asked, lowering the gun. He stared at me. I saw flashes of red in his eyes and I wondered if he had slept at all in the past week.

"I'm not a cop, Spencer."

Spencer smiled and placed the gun on the desk. Obviously a little relieved, he got up and came toward me. He grabbed the tape recorder from my pocket.

"I know you never go anywhere without this." He pulled the tape out and placed both on the desk.

"You know me pretty well. I'm wondering if I know you at all."

"Sit down, Luc. I have some things to tell you." I noticed Dr. Waldhanz had situated himself at the door. Guarding it.

"Some?" I asked, heading toward the couch. "I think you have a hell of a lot to explain."

"I'm sorry I had to meet you this way. I couldn't exactly call you on the phone or stop by the house. Not only are the cops watching the house, but you started a multimedia frenzy out there. Everyone is looking for me."

"What did you expect, Spence? You left with no notice. Did you expect me to just leave it to the fucking cops?"

Spencer laughed. "Of course not. I don't mind the publicity. And I am really glad to see you."

"Could have fooled me. What's with the gun?"

"Picked it up on Friday for only two fifty." He looked at the gun proudly. "I needed to make sure I could protect myself. I'll get to that in a second."

I noticed his face soften, but I didn't say anything. Finally he asked, "How's Mattie?"

"Not good," I answered. I could see his sadness. I didn't care. I was angry with him. I wanted to punch him. No, I wanted to grab the gun and shoot him in the face. But I knew I wouldn't. He had saved my life once and that was enough.

"She's scared that something horrible has happened to you. She hasn't been eating. And the only way I can get her to sleep is to drug her. She's all cried out but she refuses to let up. She blames herself."

"It's not her fault," he started. I saw the tears come to his eyes. "Take care of her, Luc. I expect you to do this for me. For her."

"I can only do so much. You're her husband. She needs you home."

"I can't. Not yet. Trust me, it's safer that she doesn't know where I am. I don't want her to be a target, too."

"Tell me what the hell is going on."

Spencer looked at his doctor then back at me.

"I was working a case for this guy named Angel Martinez. He was arrested illegally. He was never read his rights and he was beaten after the handcuffs were on. He wanted to sue the department." He shook his head as he thought of Angel.

I waited for him to continue.

"I explained that cases like this weren't getting that much attention lately. But I told him I would do my best. Then he disappears. This is Thursday. I talk to his mother and she tells me he went into hiding."

"I know this much. I spoke with Angel's mother yesterday. Why are *you* hiding?"

"On Friday, two detectives questioned me about Angel's disappearance, but I refused to tell them anything. Then I realize I'm being followed. I didn't panic at first. I knew I didn't do anything wrong.

"Then on Monday, I got a call from Angel. He says he needs to meet me. Says he is scared. He tells me he's at a friend's house. But I need to make sure I'm not being followed. I told him I couldn't meet him because I was being watched."

"Did you go see him?" I asked.

"I waited in my office all night. I don't remember what time it was, but the detectives that were sitting outside came into the building. I went down the stairs and ran for my car."

He got up from the chair and looked out the window. "I didn't think how that little action changed everything. I assumed I would talk to Angel, get him somewhere safe and then be able to go home and be with Mattie. If I had known what was going to happen, I wouldn't have gone. I wouldn't have left Mattie this way."

"What happened?"

He didn't look at me. He kept his eyes focused on the windowpane. I glanced at the doctor. He was watching Spencer, too. No one seemed interested in the gun, except me.

"Angel was dead when I got there. I didn't even realize it was him at first. I didn't recognize him. There was so much blood. The fence was covered."

"Did you go straight to the house?"

"What?" he asked.

"Angel wasn't shot until after two, Spencer. You need an alibi. Tell me where you went first?"

"Oh, yeah." Spencer looked away, thinking. "I, uh, went to see Angel's mother. I wanted to tell her everything was going to be OK. I got to Angel's friend's house around three o'clock."

Spencer rubbed his eyes and continued, "Shit. I was scared and I took off. I spent the night at the UCLA library. It was the only place I could think of going."

His story seemed forced, but I said nothing and let him continue. The doctor remained quiet.

"Then Wednesday, I saw my picture on the news. I knew immediately it was your doing." He attempted a half smile. "I left the car in the parking lot at UCLA all day. I figured with school in session, there was a chance no one would notice it. But I knew I had to ditch it soon. The next morning, I drove to LAX and left it there. I hoped it would make the detectives think I left town. I wanted them to spread their resources thin. The thinner, the better for me. I just needed to buy some time. I walked a block and called Dr. Waldhanz to pick me up."

The doctor smiled at this. He was probably so proud that his client trusted him so much. I thought it was pathetic but didn't offer my opinion.

"Did you know where he was when I visited?" I asked the doctor.

He shook his head. "He called after you left. I informed him you had stopped by. He wasn't surprised."

Spencer continued. "He's the only one I trusted who wasn't being watched. I have to assume they have Mattie and you being followed."

I nodded. "I got confirmation that they are watching her. Nothing concrete on me."

"Well, the cops know you're following leads. I'm sure they followed you here. But since you already made one trip here, they'll think it's just a follow-up. I hope I haven't put Dr. Waldhanz in any jeopardy."

"I hope not. The deputies searched the house. Was there anything there?"

He shook his head, thinking. "No."

"What about the file on Angel? Do you have it?"

"No, I left it on my desk at the office."

I shook my head. "It's not there."

"Then the cops have it," he suggested.

"I don't think so. The firm wouldn't let them in your office." I was now convinced there was something about this case that someone wanted kept quiet. "What's in the file?"

"We have a strong case. I have Angel's notes. His arrest record and a medical report from the doctor in the ER."

"I should be able to get the information. Do you realize the sheriff's department thinks you killed Angel?"

"What?" Spencer jumped up from the chair. "They're going to frame me for his murder?"

"Not if I can help it. Do you have any idea who would want Angel dead?"

"Other than the sheriff's department? No."

"OK. I'll get the information on the case and meet with the department. There isn't a warrant out for you yet. But I still think you should stay out of sight for awhile."

"Of course. There's no way I'm coming out until this is all over. In fact, I need you to promise that you won't tell Mattie about this meeting. It's better that she doesn't know."

"Better for who?" I asked. There was no way I was going to promise that. I was angry that he would ask me to lie to Mattie.

"For everyone," he said. "I know she's worried, but it will be over soon."

"She's more than worried. She's hurting, Spence. She has been interviewed several times already. Several have insinuated she was involved. And they have brought up issues she would rather not discuss outside your marriage."

He immediately looked away, and I knew he understood me. He was quiet for a long time before he spoke. He was holding back tears.

"Luc, I didn't sleep with that other woman." He looked me in the eye and I believed him.

"I know. I met Mary on Wednesday. Her story was full of holes. Why did you tell Mattie you did?"

He looked at his doctor. Dr. Waldhanz nodded at him.

"I didn't want to hurt her, Luc. But I wanted to get her attention. It was the wrong thing to do, I admit that. But at the time, I thought it was the only way to get her to agree to counseling."

"Why did she need counseling?"

"She's not in love with me," Spencer whispered. I could barely hear his answer. He was serious. I laughed out loud, and Spencer just stared at me.

"You are so wrong, Spencer." Both Dr. Waldhanz and Spencer were now staring at me. "I know that woman better than anyone. She loves you. I know that."

"I'll admit she loves me, Luc. But she's not *in* love with me. She never has been. She's in love with someone else."

I shook my head and stood. "No way, Spence. She's not like that. I don't care if Mel Gibson asked her out, there is no way she would cheat on you."

Spencer sighed and looked again at his doctor. I wondered what the looks were for. Finally, he looked at me and said, "She's not in love with just anyone. She's in love with you, Luc."

CHAPTER 21

▼

Sunday, November 7, 2004
11:10 PM
Santa Monica

"That's a crock of shit!" I yelled at Spencer. It wasn't possible.

Spencer only shook his head.

"You've gone totally fucking nuts, Spencer. No wonder you're sitting here with this shrink."

"I'm afraid it's true," Dr. Waldhanz said.

"Did she tell you this?" I growled, turning toward the doctor.

"Not in so many words," he answered stepping back.

"Not in so many words," I repeated, dismissing him. I turned back to Spencer. "This is the excuse you're going to use to hurt her?"

"I don't want to hurt her, Luc. I promised you I would do my best to make her happy. I realized I couldn't do that."

"So you take off? That's bullshit. Is any of what you've told me true? Or was this just an excuse because you couldn't fix the marriage you fucked up?"

Spencer sighed. "I need you to believe me, Luc. I helped you once, without asking any questions. I need you to return the favor. I need you to trust me on this."

I stared at him but said nothing.

"I'll worry about Mattie as soon as this mess is cleared up. Let me handle it, though. She deserves that much."

I grabbed my tape recorder from the desk. "She deserves a hell of a lot more than that, Spencer." I stormed out of the office. Neither of them tried to stop me.

The drive home was longer than I had wanted. The car was too quiet. I opened the window and let the air chill my face. The oncoming traffic blinded me as I drove. Keeping one eye on the speedometer and the other on the rearview mirror, I tried to calm my rising anger.

I tried to focus on the mystery that had driven Spencer into hiding, but the thoughts of Mattie kept returning.

I pulled into the driveway just after midnight. Bill had already left. The porch light was the only light still on. It was too late to wake her.

In the dark kitchen, I paced the floor and debated whether approaching her on the topic was even a good idea. After three hours of debating, I decided it wasn't my place to start asking questions. The answers weren't going to change anything.

I decided to keep my meeting with Spencer to myself. Mattie would only be worried and I wanted to make sure the cops stayed far away from him. I had no idea what was going on, and I wasn't about to throw away my only ace in the hole.

I needed time.

Because there was no way I could sleep and no way I could leave the house again, I called Orin at home. I decided to call from outside, just in case the house was indeed bugged. He was pissed at being woken, but he told me he had found the arrest report on Angel and was still digging for the medical report.

On a hunch, I asked him to check any cases in the past three years for Lito Figueroa. I explained the nice house in Whittier and my concern that Lito and possibly Angel were involved in something much more dangerous than selling pot or lying in court about it. Orin was immediately interested and agreed to continue looking.

I pulled out my notebook and wrote "Angel Martinez" and underlined it twice. He had to be the center of the problem. His death had caused Spencer's disappearance.

The most probable reason for Angel's death was drugs. Underneath his name, I wrote "deal gone bad?" A rival drug dealer or gangbanger could have taken him out. It was logical with the life he led. But how had they found Angel? I crossed out the line.

The obvious suspect with the easiest access to Angel was Spencer. I didn't want to write his name down, but I did anyway. He had the opportunity and access. But Spencer didn't have it in him to murder someone. Nor could I find a real motive for Spencer to take out Angel.

I wanted to scratch his name out. But I had to look at this logically. Most everyone is capable of murder if the correct buttons are pushed. And he had obviously been keeping things from me already. I had no idea who to trust anymore, so the name remained.

Thinking of motive, I wrote down "Sheriff's Department." They had the most to lose from a lawsuit. Either the officers themselves or the department in whole would want the case settled quietly or better yet, to disappear completely. I made a note to talk to John again as my cell phone rang.

"Found an interesting case on your Lito Figueroa about three years ago," Orin now sounded awake, excited. "He sued the LA sheriff's department for harassment and civil rights violations. It never went to trial. The case was settled quietly for a cool two million."

"Good for him," I said. "What's the link?"

"Two cases against the sheriff's department within three years. Sounds like the beginning of a pattern. I'm looking into other cases."

"Who was the lawyer?"

"I don't know. I haven't been able to get a copy of the case yet. Give me a few hours."

"How did you get this information?" I looked at my watch. His speed was amazing.

"I have a friend that works at the courthouse. He said some detective came in a couple of days ago and asked for the case. He told me the case had been misfiled and it took them over an hour to find it. The detective took it with him, so he doesn't have the file. But he remembered Lito's name when I called. He thought it was weird that they were looking into a three-year-old case that settled out of court."

I felt we finally had a break. Lito sued the department and got a hefty award. Angel turns around and tries the same thing and ends up dead. Lito soon follows.

Maybe the county was tired of paying. Or the department was tired of covering up for its deputies. Now the cops had taken the case file. I was starting to believe Spencer was right. The department had the most to lose if Angel spoke out. And they had just taken the evidence. I circled the last line in my notes.

I instructed Orin to find out more about Lito's case. I wanted names of all those involved, including the judges on each and the deputies charged. I wanted to know everything about everyone. Their personal and business dealings and any secrets they wanted to keep hidden. I needed a better connection between the two cases.

I felt I was getting closer. But I was still a step away from bringing Spencer home. The detectives blamed Spencer. Spencer blamed the department. I needed someone else to blame.

CHAPTER 22

▼

1999
Malibu

Luc watched her from his car. She was wearing white. White always looked good on her. The cutoff shirt and short shorts revealed a little too much of her long, lean legs and flat stomach. Her hair was pulled back from her face, just the way he always liked it.

It had been almost a year since he had seen her. He wasn't sure what her reaction would be. She looked stunning, beautiful, sophisticated, yet fragile. And his guilt ate at him.

And her eyes looked sad. He put out what was left of his cigarette and grinned. He knew he could change that.

Mattie was carrying a large box from her car toward the open front doors. She hadn't noticed him pull into the driveway behind her. As he stepped out, the afternoon sun warmed him.

Mattie turned toward the sound of the car door slamming.

"Put that box down before you hurt yourself," Luc called out. "And put some clothes on. The neighbors are enjoying this way too much."

He was pleased to see a huge smile spread across her face. She dropped the box and came running toward him.

"I hope that was clothes in that box."

"Luc!" she screamed as she jumped into his arms. "I'm so happy to see you." She kissed him on the lips and he pulled away quickly.

She looked past him, eying his new Audi. "Where did you get that?"

"I stole it from one of your new neighbors. They don't deserve it."

She punched him in the shoulder and he pretended it didn't hurt.

"I needed a car," he said, looking at his new car. He was proud of it. Even more so because he knew she would be happy that it was paid for with clean money, money he had worked hard for.

She frowned. "What about the motorcycle? I thought you looked cute on it."

He laughed. "I still have the motorcycle. But if you call me cute again, I'll sell it." He pulled her toward the car. "I needed the car to bring your housewarming gift over."

He opened the passenger door, and a puppy jumped out. The little German shepherd bounded toward Mattie.

"Ahhhh!" she squealed as she fell to her knees. He smiled as the puppy licked her face. "Where did you get him?"

"I stole him from your neighbors, too." He handed her the leash. The dog continued to squirm with delight.

"You need some security here. A single woman living alone and all."

She smiled up at him. "Malibu is very safe. You don't need to worry about me. So how are you?" She looked him over.

He smiled. "I'm sober."

"For today?" she asked tilting her head.

"No, really. Four months. No alcohol. No drugs."

"Wow. I never thought I would see that day."

"Me neither." Being reckless was one thing. Luc had hit rock bottom and realized too late that he had lost all control of his own life. He knew if he were going to face Mattie after what he had done, he would need all the control he could get.

He looked up at the house. "So show me this new house."

She led Luc and the puppy into the house. He glanced around the empty living room.

"You'll need some furniture, Mat. And you should frost these front windows. You don't want peepers looking through here."

She smiled as she looked around the large room. "I was thinking about putting a large leather sectional over there," she pointed. "And maybe—"

"Mattie, you don't need to worry about the decorating," Luc interrupted. "Get a professional to come in here and decorate for you."

"Says the guy with newfound money."

He pulled her into his arms and hugged her.

"The house is beautiful. You should be proud. I know how hard you worked for that trust fund."

She pulled away and punched him again in the arm. He laughed through the pain. He knew he would wake up with a bruise. But he would never complain.

"Come on," she grabbed his hand and pulled Luc and the puppy up the spiral staircase. "You have to see the balcony."

She pushed open the double French doors that led out to the balcony. It overlooked the Malibu shoreline and beautiful Pacific Ocean. She leaned against the railing and looked out toward the ocean.

Luc watched her as she closed her eyes toward the sun.

"What does this remind you of?" she asked, her closed eyes, still enjoying the warmth of the sun.

The breeze rustled her hair. He couldn't take his eyes off of her. Nor could he respond.

Her eyes fluttered open and looked at him. "Luc?"

He couldn't speak. Instead, he turned his face to the ocean. The setting sun had turned the horizon a brilliant orange that cascaded against the blue ocean. He looked down the deck and watched the swells roll in. A small company of surfers in multicolor wetsuits sat on their boards waiting for the right moment. He remembered to breathe.

"Doesn't it remind you of the tree house? Of being completely alone, just the two of us?" she continued.

He nodded but didn't look up. She turned her face back toward the setting sun.

"Are you seeing anyone?" she asked.

He cleared his throat, which had gone dry. He suddenly wanted a beer. "I'm single for now," he said. "You?"

"I have a big house and just me to fill it," she said. He could hear the sadness, the loneliness. And felt the guilt.

"You can't blame me. I swear I'm not scaring them off anymore."

She laughed. "It's still your fault. I haven't found one guy that can compare to you."

He grinned and winked at her. "That was my plan. I'm just so damn loveable."

"Did you love her?" she asked, suddenly serious again.

"Who?" he asked, confused with the change of subject.

"Carmen?"

He shook his head, looked at her. "No. Why?"

She turned away. "You changed after you broke up with her. First you disappeared for two weeks. You missed school and didn't call to tell anyone you were OK. You didn't even call me. I had to hear from your roommate."

"That wasn't about her. It was about me. I just needed some time to myself."

He knew he should tell her what he had done, but he couldn't. He couldn't bear to have her disappointed in him.

"I thought you were having a hard time with the breakup. I tried to contact you, but every time I called, your roommate told me you were out. You didn't even tell me you were graduating. Are you avoiding me, Luc?"

"I'm sorry." It was all he could offer. "I'm here now. You know I would never make you move on your own."

"A friend will help you move," she mocked.

"But a real friend will help you move a body," he muttered, cringing to himself.

"You need to stop pushing yourself away from everyone. Promise me you won't disappear like that again."

"I didn't realize you loved me being around."

"You know if you let that hard exterior down for just a bit," she said, knocking on his chest, "you just might experience love."

"No way, Mat. I'm not cut out for love. It's not in my genes. It's a survival thing." He thought of Joey. "No one can hurt me if I refuse to let them in."

"It's not always about pain, Luc. You may like the feeling."

"I wouldn't know. I've never been around love. I probably wouldn't even recognize it." He folded his arms over his chest. "What about you? Ever been in love?"

She smiled. "Of course. Right now, I'm madly in love with Charlie."

"Who's Charlie?" he asked.

She laughed at his stern face and leaned down to pick up the puppy.

"I think I'm going to name him Charlie. What do you think?"

He grinned as the dog tried to squirm from her arms. "He needs a tougher name than that. How can I expect him to protect you from all the evil out there?"

She put the dog down and looked at Luc. "I don't need protection, Luc."

"You may not want it, but you need it."

"You may be surprised by my wants and needs."

She turned away from him, but he thought he saw anger flash in her eyes. He had wondered if she still had those emotions in her.

He looked at her as she searched the skyline. The private beach below did remind him of the tree house and his many nights spent gazing out at the Manhattan Beach Pier and the ocean beyond. With her. Their beach, their tree house, their memories.

Suddenly he was thinking back to that kiss at the prom. The passion she offered. The heat he had chosen to protect himself from.

He turned his back to her, trying to erase the memory. Like so many times since, he shrugged off the feeling. He allowed the silence to surround him.

"Would you like to stay the night?" she whispered.

It was a simple question and he knew she meant it innocently. But he wanted more than what she was offering him now. He shook his head violently but the images wouldn't disappear. He couldn't breathe. He had let his wall down and she had attacked him without realizing it.

"No," he muttered before he could change his mind. He hurried through the French doors and away from the burning sun.

CHAPTER 23

▼

Monday, November 8, 2004
9:30 AM
Malibu, California

I awoke to the sound of knocking on the front door. It grew louder as I pulled myself from the bed. Mattie's door was still closed. As I walked to the door, I scanned the house.

Charlie growled at the closed door. I yelled at him to behave and he retreated upstairs to guard Mattie's room.

Bill Connor was standing at the door with another man. Another lawyer? He looked familiar. But then again all lawyers looked alike to me.

"Good morning, Luc," Bill said. His tone was serious. I noticed he didn't call me son.

He looked me over. I had slept in my clothes. I knew I looked like the bum I felt like. I didn't care. I felt like shit. The dreams tore into me, like bear claws. If I didn't fix this mess soon, I knew I wouldn't survive.

"Morning, Bill." I allowed both men to enter. "Let me make some coffee." And wake up.

I started the coffee and returned to the living room where Bill was making himself comfortable on the couch.

"Is Mattie up?" he asked.

I shook my head. It throbbed as I did so. I rubbed my eyes to ward off the oncoming migraine. I tried unsuccessfully to remember the last time I ate something.

My eyes focused on the man standing next to Bill. He wore a black Armani three-piece suit, a red tie, and a gold Rolex on his wrist. His salt-and-pepper hair was unnatural. Dyed black hair with the salt added for personality. He reeked of cologne that made my already tired eyes water.

Definitely a lawyer. And a rich one at that. He was the type I would have robbed on the streets of DC. I wondered what type of car he drove. Probably a Jag or a Rolls. He would need luxury. And he would want flash.

His face was tight as his eyes scanned the room. He seemed more interested in the house than me. I didn't appreciate the lack of respect. When his eyes finally turned to me, they didn't waver.

I didn't like him. But then again, I didn't like many lawyers.

"You remember Edgar Twaine. He's an associate at my firm," Bill said.

I shook his hand and waited for Bill to explain why he was here. Edgar sat down next to Bill, his eyes still studying me.

"Edgar handled the LA County corruption case three years ago. He was lead counsel." Twaine threw a crooked grin at me. He was obviously quite proud of that.

"Oh, of course." The name had slipped my mind, just as easily as that life had.

It had seemed like ages ago. George Pinkle, a rising porn actor and producer of fluff films, was arrested on charges of domestic abuse. His ex-girlfriend had reported the incident to the sheriff's department. They rushed into action, busting in Pinkle's door. They handcuffed him, searched his home, and finally tossed him in jail.

He claimed he was never read his rights, never shown a warrant, and was refused the right to call his attorney. He spent a night in jail and upon waking learned that his ex-girlfriend had dropped the charges. He was released without apology.

Upon returning to his home, he found his place turned upside down. Worse, he discovered a briefcase that had been full of cash; ten thousand to be exact, was missing.

George contacted Connor & Associates and within twenty-four hours, they sued the sheriff's department for civil rights violations. Unfortunately, they didn't have the evidence they needed to accuse the department of theft, so Bill regrettably left it out of the lawsuit.

But the theft bothered Bill. The department was guilty of misusing its authority. That happens everywhere. But deputies committing theft seemed a much worse problem. He wondered how widespread the criminal behavior of the department was.

But if Bill was going to get any information, he needed someone who knew the department as well as the criminal mind. So he called me.

I told him I would find out what I could. He handed me a mini tape recorder.

"No cop is going to admit to stealing money with a tape recorder in my hand."

"Then don't let them see it," he said. "If anyone can do it, you can."

The *Reporter* refused to give me the story, but I didn't care. I was already well-known by the department. And I had contacts in the department that would have to talk to me. And I had no problem stealing a story from another reporter.

Sergeant Keller and I had a long-standing relationship by this point. We had met a year earlier at a local bar he frequented. I wanted a quote for a story on a drug bust. So I found him.

I didn't care that it was a gay bar. My future at the *Reporter* was on the line. I approached him and struck up a conversation with him. He thought I was hitting on him. When I questioned him on the gang bust, he freaked. Worried that I would out him, he gave me the quote. He became my anonymous source in the department, probably against his own wishes.

I called Keller and tried to set up an appointment, but he wouldn't take my calls. So I cornered him at his favorite bar. He didn't want to be seen talking to a reporter, but I reassured him with lots of alcohol—and the threats of printing a wonderful story about homosexuality in law enforcement.

We talked mostly about sports, since I couldn't exactly talk about girls. He began to look comfortable. Just when he was off guard, I brought up the Pinkle case.

"Did the cops get anything interesting from the porn guy?" I asked.

He shifted slightly and looked around the crowded bar. I laughed at his uneasiness. Ignoring the "no smoking" sign, I lit a cigarette and offered him one. He declined.

"Off the record, of course. I couldn't print that shit anyway. I was just wondering what kind of kinky shit they found at his place."

He laughed when he understood what I was asking. Maybe he thought I was gay, too. I didn't care. I just prayed the recorder still had tape left.

"I heard he had a lot of sex shit—tapes, magazines, the most amazing little toys." He shrugged. "Unofficially, he had a lot of money, too."

It wasn't good enough so I pressed further.

"Money? Big-time money?"

"Yeah. The deputies that arrested him said they found a couple of grand in cash just lying in his living room."

"Really?" I tried to look shocked. "What happened to it?"

His eyes narrowed as I blew smoke in the air. He still couldn't tell if he could trust me. I was still a reporter. I grinned. He shrugged. I had kept his secret for almost a year.

"They found it in a briefcase. Rumor is it never made it down to evidence."

I knew it wasn't enough to convict anyone but when it was played in court, it made headlines. Mine being the largest.

It not only helped break the case open for Bill's firm, but it also drew mass hysteria from the public. My weekly feature stories buried the department.

The county opened a full-scale investigation into the deputies involved and the department as a whole, which resulted in a mass layoff, including Keller. The sheriff was ousted and Maclay was elected to replace him.

My stories had everything that a struggling newspaper and second-rate journalist could ask for: money, violence, sex, and above all, corruption. They practically threw the Pulitzer at me.

Edgar Twaine had been handed an open-and-shut case. The biggest case of his career. It made him famous in LA. And now, I knew exactly why he was here.

"Mattie told me the detectives were in the house on Tuesday. Without a search warrant," Bill started. He looked at Edgar.

"I am concerned about Spencer's civil rights, as well as Mattie's," Edgar finished for Bill.

"I understand your concern, but they have apologized and are trying to cooperate with me to help find Spencer," I said.

This was the reason I hated lawyers. The sharks were circling already, looking for new blood and more money. It made me sick. Edgar made me sick.

"But it was an illegal search, Mr. Actar. And it is my understanding that these specific detectives have been involved with previous misconduct. Do you know if they found anything? Did they find anything in the house? Did they remove case files or legal documents?"

"I've been told they didn't find anything." My concern drifted to the misconduct of Detectives Hatcher and Medina. Maybe this shark was right. Maybe I should have been more worried about the officers in the house. I would have to question Carliss.

My current assumption was that Angel Martinez had been killed because of the case against the sheriff's department. Now Spencer was running, scared for his life, too. Was the sheriff's department trying to hush the case or fix a wrong?

"What were they looking for?" Edgar asked.

"The obvious—any information that would tell them why Spencer disappeared and where he may have gone."

"I understand from Tim Robinson that the firm suspects the deputies broke into Spencer's office the other night. They have no proof and it appears nothing is missing. But it makes you wonder if they are trying to set Spencer up."

I didn't offer that I was responsible for the break-in. Nor did I want to get into the Angel Martinez situation. It was bad enough that Spencer had disappeared voluntarily. I didn't want to make it worse by telling them he was already a suspect in a murder investigation.

Edgar looked at Bill for support. "I really think we need to send a message to the sheriff's department immediately and ask for anything they may have recovered to be returned. There could be personal information or worse, client-privileged documents."

I watched the lawyers as they discussed the situation. After a lengthy discussion of what route to take with a lawsuit, I finally interrupted.

"He's not a suspect. The deputies are trying to help us find him." I hoped I was right.

"All the more reason to keep a close eye on them," Edgar suggested.

"Why don't we wait on any legal maneuverings until we know more about the situation?" I suggested. "Mattie doesn't need this right now." I directed this to Bill.

"I think our priorities should be on protecting Spencer's innocence," Edgar said, challenging me.

"I don't give a fuck what your priorities are. My priority is Mattie."

"And I appreciate that," Bill said, his voice calm as he stepped between us. "But we still need to find Spencer."

"I'll find him. I am working with the detectives and Mattie to find him. Please leave this to me. For Mattie's sake."

When it came to his daughter, Bill knew I always did what was best for her. He finally agreed to leave the investigation with me. Edgar didn't look happy.

"Please keep me updated. If you hear anything, call me immediately. I can help with any legal issues that arise." Edgar held out his business card. "Or if you want me to talk to the department for you."

"I have them under control," I answered, refusing the card.

Bill and Edgar let themselves out. After checking on Mattie, I decided I needed some air. I instructed Charlie to keep guard on Mattie and slipped out of the house.

My thoughts drifted again to what Edgar had said, that the detectives had been involved in misconduct. What did that mean? Could they have been following Spencer to scare him off or were they really looking out for Angel? I went with my gut and knew I couldn't trust either of them.

I wondered how deep Detective Ward was involved. He had been less than generous with his information. He only revealed what he had to when I cornered him. I no longer felt I could trust him, either.

It was something I should have done a long time ago. I called Big Jim and asked him what he knew about Detectives Hatcher and Medina.

"I never heard of them, but I can ask around," he offered.

"Thanks, Jim. What about a Detective Ward? He's homicide."

"Yeah," he laughed. "I know him. He just made detective last year. Robbery-homicide, out of Industry Station, I believe. He has one of the best close rates over in homicide. He usually works alone. And he isn't well-liked."

"Why?"

"Rumor is he made detective by fuckin' the sergeant. She's gorgeous but very married."

"Is it true?" I asked.

"Oh, he fucked her, alright. He was investigated by internal affairs and got slapped on the hand. They claim he passed the detective test with flying colors. Although, I think he got more than a signing bonus with her on his lap. You have to give him props for that one."

The information was useful, but I wasn't ready to offer the props just yet.

"What did you find out about Angel?" I asked.

He paused. "Can you meet me here in about an hour?"

I checked my watch. Angel's funeral was in less than an hour and I needed to be there, wanted to be there. I agreed to meet with Jim afterward at Paradise.

CHAPTER 24

▼

Monday, November 8, 2004
11:00 AM
Lynwood, California

"Makes you appreciate your life, doesn't it?" Orin asked.

Orin and I stood at the back of the church and watched the mourners. I scanned the crowd for anyone out of place. Orin was looking for people to interview.

Ana Martinez stood in the front pew. The priest consoled and she nodded. Her eyes never left the casket. I felt sorry for her. I wondered if anyone outside those church doors cared about her.

Ignoring Orin, I watched as several young men approached the closed casket. I felt a little uncomfortable in the church. It wasn't the occasion or the people around me; I just didn't belong here.

"Every morning I wake up wondering how I survived another day. Why aren't I dead and buried already?" I asked.

"Maybe God has bigger plans for you. Have you ever thought that your life was tough because God thought you could handle it?"

Orin wrote something in his notepad. I had forgotten mine.

I smiled. "I'm not a religious man, Orin. The only other time I've been in a church was Mattie's wedding. And she had to drag me kicking and screaming."

Orin looked up at me. "You don't believe in God?"

I looked at the man hanging from the crucifix and thought of all the bad things I had done in my life.

"I never cared. I always felt that God in some way had looked the other way when it came to my life, so I had no problem looking the other way when it came to his."

Orin continued to watch the small crowd at the front of the church.

"I've done a lot of bad things in my life," I said.

Orin nodded. "It's not too late to ask for forgiveness."

"You're assuming I regret my past. I don't. I lived my life the only way I could. I could fight or I could die."

Orin grunted. "Fight or die. What happens when you stop fighting? Nah. You forget the other option—to live."

The organ rang out, making several people jump. Then it faded into a soft melody and covered the sounds of weeping. I wondered which was more depressing.

"I'm proud of what I've become. And if I had to do it all over again, I would do the same things. What I don't understand is why I'm not lying in that casket. Why am I still alive?"

"Ah, the age-old question," Orin said finally, smiling. "Why are any of us here? You're in the right place to look for answers. I suggest, since you are looking for a meaning in your life, you take a look at religion. It may help you answer some of those questions—"

"You know, Orin, I've always hated your speeches."

"And yet you continue to come back for more. Sometimes the longest road out is the shortest road home."

"Orin, I don't want him ignored." I said, glancing back at the casket. "He will be because it's the easy thing to do. But he deserves more."

Paradise was right off the 10 Freeway in West Covina. I found it easily, even though I had never been there before. I knew I would be much more comfortable there than the church I had just left.

Still early, the place was empty except for a few lone regulars. Most kept their noses in their beers and ignored the women in skimpy bikinis walking around. They were waiting for someone specific to come on stage. Music blared from the stage.

Not quite a strip club, the woman who danced here were a step above strippers. They kept their clothes and their dignity on. It was only a half-assed way around the laws since the men still fantasized about the women but were now able to do so with a beer in their hands.

Finding a booth in the back corner, I sat down. There was a candle lit on the table and I blew it out. I wanted the darkness, away from the noise. A waitress wandered over, glancing at the candle that still smoldered.

"What can I get you?" she asked.

"Just a soda," I said.

"Two-drink minimum, hon."

"Just a soda," I repeated.

She walked off just as a young blonde moved in. Her lips were painted fire engine red to match her acrylic nails. She wore a G-string and a bikini top that barely covered her nipples. Her tits were fake.

"Are you here just for the dancing, sweetheart?"

"I just want to be left alone."

"Then why did you come to Paradise?" she asked, suddenly interested in me.

"Business." It was a rough, deep voice that answered for me. I looked up and saw a big black man standing above me. The eyes that drilled into me were the eyes of death itself.

The dancer flashed a smile. She kissed Big Jim on the cheek and walked off without another word. He didn't even flinch and kept his eyes on me.

He was smaller, leaner than I remembered. He gripped my hand and shook my arm, showing me the strength had never left. He had kept up with the vigorous workouts we started in college.

His bulky arms were covered in tattoos. A skull on his right forearm stared with fire spurting from the empty eye sockets. His left arm was adorned with his weapons of choice: a six-inch blade, a shiny AK-47 and a recently added sawed-off shotgun. These were just the tattoos visible under his Paradise polo shirt.

When Jim was only sixteen he had killed a man in a fight over a parking spot. He said the killing was not premeditated, and he wasn't sure how he felt being able to take a man's life so easily. In remembrance of the man and the life he took, he had a picture of the car tattooed on his chest.

It soon became a tradition to have a symbol of the dead tattooed on him. With every death he delivered, another tattoo was added. Only a few knew of this tradition. I was one of the few. Not sure if that made me lucky or not.

"How ya doin'?" he asked, dropping into the booth. I felt the entire room shift.

The waitress that took my order came over and dumped a soda in front of me. She gave Jim a shot of something. I instantly wanted to trade mine in.

"I'm fine. Are we OK here?" I asked as soon as the waitress walked away.

"Yeah, this place is clean. I have a guy at the door watchin' for cops."

"Was he following me?" I asked, looking over at the man in the doorway. He looked Samoan. His arms were bare, unlike Jims. He had long black hair that hung in a single braid down his back. His eyes looked through me, threatening not just myself but everyone around me. He was scary, and I didn't scare easily. I knew he could kick my ass, so I turned away.

Jim smiled and I knew the answer. He wanted to protect himself just as much as he wanted to protect me. I needed to get better at detecting a tail.

I waited for Jim to drain the shot.

"What do you have on Angel?"

"He was dealing. Worked for a guy named David Chavez Castellino. He goes by the name of Chavez and handles the dealers in Lynwood. I talked to the guy. He said Angel was gettin' out. He said he had a big payoff coming and wanted a clean break."

"Chavez? He has the Lynwood territory now?"

I watched him raise his eyebrows.

"You know Chavez?"

"Yeah. He was a small-time supplier when I was running. He used to work the South Bay. Did you mention my name?"

He lit a cigarette and offered me one. I was tempted but shook my head. The adrenaline shooting through my body was enough of a buzz. He looked at me a long time before answering.

"I told him a friend wanted to know. I don't mention names. He is one of the larger suppliers in LA County now. I'm guessin' you're not a fan."

I shrugged. "I never liked dealers."

"What happened?"

Jim stared at me, waiting for a response.

"It's not relevant."

I stared back.

"It is if you want more information. I need to know what I'm gettin' in the middle of."

I let the silence drag on as he sucked on his cigarette. Even though I knew he would have no hesitation in killing, I also knew I had nothing to worry about.

My past was not something I discussed, even to the few friends I had. But then again, I suspected Big Jim knew more about me than anyone else.

"He took out a friend of mine awhile back," I said finally. "And I hear he doesn't like to dig his shit out of a burned-out trailer. Revenge is sweet, but I don't forget that shit."

"Worried he may come back to even the score?"

I shrugged. "Right now, I'm more concerned about the cops killing me than Chavez."

He nodded and slowly blew out smoke. I wasn't answering any more questions. And he wouldn't ask any.

"How did Chavez take Angel's departure?" I asked.

"He doesn't worry about small-time like Angel. He's got plenty of others ready to take his place."

I knew it was true. I had once been in his exact position.

"Does he have any idea who would want to take him out?"

"No. But he promised me he didn't whack him. If Angel had pissed him off, he would have made him hurt before taking him out. A clean point-blank shot to the head doesn't sound like any of the bangers I know."

"That's what I thought, too. Besides, Chavez is a lousy shot. Even at close range. What about Figueroa?"

"He was harder to find information on. Looks like he's been out of the trade for at least two, probably three years. No one knew anythin' except he likes to party with some high-end shit and has lots of cash to throw around. Rumor is it's all clean."

"I just found out he sued the sheriff's department and got a hefty award. Harassment, brutality, that kind of shit. Ask around about it. I want to know if it was legit."

"Hmmm. Good for him. I'll ask around. Do you have a piece?" Jim asked, shoving the cigarette into the table.

I shook my head.

"You want one?"

I thought of Mattie first. She would be pissed if she found out. But I also thought of Spencer's gun. And the deaths of Angel and Lito. And I thought about Chavez. I still had a score to settle with him.

"Whatcha got?"

Jim slid over a gun under the table. I grabbed it and stuck it in my jacket pocket without looking at it.

"What you got there is a Browning nine millimeter. Fifteen in the magazine, fully loaded."

"American made?" I asked.

He grunted. "Since 9/11, I only use American. I don't want to fund those asshole terrorists. It's clean. Don't worry."

"Thanks. I appreciate it. What do I owe?"

He stared at me, contemplating.

"Nothing. It's been taken care of." He looked around the club. I wondered if he was waiting for someone. "What do you think of this place?"

I smiled, realizing he knew about his sister after all.

"Nice place. Your sister seems to be doing well for herself."

He grunted and returned his eyes to me. "I owe you."

I shook my head. "I have a feeling we're even."

CHAPTER 25

▼

Monday, November 8, 2004
2:25 PM
Commerce, California

I needed to talk to John Carliss. He was the only person left in the sheriff's department I could trust, who wouldn't lie to me. I drove to the Malibu sheriff's station and asked where Carliss worked. They directed me to the homicide bureau in Commerce.

I called first and learned that Carliss was out on a call. I alerted the receptionist that my call was about a current case and could be crucial. She promised to relay the message and my name as soon as she could.

Carliss called within ten minutes. He didn't sound happy to hear from me, but he agreed to meet me at a diner near the department.

He was already ordering when I walked in and spotted him hiding in a booth. He looked pissed and grunted when I slid into the seat.

"What the hell do you want now, Luc?" he asked after the waitress took my order.

"I have some questions and I don't want the information getting around. I also want honest answers."

"I ain't telling you shit. You screwed the department. You're on your own."

"What are you talking about?" I asked.

"Considering you have your lawyer running amok, I am no longer willing to help you. Neither is Ward or the rest of the department."

"What lawyer?"

"Twaine. He's making threats to my detectives for information about Spencer's disappearance and the resulting investigation. Threatening my officers with lawsuits and life behind bars. He's becoming more of a nuisance than you."

"Edgar Twaine? From Bill Connor's firm?"

"No other. Call off your lawyer, Luc, before this gets ugly. Then I might be willing to have lunch with you."

"I didn't know Twaine was running his own investigation. I'll stop it. Believe me."

He laughed. "Believe you? That'll never happen."

"I need to know what the case is against Spencer."

He shook his head, knowing where I was headed. "You no longer want to know where he is?"

"I know he's alive. At this point, that's enough."

"Shit." he ran his fingers through his hair. "Tell him to come forward. We need to talk to him."

"He doesn't know anything. But he's scared for his life."

"We can protect him."

"From whom?"

He didn't have an answer. "Tell me what you know first. Then I might be willing to share."

"Spencer has an alibi for the Angel shooting. He told me he went to see Angel's mother. Afterward, he went to Lito's house, but Angel was already dead. He got scared and took off."

John sighed. "I'll have Ward check it."

The waitress brought our food. I wasn't hungry, but John dove right in.

"Why were Medina and Hatcher assigned to Angel's disappearance?" I asked.

He looked confused. "I think they were next in rotation. Why?"

"What about their past misconduct?"

I have rarely seen John angry, so his reaction had me sitting back.

"What the hell are you talking about? Those boys are clean. I checked myself after you called Maclay."

"I have a source who says otherwise. And they were in Spencer's house conducting an illegal search with at least two other deputies."

"No way," he said, shaking his head. "Your source is wrong. Neither of them has had a single complaint filed against them. And they conducted a search after Mrs. Hardwin allowed them access to the house. When she asked them to leave, they did."

"The search becomes illegal when they misrepresent what they are looking for. The deputies were looking for information to incriminate Spencer, not help find him.

"As for Ward, I'm not sure which head he's thinking with. I think you should look a little more closely at your supposed clean department. I know of at least one recent case where the department admitted guilt. The county paid a cool two million to keep it quiet."

John didn't respond as he picked at his fries. I told him about Lito's case.

He stared at me trying to figure out if I was telling the truth. He didn't want to believe me, but he also knew I had no reason to lie to him.

"I'm guessing there are more," I said, hoping I was on the right track. "So I am going to keep digging. I am starting to think the sheriff's department got a little tired of dishing out money. And now people are ending up dead."

He sighed as he wrote in his notebook. "I'll check with Detective Ward."

I leaned back and looked at John's empty plate. I pushed my untouched food at him. He still looked hungry.

"Johnny, the media will have this story if I don't get what I want."

"What do you want?" he asked.

"First, I want the surveillance on myself and Mattie ended. Second, I want an assurance from you that if there is a raid on the house or an arrest warrant issued for Spencer, that you'll tell me before it's processed."

He laughed. "Do you want the moon and stars, too?"

"And my last demand—I want you working this case. I want you in charge of every aspect. I don't want to see Hatcher, Medina, or Ward near me, the house, or Mattie."

"I'm not a detective. I don't run investigations, Luc—"

"I know you have to go up the chain of command for this. I'll be making my own call to Sheriff Maclay issuing the same demands. I expect to hear back from you before 6:00 PM tonight. Otherwise, you can see my press conference live."

"Why me?" John asked as the waitress cleared the table. She eyed my untouched plate. "You don't even like me."

"You're right. I can't stand you. But you're a good cop."

He cocked his head and grinned as he tried to figure out the reason for my compliment. "And how do you know that?"

"Because I've had you watched since you entered the force. If you had crossed the line just once, I would have been there to bring you down."

He laughed. "You're never going to forget that one innocent kiss, are you?"

"Are you going to forgive me for breaking your nose?" I asked.

"No."

"Besides, I like to finish what I start. And your father interrupted me."

"You've had ten years to kick my ass," he said, rising from his chair. "What are you waiting for?" he taunted.

I looked up at him but remained sitting. I was tempted but realized my anger toward him had disappeared a long time ago.

But it was still fun to antagonize him.

"Mattie made me promise not to touch you. But that doesn't mean I won't put you behind bars the first chance I get. They'll be plenty of guys that will do my beating for me."

He laughed again. "I can guarantee you'll be behind bars before I ever will. You can get the bill. I wouldn't want to misuse department money by feeding a criminal."

"Six o'clock, Johnny. These people won't be ignored."

He looked at me. "Tell me, Luc. Who exactly are you fighting to protect here? Mattie? Spencer? Angel?"

"All of them. No one else will."

I paid the bill but remained sitting at the table. I thought about ordering more food but knew I wouldn't eat it. My mind was moving too fast.

I still hadn't heard from Orin, so I called his cell phone. I got his voicemail and hung up. I called his office. He was out so I left a message for him to call me. I hoped his disappearance meant he had found a good lead. I tried not to think that it could also mean he was in danger.

CHAPTER 26

▼

Monday, November 8, 2004
3:00 PM
Santa Monica, California

Bill Connor was only eight years old when his mother shot and killed a man. Only eight when he watched that man die.

Seeing a man bleed to death in front of you is hard for any child to forget. But Bill found it much harder to forget the sight of reluctant police officers arresting his mother.

After years of abuse, Bill's mother, Madison Connor, fled with her only son to LA when he was six years old. Fearing her abusive husband would find her one day, she bought a gun and learned how to protect herself. She would never again be scared. And she refused to be weak.

She had rushed into the liquor store with her son in tow when she happened upon the robber. His gun was pointed at the woman behind the register. His focus was on the money she was trying to pull out. He never saw Madison or Bill.

She had feared for her life and the life of her son. That's why she told the jury she pulled her gun and shot the man in the head. The trial was only two weeks long, and the jury ruled it was self-defense.

Bill sat in the front row of that courtroom. He fell in love with the law and everything and everyone that surrounded it. He was in awe of the power of the judge, curious about the jury's reactions, and utterly impressed by both attorneys.

It wasn't law enforcement that punished those that broke the law. And it wasn't law enforcement that protected them. It was the courts—the judge, the jury, and the lawyers.

He vowed that his law firm would help protect those falsely accused of crimes, those mishandled by law enforcement. It didn't matter what they did for a living, nor their monetary status. Everyone deserved their day in court. Even George Pinkle, famous porn producer and actor.

Connor & Associates was located in Santa Monica. They were famous for their cases against the LAPD, the sheriff's department, and other smaller police departments in Southern California. But the bulk of their workload—and their income—came from civil cases.

The office was classy and expensive, more like a museum than an office. It smelled of pine or old books, and the dim lighting encouraged whispering.

The last time I was here, I had delivered a small tape recorder to Bill. I felt out of place then, like a fly at a funeral. I wondered if that was the feeling they were hoping to convey to their clients.

A young college student looked up from the mahogany reception desk to greet me. The desk was too big for him. His smile was even larger.

"Where is Edgar Twaine?" I felt I should have whispered the demand, which only convinced me to yell it.

The young man continued to smile, despite the change in atmosphere. He whispered, "I'm sorry, but he's with a client right now. Would you like—"

"Then interrupt him," I said, throwing a smile back at him.

The boy looked confused and played with his collar. Not sure what to do, the boy finally picked up the phone. Before dialing, he asked, "Can I tell him your name?"

"I'm the one who brought him his biggest fucking case on a silver platter."

He stared at me for another minute before whispering into the receiver. Not liking the response, he dropped the phone back into the cradle and refused to look up. The smile was now gone, replaced with anger or resentment. I wasn't the only one who didn't like Edgar.

"He'll be out in one second," the friendly boy muttered.

"Which office?" I asked. I didn't want to wait.

"He'll be out in a second," he repeated.

I walked around the desk just as Edgar was walking down the hallway with a bald, stocky man. Edgar spotted but ignored me as I approached them and continued talking to his client.

"Excuse me," I interrupted. "This is important. Get lost," I told the man.

Edgar finally turned to me; and fire sprang from his eyes. It reminded me of Big Jim's tattoo. I thought I actually saw steam blow from his ears. I grinned.

His client looked confused but didn't walk away. I pulled out my wallet, grabbed several large bills, and stuffed them into the man's hands.

"Get a new lawyer," I said, then pushed the man away.

"We need to talk," I said.

Twaine turned his back on me and walked down the hallway. "Have they found Spencer yet?" he asked as I followed him into his office. His voice was much calmer than I had expected.

"I believe I told you I would handle the detectives." I slammed the office door behind me. "Was I not clear?"

Edgar turned, then motioned to the black leather couch. "Sit. I'm assuming there is no new information."

"No, there isn't. I would have more if you had stayed out of my business."

"Now, Luc. Stop acting like a child and sit down."

It was just stern enough to make me stop and look at him. I glared at his beady eyes. He was controlled and I hated him for it.

"What the hell were you thinking harassing the department?"

"Spencer and Mattie are personal friends of mine. I was trying to protect Mattie."

"No, I protect Mattie. Not you. All you did was fuck up my investigation. I told you I would take care of it—"

"And you told me you would keep me updated," Edgar snapped.

"There was nothing new to report," I barked back. I hated to be interrupted.

I decided it was time to sit down. I pulled the gun from my pocket and laid it on my lap.

He glanced only briefly at the gun then sat down behind his desk. He didn't seem bothered by the gun and that annoyed me. I looked for any sign of fear and found none. Instead, he played with a gold letter opener.

"Your lack of information led me to *correctly* assume your links to the sheriff's department were insufficient. You had no plan when we previously spoke. I wanted to make sure the detectives were handling this case properly. And I presume you still have no plan. You are obviously incompetent in handling this issue. I believe I should take over from here."

"This isn't a repeat of three years ago. You don't get to ride on my coattails this time around."

He jumped from his seat, the letter opener falling to the desk.

"How dare you say I rode your coattails! The Pinkle case was *my* case, not yours. I spent seven months working that case before it even went to trial. You spent an afternoon in a gay bar."

"You didn't get a Pulitzer," I said, smirking at his anger.

"Fuck the Pulitzer. I got a million dollars. You got shit!" he yelled, pounding his desk.

"It's always about the money with you guys."

"That's right, Luc. It *is* always about the money." Edgar brushed at his suit to calm himself. He sat back down and picked up the letter opener again.

"Stay out of my way. And let me handle the cops."

"I don't trust them, Luc. Did you know they have deputies watching the house? Watching Mattie?"

"Not anymore," I said.

He contemplated this as he played with the letter opener. I saw a quick glance at the gun.

"Then I suggest someone should be watching out for her safety."

I didn't like the way his words sounded like a threat.

"I will take care of Mattie's safety. You stay the fuck away from the detectives. How's that for a plan?" I tucked the gun in my pocket and walked out.

Big Jim called as I left Connor & Associates. He didn't have good news.

"You have a tail. A blue Camry. Woman driver."

"Shit." I scanned the parking lot as I approached Mattie's car. I didn't see the Camry. Nor did I see Big Jim. "Cop?" I asked.

"I don't think so. It's not a pro."

"Can you take care of her?" I asked, driving out of the parking lot.

"Cell phone, sweetheart," he reminded. "Don't do anything stupid."

"Tell me how to lose her."

"Don't bother. If she were a threat, she would have made her move by now. And I can learn more about her if you don't scare her off."

"Thanks, Big Jim."

"Hey, that's what friends are for."

CHAPTER 27

▼

Monday, November 8, 2004
4:40 PM
Malibu, California

I tried not to worry about the woman following me. I felt better knowing Big Jim was watching my back. I needed to concentrate on Angel's murder and clearing Spencer.

I called Orin as I watched the streets outside Mattie's house. He had struck gold. At least he was bragging he did. He had information but wanted to see me in person. We planned to meet at his office in a couple of hours. There was no way I was discussing anything from the house. And I wanted to wait for the call from John. And the clock was ticking.

Mattie was ordering pizza. I left her alone in the kitchen and made a quick call to Sheriff Maclay's office. To his voicemail, I repeated the information on Lito's and Angel's cases and gave him my requests. I felt like a kidnapper listing my demands. If they weren't met, hostages would start to die.

Mattie joined me on the couch when I was done and put her head on my shoulder.

"He's not coming home, is he?" she asked.

"Mattie, you need to keep a positive attitude." It was the best I could offer at the moment. It was stupid of me to not think of the truth.

She shook her head and I saw the tears start to fall again. I hated women who cried, but nothing tore at me more. I wondered what had ever happened to the strong little girl I knew in grade school. When had she become so passive and defenseless?

I was surprised to see how much it pissed me off. I pulled her up and out of the living room.

"Where are we going?" she asked, wiping her eyes.

"I want to take Charlie for a walk. Come with me." I called Charlie and opened the back door. He bounded out and I followed, pulling Mattie out with me.

"Mattie," I whispered, "Spencer's alive. I saw him."

"What?" She searched my face, waiting for some explanation.

"He's in hiding. For his safety and yours. We need some time to sort some things out. Until then, we have to pretend he's still missing. I don't know if the house is bugged, so watch what you say in there."

"I don't understand. Why can't he come home?" she asked.

I saw the glimmer of life come back to her face. She was confused but she was happy. I suddenly felt bad for believing for a second that she wasn't in love with him.

"He fell into something that appears to have gotten others killed."

As fear spread over her face, I regretted my words. Maybe truth wasn't such a good idea after all.

"Don't worry. I'm helping him sort it out. He misses you, and he's worried about you. But you have to stay strong. He'll be home soon."

"Thank you, Luc. I should have known you would help me, help us." She wrapped her arms around my neck and I hugged her back.

"I would do anything for you. You know that."

She fought back more tears.

"I was so scared that everyone was right, that I drove him away."

I looked in her eyes and knew there would be no more lies.

"Sweetheart, a man would have to be crazy to leave you."

Then she kissed me. I should have pulled away. I should have made sure the kiss was innocent, friendly. But when I felt her lips on mine, I faltered. I lingered too long. I tasted that familiar sweetness I remembered from high school. But it was the desire and passion in the kiss that threw me off guard.

It wasn't me that forced the kiss deeper. She kissed me deeper, stronger. I felt her mouth open and my head begin to spin. The same feeling that had left me breathless once before returned.

But this kiss was far from the innocent kiss in high school. I heard her moan and I drowned.

I wanted more. I needed more. The thought had me pulling back forcefully. I took several steps backward and stared at her. I wanted her. The thought had me reeling. I felt sick and disgusted with my weakness.

I could have survived if I had seen anger in her eyes. I would have reveled in the yelling. But the confusion I saw in her eyes clawed at me. And I knew I wouldn't survive.

Neither of us said anything. Instead of talking, I turned away. I needed to get away from her. I walked back into the house. Once there, I realized I couldn't stay in the house. In their house.

"Luc, wait." Mattie followed me inside, but I didn't stop.

I grabbed my cell phone and the keys to her Mercedes and walked out the front door, slamming it behind me. She didn't follow me out.

I drove to the closest bar I could find. It was a country bar, but I didn't care. As long as they served alcohol and it wasn't a gay bar, it would do. My first plan was to get very drunk. I threw a twenty on the bar and ordered two shots of whiskey. If things worked out, my second plan was to get laid.

I didn't care that I had been dry for more than three years. All I wanted to do was punish myself for the things that had run through my mind when I was kissing her.

Garth Brooks played from the speakers behind me. The Lakers game was playing on the big screen. People cheered then went back to their drinks, knowing the Lakers had no chance to make the playoffs without Shaq.

I was into my fourth shot when my cell phone rang. I wondered if it was Mattie. I picked up the phone, prepared to yell at her. I didn't know what to say other than I wanted to be left alone. I wasn't sure if I was happy or sad to not hear her voice on the other end.

"Luc, it's Lieutenant Carliss."

"Hi, Johnny. You better have good news for me." I said. I checked my watch. It was just before six. John had just beaten the deadline.

"Good for who? I checked the case you gave me and you were right. The case exists. Planting of evidence, harassment, and unlawful use of force. The Figueroa case was settled out of court and the county paid the tab.

"Apparently Detective Ward already started down that road and pulled the case a couple of days ago. He seems to think the case was a scam. Just like Angel's case. I'm having some deputies look for similar lawsuits in case this scam was widespread."

A tall man with a black cowboy hat bumped me as he reached for his beer. I put the phone down on the bar and poured the whiskey down my throat. I turned and scowled at the cowboy, hoping he would move away. He didn't.

"What the fuck's your problem?" he asked.

He stunk of Stetson and cheap beer.

I pulled the butt of the gun out of my jacket. "You sure you want to curse at me?"

The man's eyes crossed, and his face paled. I smiled. That was the proper response to seeing a gun. The man took his beer and moved to the other side of the bar.

"Luc?"

I tucked the gun back in my pocket and put the phone back to my ear.

"If the case was a scam, why didn't the department fight the charges?"

"I don't know that yet. But it was a civil case. No criminal charges were ever brought against the deputies. Figueroa and his lawyer agreed to that in the settlement."

"Were the deputies punished?" I asked.

"I think you'll be surprised to know that all the deputies involved were released from duty."

"Why the cover-up then?"

"There was no cover-up, Luc. The media wasn't alerted because neither side thought it would benefit anyone. The cops denied the charges but were glad that there were no criminal charges brought against them personally. The department and the county paid their tabs. The deputies left the force and were able to move on with their lives."

"What about Hatcher and Medina?"

"There is nothing in their records. I won't say your source is lying, but it looks questionable. Internal affairs never opened a case on them. They are now looking into all of their past arrests."

I wasn't sure whether to believe the information. I would process it later. I took another shot from the bar.

"What about my demands?" I asked. I hoped no one at the bar was eavesdropping. I quickly scanned the bar. The cowboy at the other end of the bar was staring into his beer. No one cared what I was doing.

"The deputies watching the house have been brought back to research this case to see how it connects with Spencer's disappearance. And I talked to Sheriff Maclay. He's made me your point person. I got what you asked for. Now I need something from you."

"What?"

"I need to talk to Spencer. No warrants. Just questioning."

"I'll see what I can arrange."

He gave me his direct number. I promised to contact him soon. I called Dr. Waldhanz and left a message on his voicemail that I wanted to talk to him again. I didn't mention Spencer.

I ordered another whiskey and looked around the bar. A young Hispanic woman sitting at the bar was watching me. She wasn't there when I walked in. I smiled and she smiled back.

She looked familiar, but I couldn't think who she reminded me of. Her eyes scanned the bar then flicked back to me every so often.

I turned back to my drink. She moved over to me and introduced herself. I quickly forgot her name. It wasn't important. I introduced myself only as Luc. The second part of my plan was moving along just fine.

"Where are you from?" she asked. I quickly wondered if she was a hooker. She had the demeanor and attitude, but her eyes didn't match. She was too pretty. Her mouth was painted red, her smile big. She had several earrings dangling from both ears. She looked too young to be hanging out in a bar picking up strange men.

"Nowhere." I waved the bartender over and ordered two more shots of whiskey. I handed him another twenty.

"Where are you staying?"

"Nowhere." I didn't want to think of Mattie. The bartender returned with the shots and I handed the woman one. She didn't drink it. She toyed with a large emerald ring on her finger. I knew it wasn't real.

The alcohol was already having an effect on me. I didn't try to hide it.

"Can we go to your place?" I asked. "I prefer not to fuck in a car."

She blinked, pretended to be shocked, and then sneered.

"Sorry. I didn't realize you were an asshole."

I shrugged and got up. I threw another twenty on the bar for good measure. Determined not to feel like a rejected jerk, I headed toward the door.

"You're too drunk to drive." The woman followed me out to Mattie's car. She was persistent. Or desperate. Or maybe liked the way I threw money around.

"I'm fine," I insisted. I leaned up against the car and looked at her. I noticed the shortness of her skirt and her long, thin legs. She smelled like lemons.

"Sure you won't reconsider? I promise the ride is well worth it."

She walked over and shoved a napkin in my palm.

"Call me when you're not so drunk and obnoxious." She walked back into the bar.

"That might be awhile," I muttered to myself. I threw the napkin in the passenger seat and got in.

CHAPTER 28

▼

Monday, November 8, 2004
7:18 PM
Torrance, California

I didn't realize where I was headed until I saw the sign for Torrance. It had been more than seven years since I had last seen the two-story apartment building. I wasn't surprised to see it had aged faster than I had.

I parked the car and walked across the deserted street toward the barren apartments. The sun had fallen past the horizon and the coming darkness made the street look like a scary movie. The cold had already started its attack. As soon as the fog rolled in, the animals would take over the streets.

I looked up at the apartment labeled 204. The numbers were barely legible, but I knew which one was mine. The apartments were vacant. An eviction notice still hung from one door.

According to my social workers, I had spent my first three years with my mother on the streets. She was an addict and probably a whore. I was never sure if it was crack or heroin, so I had tried both when I was younger. Neither stuck.

This guy who claimed he was my father took me when I was three. They were never married as far as I knew, so he could have been a john or just some guy my mom bought drugs from. Either way, I never saw her again.

The next few years, I learned what real pain was. The intense crushing of hunger ached in my stomach day after day. There wasn't a night that went by that I didn't think about eating. I ate live cockroaches and crickets when I could find them. I ate crumbs from the gutters just to have something in my mouth. The pain was overpowering. Suffocating. I didn't think there was anything worse.

My father spent those years teaching me how to shoplift and pick pockets. It was easier for a child, he explained. I spent my days stealing whatever I could get my hands on just to have it stolen from that prick.

When night came, I would find a cold corner to hide in and hope the predators would stay away. The pain in my stomach clawed at me continuously and the fear of being beaten, stabbed, or killed while I slept was almost as excruciating as the hunger.

When the social worker moved us into a one-bedroom house in Hollywood, I didn't complain. At least I had a roof over my head. I even had a mattress on the floor to sleep. And I refused to let fear run my life. I had to survive.

I learned that I needed to take care of myself if I was going to survive. And I did pretty well. I learned to steal just enough to hide and enough to hand over to my father. I kept the food for myself and handed over all the money to him. I didn't need the money. I just needed to eat. I needed to keep the pain away.

Then the asshole lost his job. I was never sure if it was because of the alcohol or the fact that he never showed up. Either way, we ended up back on the streets.

But I used the time well. I learned how to steal without getting caught. I learned how to pick a lock faster than I could lock it and use everyday items to do it. Carrying a pick could land you in jail faster than a loaded gun. There were always burglaries waiting to be pinned on someone.

And I learned how to protect myself against the scariest of criminals. I carried a knife wherever I went. I learned fast, no matter how great my aim, to never throw it. That was just an easy way to lose my weapon. When I used my knife, I was always face to face. It hardened me and made me respect pain.

I started drinking then. Not only because it was readily available from my father, but also because I liked how it numbed my emotions. I was finally able to escape the pain and fear. Years later, I dropped the bottle. I realized that feeling the pain was better than not feeling anything at all.

I lived so long on the streets that when social services found me a year later and arranged for us to move into a two-bedroom apartment in Torrance, I went from living in hell to a castle beyond my dreams. I had a room of my own. A bed with a blanket. We even had a refrigerator and an oven. It was perfect.

The apartment was cheap. That was how I met Mattie. If the apartment in Torrance had been too expensive, I would have wound up dying in some other town far away from Mattie. I would never have reached the age of twenty-nine. I would never have become anything.

My life began here. My life hadn't become easier. In fact, I had several obstacles to overcome. But it was here that I learned what hope was and how it could change everything.

I was forced to go to school. I was so far behind that I ended up in remedial classes. I couldn't read or write. But I could scare the shit out of the teachers. Or I could wink and have them loving me. But I found it a waste of time. I needed to be out stealing. School would get me nowhere.

I had met Joey first. He was dealing outside the apartments. We became friends, something I knew little about. But we became instant partners in crime. He had risen above picking pockets to breaking and entering. He had the contacts and I had the skill. We fed off each other.

Joey and I had gone out to steal from the rich Manhattan Beach residents, only blocks from our bad neighborhood. Mattie had caught me stealing lemons from her father's tree. Perched in her tree house nearby, she watched over me.

She was the most beautiful thing in the world. And I would have done anything for her. She promised to leave her privileged prep school if I promised to walk her to school every day. The fear of losing her had me making promises to do more than survive. For the first time, I wanted to live.

A "for sale" sign was stuck in the dirt like a tombstone. I wrote the number down. Maybe when I sobered up, I would call and buy the building.

The last time I came here, I came here to die. When I felt hope falling from me, and I wanted to end it here. Where the hope had first sprung.

The telephone call from Mattie that had driven me out of the dorm room that night sent me back to the streets. She had dumped Carl. She didn't want to tell me why, but I knew something was wrong. She finally told me he had hit her.

I slammed down the phone and walked out. Spencer watched me leave but didn't stop me. He knew better.

Two weeks later, I woke in that old apartment, waiting for death or the police to drag me away. It had been abandoned months earlier and I lay on the floor of my old bedroom, surrounded by my own filth. Bottles of Jack Daniel's thrown in one corner. Rats and cockroaches scurrying across me. Vomit and blood everywhere.

At the time, I was surprised that Spencer had found me. I always wondered if he realized how close I had come to putting the gun in my mouth and pulling the trigger. He had saved me that night and yet never asked what had happened to me.

I was pretty sure he wouldn't want to know.

"This barrio ain't yours anymore, *pediche*."

A familiar voice interrupted my memories. I knew who it was before I saw him. Only one person had ever called me a beggar.

Chavez had looked old when I was eighteen. And yet he looked like he hadn't aged since, just a little rounder around the waist. His black hair was slicked back and pulled to a small ponytail. White T-shirt and khaki pants worn loose and low was his standard uniform. Not much had changed.

"Chavez." I turned to face him. "How's your house?"

I kept my eyes on his hands, thankful they were still empty. But I knew it was only a matter of time. He never went anywhere unarmed.

"How's your friend?" he spat back. "Still dead?"

"I should have made sure you were in it when I burned it to the ground. But I wanted you to watch as your drugs burned up. The fire was brilliant. Lit up the whole sky. You did get to see it, right?" I smiled, remembering that night of alcohol and tears.

"Did you know I was aiming for you that night?"

"Your aim's always been as crooked as your dick, Chavez."

"What the fuck you doin' here?" he asked.

I watched a second man walk just outside the shadows and stand behind Chavez. I pulled the gun from my pocket before Chavez had a chance to react. I pointed it at his forehead and smiled.

"You were always slower than shit," I muttered.

Chavez didn't look worried. I didn't expect him to. I heard a rustling behind me and I guessed there was a gun now pointed at my head.

"You know I have you outnumbered. You touch me and you'll drop like a fly."

"Have I ever been scared to die, Chavez? Tell your boys to back off."

"Why?"

"First, because I know you wouldn't want them taking care of something you have waited all your life to finish. And second, because I need information, not a score to settle."

"Get that gun outta my fuckin' face and we'll chat."

I lowered the gun but kept it pointed at his heart.

"Don't make me shoot you in the chest. I really want to see your face explode when the time comes."

He turned his back on me just to show I didn't scare him. I thought it was pretty ballsy since I was still debating whether I would let him live.

"*Ahi te huacho*," he yelled to the hired gun behind him. "I'll take care of this *cabrón* myself." The man turned to walk off.

"And the guy behind me," I mentioned.

Chavez turned back to face me. He was smiling. He whistled and I heard the rustling move away.

"So let's talk, *pediche*."

I moved quickly and put the gun back on his forehead. I wanted him to feel the cold metal on his skull. He didn't flinch. I wondered why only cowboys seem to be scared of my gun.

I reached in with my left hand and grabbed a pistol from his waist and a switchblade from his pocket. I threw both behind me.

Feeling a little more in control of the situation, I lowered my own gun. Chavez only smiled. It only made me slightly nervous.

"I want to know what you know about Angel Martinez."

He shrugged. "He was a pusher, like you."

"Like me?" I asked, raising an eyebrow.

"Not exactly like you. He never stole from me. He worked a small territory in Lynwood. He was smart enough not to play around with my dope and he always paid me on time."

"What did he push for you?" I asked.

"Mostly pot."

"Cocaine?" I asked.

He didn't answer. I didn't need him to.

"He always paid you on time? What about when he got lifted?" I asked.

"I went to see him after he was released. Personally. Told him I didn't care how he unloaded the goods, long as I got paid. He told me he would get me my money. The following week, he paid me in full."

"How did he get the money?"

"He told me he was suing the cops. His lawyer dropped him some money. He told me he wanted out. I said see ya."

"And that was it? You ended on good terms?"

"Of course. I only get pissed off when I lose money. Which, by the way, you still owe me over two grand. And that's not counting the drugs you burned up. We had a deal."

I smiled at him. "Deals don't apply to criminals, Chavez. You know that better than anyone."

"I answered your questions, now you can answer mine. Why you askin' questions 'bout Angel? You workin' for the *puerco* now?"

"You probably should have asked me if I was working for the cops before admitting to the drugs, dumbshit."

He smiled too, as if he had a secret he was waiting to spring on me.

"I'm not scared of you, Luc. I didn't know back then what your soft spot was. But I do now. Don't think I haven't been keeping my eyes on that beautiful *ruca* of yours, Mattie."

I raised the gun back to his head. I tried to hold back the fury as I looked into his cold eyes.

"You don't want to know what I did to the last person who mistreated her," I growled through clenched teeth. My finger itched on the trigger.

"I hear her husband's missing. Guess I'm not your only enemy."

"Did you have anything to do with it?" I asked, my eyes narrowing on his face.

He laughed. "If I was gonna hurt you, I wouldn't go after the suit. I would have fucked that beautiful girl of yours right there in her quaint little Malibu home. I would have made you watch, too."

I felt my head spinning from anger as I tried to hold onto my restraint. My finger felt heavy against the trigger as I fought for control.

I was just a little disappointed as I watched Chavez's head jerk backward. His body collapsed to the ground in spasms before I even heard the shot. I jumped back so the pooling blood wouldn't find its way to me.

CHAPTER 29

▼

I spun around, my gun ready to take out anything that moved. I recognized the figure walking toward me.

"What the fuck did you do?" I asked, lowering the pistol.

Big Jim looked down at the dead body of David Chavez.

"Just did what you were too slow to do. He was reaching for a weapon."

Big Jim leaned down and pulled the six-inch blade Chavez had hidden on his back.

"Your anger always made you blind."

I looked around. Where had Big Jim shot from? What if his aim hadn't been accurate?

"He had friends," I said.

"They're being taken care of." He was calm as he looked down at the body. "Stupid piece of shit."

He kicked the limp body. I hear him mutter something about respecting women.

My head was clearing from the alcohol. The echo of the gunshot rang in my ears. I looked down the street.

"What about my tail?"

"You lost her. I got a plate number though. I'll see if I can find someone to run it after I clean this mess up."

"Thanks, Jim."

I stared down at the dead drug dealer. I wish I had been the one to pull the trigger. I put the gun in my pocket.

"You should get out of here. You don't want anyone noticing that nice car of yours."

"Shit. I'm going to be a suspect if the cops connect Chavez to Angel. I don't have an alibi." I looked at the pistol and switchblade I dropped earlier. "I need to wipe those."

Jim looked at my hands. "Why the hell aren't you wearing gloves?"

"I didn't come here to knock off a drug dealer, Jim."

"Why the hell did you come here then?"

I looked up at the apartment building.

"I needed to come home."

He laughed. "Man, you can't find home in an abandoned building. Get the hell out of here. I'll make sure no one ever finds our friend here. You won't even need that damn alibi."

"Thanks again, Jim." I said, walking back to my car. It was good to have bad friends.

It was almost ten when I arrived in Orin's office at the *Reporter*. He made no comment about the stench of alcohol that followed me in. Instead he waved me to follow him. We walked into the conference room. The large oak table was covered with old newspapers, typewritten stories, and handwritten notes.

I was astonished that Orin had found so much information. I looked at him. He was smiling at the mess on the table.

"Where do I start?" I asked.

"Let's start with Angel Martinez. We'll go back in time to the other cases later. Angel is much more interesting."

I sat down at the table and he threw some papers at me. I tried to skim the information quickly so I could process it later. We had a lot of information to cover.

Because I didn't read fast enough, Orin narrated for me.

"Angel Martinez was born on October 8, 1985, at Good Samaritan Hospital in Los Angeles."

"That's where I was born," I said absently.

Orin looked up from his notes. "Really?"

"Well, not quite. I was actually born in the alley about a block away."

Orin continued to stare at me. I realized I had never talked to Orin about my childhood.

"My mother was a street whore. She named me Luc because she couldn't spell Lucifer. At least that's what my father used to tell me."

"Lucifer? Like the devil?"

I grinned. "Leader of the fallen angels." I shrugged. "I lived on the streets with her for awhile before my father took me. Then I met Mattie."

I looked back down at the notes. Orin realized I was finished talking.

"Angel was born homeless, too. Ana Martinez had recently been kicked out of her parent's house and the father wanted nothing to do with her, let alone a baby. A nurse heard she was homeless and asked the chaplain to help her. They found her a place to live and a job close to home."

"How did you get this information?" I asked as he shifted to another stack of notes.

"His mother. I talked to her after the funeral."

He handed me some cards.

"Here are Angel's report cards." He smiled as I flipped through them. "Since kindergarten."

"Damn proud of yourself, aren't you?" I opened the first one and read the teacher's comments aloud. "Angel is a good student. He shows a thirst for knowledge and is always trying to figure out how things work."

"He made friends easily and was a good student. He excelled in English, spelling, literature, and even history," Orin continued. "At about the sixth grade, his grades in math and science started falling behind."

"I always sucked at math, too. Mattie had to help me pass algebra."

"Ana tried to help Angel," Orin continued, "but with her job taking so much of her time, he started falling further and further behind.

"The school was on track to becoming a California Distinguished School, a great honor in the education field. Unfortunately, those students failing classes lowered the school's average. Angel failed two math classes and was on his way to failing a physical science class. Suddenly he was kicked out of school."

"Fucking system," I muttered.

"The school claims they found him gambling in the parking lot. His mother doesn't think so. She tried to fight it, but Angel had no choice. He had to attend Sutter Regional if he wanted a high school diploma."

I knew the school. It was filled with teen mothers, gangbangers, and drug addicts. It was a haven for crime and punishment. It's where the dealers on the streets found their recruits. I knew there was only one path Angel could take.

"His mother said Angel started to hang out with the wrong crowd. She didn't make a big deal out of it, because for the first time in a long time, Angel wanted to go to school every morning.

"According to his friends, Angel made a killing at the school. Because he had the ability to make friends wherever he went, he found he had a talent for unloading large amounts of pot. And because he had no desire to try the drugs himself and was really reliable, the suppliers came to him first.

"When the money started coming in, he realized he could help his mom out and possibly move out of the city if he made enough money. He stopped attending classes and worked on getting a bigger clientele. He was arrested twice as a minor."

Orin handed me the rap sheet with the drug charges. Possession for a minor. Angel was sent to juvenile detention both times. The first time he spent two weeks. The second showed he was given two months and was required to visit a drug counselor.

It took him off the streets, and he lost clients. Even worse, he had lost what dope he had when he was arrested and to pay Chavez he would have to dip into his own savings.

"Last month, on his eighteenth birthday, Angel was again arrested for dealing," Orin handed me a folder.

The arrest record showed he had a shitload of pot and two rocks of cocaine. He was arrested in front of his home. The arrest sheet said he did not resist. I suspected the arrest report was not accurate.

I found it interesting that the deputies had been in the neighborhood the day he turned eighteen. He was an adult now and could be prosecuted as such.

Orin had also been able to locate his arrest picture. It was just a face shot, but I noticed he looked different than the young man in the pictures his mother displayed at the house.

He was tougher, stronger. He had a gang tattoo on his neck and a scar on the right side of his chin. If I had seen this man on the street, I would have turned the other way.

"The day Angel made bail, he walked into the emergency room at Good Samaritan Hospital."

Orin smiled as he handed me a copy of Angel's medical records. I wanted to ask how he had found them, but I knew I wouldn't get an answer. Journalists liked to keep their sources to themselves.

"He was not admitted to the hospital but the reporting doctor in the ER summarized his injuries. He had two bruised ribs, possibly broken. He had several bruises on his stomach and chest. The doctor could tell he had been in a fight. And they were consistent with being beaten with both hands behind his back."

There was a photo in this file as well. Angel's body was badly bruised. Not only had Angel been in a fight; he had obviously lost. I focused on Angel's face. There were no marks on his face. Whoever had beaten him up had stayed away from his face. Just like my father had.

"And he ends up dead a month later," I put the notes on the table and rubbed my eyes. "Why?" I asked.

Orin didn't answer.

I got up to pace. "Angel and I are so similar. We have the same background, dealt the same bad hand. Yet he ends up six feet under. Why not me?"

"You know how to bluff."

I cocked my head and looked at him. "What?"

"You got a bad hand, but you convinced everyone that you could win despite it. You survived when others would have folded."

"It's a strange game."

Orin nodded. "In poker, rarely does the best hand win."

I thought of Mattie. I shook my head. I had to concentrate on one mess at a time.

"So do you think the department is trying to cover this case up?"

"At this point, it looks that way. You said yourself you didn't trust those cops. And the case looks strong. Other than the deputies that arrested him or the department itself, there was no one that had a reason to kill Angel."

The evidence was vague, but depending on a jury, I felt the information we had would probably be enough to get the sheriff's department in a lot of trouble. I picked up my phone and called John's cell phone.

"I want to meet with the arresting deputies. The two that arrested Angel last month."

"No."

I didn't like the answer or the tone so I waited. John didn't seem to like the silence.

"Why?" John asked.

"I want to know more about Angel. I need to know how strong his case was against the sheriff's department." I didn't mention the information I had in my hands.

"There was no case, Luc."

I heard him sigh and let the silence come.

"Fine, I'll set something up tomorrow. Completely off the record. When can I see Spencer?"

"After the meeting." I hung up the phone.

Orin was still smiling. "Can I be there?"

"No."

He shrugged and waited. The silent treatment didn't work on me.

"Let's move to Spencer's involvement."

He handed me some handwritten notes. Orin had interviewed Angel's friends. Several friends were on record stating Angel was scared of the cops. He was worried about retaliation from the lawsuit. But he felt confident that his case was strong. He claimed to have a great lawyer and would be getting a huge payout soon.

He was planning on moving his mother and himself out of Los Angeles and away from the crooked cops.

The case was looking stronger. I understood why Spencer was working with Angel. It seemed like an open-and-shut case. But I was concerned with why Angel had picked Spencer to represent him. Spencer wasn't a great trial attorney. He wasn't famous for suing cops. What had drawn Angel to Spencer?

Orin handed me a single sheet. It was a typewritten article on the death of Angel Martinez. It contained the basic information on the murder I had provided earlier as well as quotes from his friends.

There was also some general information about his mother and his desire to move out of Los Angeles and away from the life of drugs and crime. There was no mention of his open case against the sheriff's department or his connection with Spencer Hardwin.

"Can I run this in Wednesday's paper? None of the other papers are talking about Angel. I don't want him to be ignored in all of this."

He knew he didn't need my permission. He could print what he wanted. Unfortunately, he also knew I would withhold additional information if he didn't play it the way I wanted it played.

"Give me until Thursday," I said. I hoped I would have something more by then. "I want to run another article with it."

"About what?" he asked.

"I want to announce that Spencer Hardwin has been found."

He smiled at me. "Has he?"

"By Thursday, he better be." I looked at the rest of the pages. "What's the rest of this?"

"This is what I found on Lito's case. The lawyer's still alive—Ron Mert."

"Really? We have a live person?" I asked.

He handed me some notes.

"He's had lots of cases against the sheriff's department. Most have been kept quiet. Several settled quietly for large sums of money before ever hitting the courts. It seems he had found his calling in suing the department and the county of Los Angeles. And his other clients are still alive, as far as I can tell."

I smiled. "Great. I want you to find these guys. And I want to talk to the lawyer."

I noticed he was no longer smiling and I felt my hope slither away.

"I've been unable to locate the lawyer."

"God damn it! Everywhere we turn, we find missing persons and dead bodies. What the hell is going on?"

"I think we stepped into some really deep shit. I'm going to spend the rest of the evening—" he looked at his watch and corrected himself, "morning, trying to find the rest of his clients. They're druggies and gangbangers, so it may take some time."

I waved at him as he got up.

"I'm going to go through the cases. I'll meet up with you later."

"Do you need a place to crash?" he asked.

"Not tonight. I'm too wired to sleep now."

Orin nodded. "Hey Luc, I don't know what your plans are, but if you're looking to stay in LA when this thing is all over, there's a job here for you."

"I don't think I'll be staying, Orin. You watched as success broke me down once before."

"Success and money does not bring happiness nor does it bring misery."

"Where the hell do you get these sayings?"

"Whatever you do, Luc, don't stop fighting."

CHAPTER 30

▼

Tuesday, November 9, 2004
10:00 AM
Commerce, California

I didn't sleep. After a night of murder, missing persons, and dirty cops, I was frustrated and cranky—but not sleepy. I didn't think I could handle the dreams anyway.

Carliss arranged for me to talk with Deputies Crane and Italsano at ten. The meeting was in a small conference room. The deputies were seated when I arrived. A union representative sat between them to take notes. Carliss was pacing behind them. No one looked happy to be there.

"Good morning, boys. I appreciate you meeting with me." Neither responded. I pulled out my tape recorder and hit record.

Carliss jumped toward me.

"No way, Luc. No tapes. This is off the record."

"OK," I said, quickly putting the tape recorder back in my pocket. I somehow forgot to turn the recorder off. I didn't care about the law or their rights at this time. I wanted information.

"I understand you two arrested Angel Martinez last month for possessing and selling marijuana and cocaine. Is that correct?"

"Yes, sir," said Deputy Crane proudly.

"Did he resist?" I asked.

"No, sir. As a matter of fact, he was very civil."

Crane smiled but didn't look at me. His eyes shifted from me to Carliss and then back. It was an obvious lie. He sat back in his seat, hoping I would challenge him.

"Did you know that Angel was planning on suing you and the sheriff's department for excessive force and planting of evidence?"

"That's bullshit," Deputy Italsano blurted out. "He can say whatever he wants—doesn't make it true. He's just a lousy drug dealer."

I smiled. "Funny thing is that Angel can't seem to say anything now. He's dead." The deputies were quiet. They hadn't heard the information. "But I have two things that can say more than Angel can."

I opened my folder and tossed them Angel's hospital pictures.

"See those bruises on his chest? Which one of you had the privilege of giving him those? Were the blows delivered before or after the cuffs were put on?"

"Shit," Crane muttered. He knew where the questioning was going. I noticed he was fidgeting in his seat. He pushed the photos away.

Carliss watched me. But he had also noticed the deputies' reactions.

"What about this?" I threw a stack of pages at them. Italsano looked at the pages. Crane refused.

"It's a medical report. You see, Angel got out of jail and drove straight to the emergency room. Said he got beat up by some cops. The doctor in the ER took his statement."

The union rep briefly glanced through the hospital records and took some notes. Crane still wouldn't look at the pages. I turned my attention to him. I could break him.

"Deputy Crane, take a look at the pictures. It looks like Angel had several bruises in his chest and stomach area. The doctor substantiated his claims that they occurred due to kicks to his midsection. No bruises on the arms. This would coincide with his arms being held, or cuffed, behind his back. Would you know anything about that?"

The union rep scribbled furiously. I heard Carliss pacing behind me. He was getting nervous, and I knew the interview would be over soon.

"We didn't touch him. End of story. Whatever he claims to have happened is a lie." Crane looked directly at me, challenging me to question him again.

"Where were you two on Tuesday afternoon?"

Italsano looked at the union representative.

The rep finally looked up and nodded. "Lieutenant, this interview is over. If a public claim is going to be made, I would like a meeting with the department to see where everyone stands on this."

Carliss nodded. It's what he was waiting to hear.

"I will have to talk to the captain." He turned to me. "Interview's over. Deputies, you are dismissed. Thanks for coming here today. Your cooperation will be noted."

The deputies quickly fled with the union rep in tow.

Carliss sat down next to me. He calmly crossed his hands in front of him and looked at the pictures lying on the table.

"Angel admitted the lawsuit was full of lies, Luc. I don't know why you're still pursuing this angle. These deputies did not kill Angel."

"I have no proof that Angel was lying about the arrest. It could be just another cover-up from the sheriff's department. If Angel's lawsuit was false, why would he call the sheriff's department and offer this information?"

"I don't know. But it looks like he was scared."

"Exactly. And right now everything points to Angel being killed because of the lawsuit. The case looks strong. And who would gain the most if Angel suddenly disappeared?"

He didn't answer. He wouldn't like the answer I had prepared.

"Has Ward found anything at the crime scenes?" I asked.

John didn't answer right away. He looked as if he were debating with himself. Finally he rose and crossed his arms over his chest.

"Not exactly at the scene, but I just found out something you might find interesting."

"What?"

"Angel's autopsy was done last Thursday. Medical examiner said it's possible the perpetrator might have grabbed Angel by the neck before shooting him between the eyes. He was able to get a partial thumbprint."

"Great!" I shouted, getting up. "Any matches?"

"That takes time, Luc. Detective Ward is still running family and friends and anyone who may have had a reason to touch him, in case it didn't belong to the shooter."

"But you had to check Spencer's prints first, right?"

He nodded. "It wasn't a match. It doesn't mean that Spencer didn't kill him, but he is temporarily off our suspect list until we find a match for the print. Ward is verifying the alibi right now. In the meantime, we would really like to talk to him."

"I'll arrange something," I said.

"Luc, don't screw with me. We need to talk to him."

"OK. I'll schedule a meeting in a couple of hours. I'll call you." I looked back at him. "And don't have me followed. I would hate to leak this medical report and the fingerprint story to the press."

I needed a shower and a shave but had no desire to see Mattie. Instead of heading to Malibu, I called Orin and asked if I could crash at his place.

After showering, I gave Orin the rough details of the interview with the deputies, off the record.

Orin hadn't been able to locate any of the clients. He was still searching. I was about to take a nap when my cell phone rang. It was Dr. Waldhanz.

"Good afternoon, Luc. I ran into an old professor of yours," Waldhanz said.

"Really?" I asked, completely confused. I waited for him to continue.

"Yeah. Do you remember Carmen? She said she would love to meet with you." I knew he was lying. Carmen would want nothing to do with me.

"I remember her," I said, hesitating.

"She said she can see you whenever you're available." The words were precise and I knew that he was delivering a message from Spencer.

"Great, I'll have to stop by and see her." I knew exactly where Spencer was.

I borrowed some clothes and a suitcase and headed to Mattie's car.

CHAPTER 31

▼

Tuesday, November 9, 2004
1:02 PM
Los Angeles, California

When I walked into the Hilton Hotel, I headed for the courtesy phone. I knew my way around. Carmen and I had spent many nights here. Spencer has refused to let me bring her back to the dorm room, since she tended to be a bit loud.

I asked for Carmen's room and was transferred. Spencer answered on the first ring.

"Are you here?" he asked. It worried me that he sounded scared.

"Yeah, what floor are you on?" I asked.

I kept my eyes on the front door, making sure I wasn't followed in. Spencer told me he was in room 608. I hung up and went to the registration desk.

I dropped my luggage in my room and headed down the hall to Spencer's room.

"What have you found so far?" Spencer asked as he opened the door.

He held the gun at his side until I closed the door. He was beginning to look comfortable with it and it worried me. I watched him put the gun on the dresser and settle in a chair at the desk.

I told Spencer everything. I held nothing back from him, even allowing him to listen to the audiotapes I had collected so far. He held back tears when he listened to Ana talk about her son. I saw anger when he listened to the deputies that had arrested Angel.

"Angel's case was solid. The arrest report and the medical records are pretty clear. I even had pictures to support the beating claim."

"The deputies are positive he was lying. Angel supposedly called them and told them he was going to lie about the lawsuit."

"I don't understand. Their theory doesn't make any sense. Angel supposedly lies about the case. He then decides he doesn't want to lie and calls the cops. Then he takes off?"

"They claim he was scared of you. And then of course that points to you killing him."

"If he was so scared of me, then why did he call me?"

My cell phone interrupted us. I picked it up, assuming it was Orin with news of a potential witness. Instead it was Carliss.

"Luc, where the hell are you?"

"I'm fucking your mother. Why?"

"What happened to my meeting with Spencer?"

"Oh yeah, that. I decided to postpone due to some last minute developments."

"What developments?"

"Well, I don't think the cops are being totally honest with me about this case. I think Spencer had a good strong case against the sheriff's department and Angel was on the verge of winning a big settlement." I started to pace the room. Spencer watched me.

"You can't hold Spencer hostage from us. We need to speak to him. And I mean now."

"You can talk to him, when I'm confident he's safe."

"Damn it, Luc. I didn't want to do this, but you're not making this easy for me. I'm going to have to put a warrant out for his arrest."

"You don't have enough for a warrant, Johnny. You told me he wasn't even a suspect anymore. If you get a warrant, I hold a press conference."

"Things have changed."

"What changed?" I asked, stopping in my tracks.

"We just learned that Spencer bought a nine millimeter handgun on Friday."

I looked over at the gun on the dresser. "So what?"

"So what?" he yelled. "His client claims to be scared of him. Less than a week later, he is shot with a nine millimeter in the head, and you say so what?"

"It's circumstantial and you know it."

"His alibi doesn't check, Luc. Angel's mother said she didn't see Spencer at all on Monday. We need to speak to him, and we need the gun. We have two deaths and a missing person case that is taking up precious news space. Maclay wants this cleared up now."

"Is he a suspect?" I asked.

"You're damn right he is."

"Then he stays in hiding until I can convince you he is not involved with either death. And remember our deal. You break your end, I go to the press."

"Luc, I can have you arrested for obstruction of justice. I won't bail you out this time. And the media won't be able to save your ass, either."

"You have to find me first," I closed the cell phone and smiled.

"What's going on now?" Spencer asked.

"Well, within the hour, we'll both be fugitives from the law."

I took the nine millimeter from my pocket and placed it next to his gun on the dresser. I looked over at Spencer, then back at his gun. I didn't like how things were adding up.

CHAPTER 32

▼

Tuesday, November 9, 2004
2:30 PM
Los Angeles, California

"When did you buy the gun, Spencer?"

"What?" he answered too absently.

"When did you buy the fucking gun, Spencer?" I asked again. "Don't make me repeat myself."

"Friday," he said, detecting my anger. I could see the fear in him and hoped it was because of me.

"Why? You said you didn't start worrying about the detectives until Monday when you got the call from Angel."

I picked up his gun. It was a nine millimeter, similar to my Browning, but probably not American made. I removed the magazine and was relieved to see the magazine was still full. On the right side, the serial number was scratched off.

He dismissed my question with a shrug, and he wouldn't look at me. I didn't like it. Spencer's case was strong. But Ward's case was getting stronger.

"Why did you buy the gun, Spencer?"

"To protect myself. I told you already."

"Spencer, you didn't hear from Angel until Monday. Why did you feel you had to protect yourself on Friday?"

"I wasn't worried when the detectives questioned me. But I called a friend of mine and he suggested I get a gun to protect myself just in case. He guessed the deputies were behind Angel's disappearance and I might be next. It scared me, but I knew I hadn't done anything wrong. I bought the gun and kept it at the office. It was just for protection."

"What friend?" I asked, concerned.

"Edgar Twaine. He's a lawyer at Connor & Associates."

That explained the call to Bill's office on Friday. It bothered me that Edgar had failed to mention this to me.

"How did you get the gun?"

"He told me the name of this guy. He came down and I filled out all the proper paperwork. He even told me I could waive the waiting period because I was a lawyer. It was legal."

"You are so fucking naive, Spencer. The gun is hot. There is nothing legal about it," I muttered, realizing this was about to get ugly.

"What?" he asked, looking up.

"Did you have the gun when you saw Angel?" I asked.

"Of course."

I wondered how Ward had found out about the gun. If it wasn't a legal purchase, someone had tipped him. Or Edgar had mentioned it.

"Carliss said your alibi didn't pan out. You didn't go see Angel's mother, did you?"

Spencer turned away from my gaze quickly.

"Damn it, Spencer. If you did something wrong, tell me. I just need to know. I can't help you unless I know how much shit you stepped in here."

"I didn't go see Angel's mother. I went to see Twaine."

"Twaine? Why?"

"I didn't want to tell you before. I'm sorry. I'm so sorry." Tears spilled from his eyes. He dropped his head in his hands so I couldn't see his face.

"Tell me—now."

He sniffed, but the tears kept coming.

"Twaine was filing divorce papers."

"What?"

"I know it was bad timing. That's why I had to stop by and see him. He called me and told me he was going to file the papers that morning. I told him to wait and to not mention our meeting to anyone."

"Someone knew about your meeting. And that someone may be trying to set you up."

I needed to make sure Mattie was safe. I called Bill and asked him to stay with Mattie. I needed backup until this was cleaned up. He promised he would stay the night. I was relieved he didn't question me. His concern was always for Mattie.

As Spencer broke down crying, I dialed Orin's cell phone.

"Please tell me you have some news," I begged.

"I may have something. Can I meet you in an hour?" Orin sounded like he was driving.

"Yeah, I'm in room 602 at the Hilton."

"Do you have anything for me?" he asked.

"I do. The sheriff's department is about to name Spencer a suspect," I said. Spencer jumped up from the bed and stared at me.

"Can I print that?" Orin asked.

"Not from me. But you can hound the department to see if they'll issue a statement. You can even ask them about the Angel connection."

"Why?"

"I need the media watching the cops. Keep them busy. And keep them away from me."

"And if I get them to admit to Spencer being a suspect?" Orin asked.

I laughed. "If you get them to admit that, you can print whatever the hell you want."

I hung up the phone and Spencer stared at me. "What are you thinking giving that information to the media?"

"Orin can't print the information without corroboration from someone in the sheriff's department or you could sue for libel. He won't get the information from the sheriff's department until a warrant is issued. John can't issue a warrant without me."

"So why tell the media anything?"

"I need as many people as possible watching this case."

"This is getting way out of hand. We need to find out what the hell is going on."

"Yes, we do." I turned to him. "Let's start with you telling me the truth."

I was pacing in my small room when I heard a knock on the door. I was expecting Orin. I opened the door to find John Carliss with his gun in my face.

He was wearing jeans and an LA County Sheriff's polo shirt. He quickly stuck his foot in the doorway so I couldn't close it on him. I looked down the hall and was glad to see he was alone.

"Come on in, Johnny," I said, ignoring the gun. "How did you find me?"

"I'm good at my job," he said, holstering the weapon. The door slammed behind him.

"We had an agreement. I told you I didn't want to be followed."

"I didn't break the agreement. No one was following you." His hands clenched at his side. "I triangulated the position of your cell phone and canvassed the neighborhood. Once I saw the hotel, I figured you would be hiding out here. The desk clerk was all too happy to identify you."

"I can't help it if I make a great first impression." I smiled and sat on the bed. "Where's Spencer?"

"He's here." I had barely said the words before John snatched the radio off his belt.

"Hatcher, check registration for a Spencer Hardwin." He noticed me watching him. "He probably didn't register with his own name, so show the lady the picture. If she can't find him, have her go through all the men that checked in today."

I knew he wouldn't find Spencer. I must have been smiling because he added one more thing.

"If you still can't find him, check all the men that have checked in since Monday and are still here."

I knew that Dr. Waldhanz had checked Spencer in two days ago as Carmen, his daughter. It would take the deputies all night to find him. I wondered when they would get frustrated enough to just ask me.

"And when Detective Ward gets here, send him to room 602."

"Am I under arrest?" I asked when he tossed the radio on the bed next to me.

"After I kick your ass," he said. From the look in his eye, he was ready for a fight. His fists were still clenched. I didn't stand up.

"You know you didn't come out on top the last time, Johnny. Since I put my gun down the last time, I am going to have to ask you to put yours down now."

The mention of his gun must have reminded him that he was still a cop and he could get in a lot of trouble for touching me.

I was only a little disappointed when the rage left his eyes and just a little thankful since I remembered how well he could fight.

"This is your fault. You specifically asked for me to be on this case. Now my job is on the line. I won't let you screw with my career, Luc. Tell me what the hell is going on before I drag you down and throw you in a dark cell."

"I'm sorry, Johnny. But Spencer isn't guilty of this. I'm positive about that. I just needed to buy some time for my information to get here."

"What information?" he asked. "No more bullshit. I need to know everything."

We both jumped at the knock on the door.

CHAPTER 33

▼

Tuesday, November 9, 2004
2:42 PM
Los Angeles, California

"We have a suspect," Orin said, looking from Carliss to me. He had folders in his hand and a cell phone plastered to his ear. He hung up the phone and walked in.

He dropped the files on the dresser and looked at me. Since I didn't say anything, he continued.

"A Ron Mert. He was the attorney in several cases against the sheriff's department. And I think many of them were bogus, including Lito Figueroa's case," he explained to Carliss.

Carliss shook his head and looked at me. "Ward's been following the same leads. You should have been working with him on this, Luc."

"But does Detective Ward have a witness?" Orin asked proudly. His eyes sparkled and I knew he had the information we needed.

There was another knock on the door. I was starting to get really tired of the interruptions. I opened the door and allowed Detective Ward in. He had ditched the jacket and his sleeves were rolled up. There was sweat on his brow and I wondered if he had been running.

I smiled at him but he scowled back at me. He ignored the others in the room. I guessed he wasn't too happy with me. It was just too easy to pass up.

"Not much of a detective, are you, Ward? You are the very last person to find me."

"I am beginning to really hate you, Actar." He closed the door behind him. "I have been more than generous with my information and instead of reciprocating, you went over my head."

"Generous?" I said. "You held back every piece of information you had."

"I gave you Angel Martinez!" he yelled back. "You know you had shit before that."

"How long have you been looking at Ron Mert?" I asked. "Were you going to tell me or were you planning on helping him with the cover-up?

"Fuck you!"

"Keep your dick in your pants, Ward. It's not going to get you any promotions in here."

He moved closer to me. I could see the anger boiling over in his eyes. I had touched just the right nerve.

"Back off, Detective," Lieutenant Carliss snapped. I'm sure he would have loved to watch, but he just didn't want the hassle of a cleanup. "We have a lot to cover."

Ward stepped back but kept his eyes on me. I had obviously hit a sore spot. I made a mental note to get the full story of Ward's extracurricular activities in the department.

I turned back to Orin. "Who is this witness?"

"What witness?" Ward asked. "A witness to what?"

I looked back at him.

"While you were out hitting on other detectives, we did some investigating of our own."

"Shut up, Luc," Carliss said. He was getting impatient with me. I only grinned at him.

Orin took a look around the room and knew he would have to ease the tension.

"As the Irish say, the end of a feast is better than the beginning of a fight. I found Judy Keen. She was a prostitute that was arrested last year. The arresting deputies asked her to become an informant and she refused. She was thrown in jail and released the next day.

"The word on the street was she talked, so when she got out, she got her face beat in. A friend on the street told her to hire a lawyer and sue the cops. She didn't think she had a case, but the friend told her to go see Ron Mert.

"Mert listened to the story and suggested a spin. If she was willing to testify that the cops did the beating and not her pimp, he could get her some quick cash. She agreed.

"It was easy," Orin continued. "Mert handled the paperwork. All she had to do was see a doctor and get a copy of the notes. The case was settled without her having to say a word or having to face the deputies. She got a hundred thousand dollars."

"Is she willing to testify to this?" Carliss asked, pulling his notepad out.

"Of course. She's scared of him, but she's also broke. She spent all the money putting drugs up her nose and she begged for more. He refused to see her."

Ward's cell phone rang and he walked to the other side of the room to talk privately. I wondered if they had found Spencer yet.

"Where is Keen now?" I asked. I didn't want to lose the only lead we had.

"Actually, she's in jail. She was arrested on a drug charge this morning."

I looked at Carliss. He grabbed his radio. "I'll make sure she's safe."

Detective Ward got off the phone at the same time Carliss finished checking on Keen.

"She's fine," Carliss informed us. "I have someone watching her. We'll head over and conduct a full interview when we're done here. What do you have, Ward?"

"Despite my lack of investigation skills," he shot a glance at me, "we got a witness to the Figueroa shooting."

I smiled at him. "The nosy neighbor to the right?"

"How did you know?" he asked.

"She was watching us when we visited Lito's dead body."

He turned back to Carliss, trying his best to ignore me. "She just identified a picture of Ron Mert."

"What about Angel?" Orin asked.

Ward looked at Orin, then at Carliss. He was unsure whether he should be answering questions from a reporter. He finally shrugged.

"Ballistics confirmed the same gun was used on both Martinez and Figueroa. Same shot through the skull. I have to assume at this point that Ron Mert took them both out. We'll see if the fingerprint on Angel's throat matches."

"Great. Then we need to pick up Mert." Carliss looked at Ward.

"With the positive ID, we issued an APB. Hopefully we'll pick him up before nightfall," Ward said.

"OK. So we know Ron Mert was making money with false claims against the sheriff's department. We have Judy Keen to corroborate this. Lito's dead and can't tell his story. How does Angel fit into this? Mert wasn't his attorney."

We were missing something, the link.

"We need to connect Angel's case to Ron Mert," Carliss thought aloud. "We need someone to corroborate Angel's story about the case being a scam. Angel can't tell us about the scam. He didn't tell his mother—"

"No," I interrupted again. "If he told anyone, he told his best friend, Lito. He can't corroborate the story."

"What about a girlfriend?" Orin asked.

"Girlfriend?" I asked, looking at Orin. I was surprised I hadn't thought to ask Angel's mother the possibility of a girl in his life.

Ward looked at me, cocked his head and grinned.

"Not such a great detective yourself, huh?" He turned back to Carliss. "He had a girlfriend. I've been unable to locate her. I'm meeting with her family in an hour."

"I want to come," I insisted.

"No. You'll want to stay with Spencer." Carliss stared at me, begging me to challenge him.

"Is Spencer off the hook?" I asked.

Carliss nodded. "We have Mert for both murders. But we need to hear Spencer's story. Can we see him now?"

I smiled and opened the door. Everyone followed me.

CHAPTER 34

▼

2001
Los Angeles

Luc sat in his new office—eight floors up, overlooking the LA skyline. He ignored the papers covering his desk. There was only one he wanted to read. He glanced again at his article. He was proud of it. More than he had been proud of anything in his life. He was somebody. People would recognize his name. His editors were already talking Pulitzer Prize.

He owed it all to Bill of course. And to Mattie for saving him.

When his phone rang, he thought briefly of letting the voice mail pick up. He was tired of fielding questions from other reporters. And he still had several follow-up stories to write. But he hit the speaker button with just a hint of a smile.

"Congratulations, Luc," Mattie said.

The sound of her voice danced through the speakerphone. Luc picked up the phone. He didn't want to share her voice with anyone. He closed his eyes, the smile disappearing.

"Hi, Mattie," Luc said. "How's Dad?"

"He's going to be busy for a while. He has decided to sue the county and the department."

"That's great."

Luc pulled off his jacket and threw it on the desk. He reached for his coffee, then realized he had left the lemon in the kitchen.

"Dad is having a little party to celebrate tonight. He wants you to be there."

"I'll see what I can do." He looked at his calendar. It was already full. He would have to move things around.

"Good. I want to see you, too. It's been awhile."

"I've been busy—the story, the career." Luc sipped at the black coffee. He needed a drink, something stronger. Sweat beaded at his temples.

"Too busy for me?" she teased.

"Never. I'd give it all up for you." And he knew it was true.

It was too hot. He felt his body boiling. He reached for the window.

"You've been avoiding me again, Luc."

"I'll be there." He cleared his throat. He didn't want to get into that discussion again. "Will Spencer be there?"

"I have to call him next. We've been busy with the wedding plans. We both can use the break tonight."

The wedding was less than a week away. She would be Mrs. Spencer Hardwin. Mattie would be gone forever. He wondered where that left him.

"I have to go, Mattie. I have to finish this story."

He heard her sigh. He tried to take a deep breath, but his lungs caught. He wanted a cigarette. He dismissed whether it was because he needed the warmth or the drug. Nothing would comfort the pounding in his head.

He was losing. And he knew it. It was better to stop fighting it. He had to let it go. This was one fight he couldn't fight.

"Good-bye, Mattie."

Luc hung up the phone. His head hurt. His body ached. He grabbed his jacket and marched out of his office. He needed air. He ran into Orin as he eyed the elevator.

"Where are you going?" Orin asked.

"I gotta get out of here. I can't do this anymore." Luc slapped at the down button. He couldn't breathe. He pressed the button again.

"Do what?" Orin asked.

"Be successful. It feels worse than living poor."

The chill pierced through him. Not wanting to wait for the elevator, he ran for the stairs. He would feel better once he hit the streets again.

CHAPTER 35

▼

Tuesday, November 9, 2004
5:50 PM
Los Angeles, California

A pounding in my head woke me from the nightmare. I tried to get up, but my body felt heavy. The alcohol still tortured me. I wished I were dead. Anything was better than this.

I looked at the clock. It wasn't even six. I had escaped the cross-examination of Spencer. Ward had left to meet with Angel's girlfriend's family. Orin had to return to the office to try to write his stories before his deadline. And John worked to secure Spencer in his room. I needed sleep more than I would admit.

Spencer was indeed off the suspect list. The murders of Angel Martinez and Lito Figueroa were chalked up to Ron Mert, someone Spencer had never even met.

Carliss was committed to finding him. I was convinced he would. But the fact that Mert was still unaccounted for meant Spencer would be hidden in the hotel for another night. Surprisingly, he wasn't too upset with the idea.

Ward was also working just as hard to find Angel's girlfriend. He suspected she would have a lot to say on Angel's behalf. He wouldn't admit it, but I knew he was worried about discovering another body. He wanted to find her alive. I wasn't sure if he would.

The knocking came again and I realized it came from the door, not my head. I rolled out of the bed and hobbled to the door. Opening the door of my hotel room, I rubbed my eyes. For a second I thought the angel standing in front of me was an illusion. I tried to remember what potion I had drunk.

"How did you find me?" I asked, yawning.

"I just talked to Spencer." Mattie pointed down the hall. "John brought me. Can I come in?"

I left the door open and turned back into the room. I heard her close the door behind her. I sat down on the bed. I couldn't look at her so I stared at my empty hands.

"I wanted to thank you for helping Spencer."

I nodded but didn't say anything. I wasn't sure if I was ready to talk to her. Unfortunately I didn't think I had a choice.

"Luc, we need to talk about the other night."

"There's nothing to talk about, Mat."

"Yes, there is." She sat down beside me. I immediately felt uncomfortable with her so close to me. But I refused to get up. I didn't want her see any weakness.

"Look. My emotions were all over the place. I was a wreck. Then I was happy that Spencer was alive. I don't know what happened. It was a mistake. And it didn't mean anything."

"Didn't mean anything?" I finally looked at her. "I'm not stupid, Mat. Spencer told me how you felt. I didn't believe him. But that kiss told me everything. You can't continue to lie to me."

She looked away as I stood up. This was worse than the nightmare. The hell had returned. I couldn't breathe. I needed air.

I needed a drink. I got up and poured myself a scotch. I didn't have any ice so I drank it straight. She didn't speak in the silence.

"When did you know?" I finally asked.

She still wouldn't look at me. "I've always known."

"Damn it, Mat! Why didn't you tell me? Why the hell did you marry Spencer?"

"I tried, Luc. But you never looked at me that way. I married Spencer because I love him. Believe it or not, I do love him. I thought I could be happy with him. I thought I could get over you."

"I'm leaving tomorrow. You won't ever see me again. Maybe that will make it easier. You need to fix this with Spencer, without me." I couldn't look at her as the words left my mouth.

"No, Luc. I don't want you to leave again. If you want me to choose between you and Spencer, I choose you."

"Damn it, Mattie. Spencer is perfect for you. He loves you. He has a great career, and he comes from a respectable family. He's wealthy and can take care of you. Don't throw that away."

She stood and glared at me. I could see the anger in her eyes. It had been a long time since I had seen her angry.

"It really pisses me off that you constantly put me on this pedestal and expect me to pretend to be this angel. But what pisses me off more is that you constantly put yourself down. No matter how much money you make, no matter how successful your career gets, you still only see yourself as that poor little kid that had to fight to survive."

"I *am* still that poor little kid!" I yelled. "No matter what you see when you look at me, I am still that same person. I may have once had a successful career. But I am still the same. People don't change."

"I did," she muttered, looking away.

"I never changed. I never will. You have to deal with it."

"So you're just going to run away again?" she asked. "Just like the last time. Run away because fighting is too hard?"

"I'm not running. I'm trying to survive."

"What about me?" she asked. Her arms reached for my chest.

"Mattie, you're married." I pushed her hands away, surprised that I still had some fight left in me. "And I can't be who you want me to be. You need to leave."

She turned before I could see the tears fall from her eyes. She ran out of the room. I was angry with myself for making her cry. I slammed the door behind her.

I spent the next two hours on the phone with my old assistant at the *Washington Post*. I wasn't about to let the *Reporter* get all the glory. I wanted to get my own story published. It was time to start looking after myself.

After I sent my revised draft to the editor, I sent all my contact information to the fact checker and waited for a release.

Within an hour, my story had been confirmed and the *Post* was preparing for placement. I hoped for the front page above the fold. Just like old times.

I knocked on Spencer's door an hour later. He was done with his interviews, but there was still a deputy stationed at his door.

"Are you going home tonight?" I asked. I grabbed a beer from his minibar.

"No," he said. I nodded but didn't press. "What about you?"

I wondered where home was.

"I have a flight to DC tomorrow night. It was the earliest I could get."

He looked at the beer in my hands.

"Why are you so mad at her?"

"I'm not mad at her. I'm mad at myself."

"Why?"

"Her life is a mess. I thought she was happy. She had turned out to be the woman everyone expected her to become. I didn't think she needed me anymore."

"She'll always need you, Luc. And I don't think it was your responsibility to make sure she grew up right. And it's not your responsibility to make sure she's happy."

"Yes, it is. It's always been my responsibility." I looked at him. "She kissed me, Spencer. And I didn't stop her."

"I know. She told me."

"And you can sit here and act like we're friends?"

"We are friends, Luc. We've been through too much. No matter what happens between Mattie and me. And no matter what happens between you and her."

"That's adultery, Spencer. I won't let her do that."

I was surprised when he laughed.

"You won't let her? I guess I should be glad you're still thinking about her first."

"Who else would I be thinking about?" I asked.

"What about you, Luc? How do you feel?"

"I don't know," I lied. Mattie was the only person that ever mattered. "It doesn't matter."

He nodded. He let it go. "I told Mattie I was filing for divorce."

"What? Why?"

"I can't do this anymore. I made a promise to you that I would make her happy. But all I do is remind her how unhappy she is. I don't want to be the one to make her unhappy. I love her too much for that."

"I can't believe all this."

"You can't keep ignoring her."

"I don't have a choice!" I yelled.

"You've always had a choice. You just need to open your eyes to see it. Maybe you should be with her tonight."

"She's your wife, Spencer." I handed him the beer. "Maybe you should be with her." I slammed the door on my way out.

CHAPTER 36

▼

Wednesday, November 10, 2004
7:00 AM
Los Angeles, California

I refused to sleep. The room was too small, too cold. Much like the old Torrance apartment. I felt trapped here.

I spent the entire night looking out the window expecting some sort of message to come flying down to me. But I knew it wouldn't come from above. I looked to the streets below.

I was born on those streets. I grew up in LA. But I never lived here—I only survived day to day, hoping one day to find a way out. Like Angel, my only goal was to escape the hell I was thrown in. I had survived. I had escaped.

But it wasn't the streets that I had to escape. That was easy compared to looking into Mattie's eyes. My heart had died, but I had to keep breathing. When I watched her get married, I knew I had to leave. This was a hell I couldn't survive. I did the only thing I could—I packed my shit and said good-bye to everything.

I watched as the streets of Los Angeles sprang to life with the rising sun. Like ants rushing in a rainstorm, cars sped off toward their destinations. Children walked to the waiting school bus. Students listening to their iPods or talking to their friends walked toward the campus. Smiling. They weren't trying to get out of LA. They were living here. They were happy here. I had once been happy here.

I looked at the city skyline and wondered when this amazing place had transformed to hell. I had loved Los Angeles when I was a child. The beautiful weather, the melting pot of people, and the hope. The hope of life, the hope of surviving. This was home.

I didn't want to go back to Washington DC. I had left three years ago, hoping to put my past behind me. To put Mattie behind me. To put the pain behind me. Now she was getting divorced. But it didn't change the fact that I couldn't be with her.

I sat on the bed with an empty beer in my hands. I thought about Mattie, and I thought about Angel. But mainly I thought about my past.

Mattie was right. I still felt I was the poor little kid from the wrong side of town. But I was proud of that. I never pretended to be anything other than who I was.

My success in life came because I had fought hard to make sure no one could push me back down. I didn't go to college to prove anything. An opportunity arose. I saw the path I needed to take to escape and I took it.

I was successful at my job because I had to be. I had to survive, to escape the streets, to escape the pain. There was no way I was ever going to be hungry again. No way would I ever be homeless. No way would I let someone else control my life.

I was surprised when Ward knocked on my door at seven. He looked tired and I knew he had been up all night, too. Neither of us felt like fighting, so I let him in. He handed me a copy of the *Reporter* and helped himself to a beer.

The top story was about Spencer: "Missing LA Lawyer Found." I scanned the article and found nothing I didn't already know.

Orin had a breaking story. I knew he would be busy fielding calls from the other LA papers and I had to smile. That had once been me.

At the bottom of the front page was the headline "Angel Found Dead in LA." The editorial had Orin's byline:

> An Angel died last week in Los Angeles, without a word from the media. His mother, Ana Martinez, said Angel Martinez was an intelligent student, a hard-working teenager and a loving son. The Los Angeles County Sheriff's Department declared Angel Martinez a drug dealer that appropriately died with a bullet in his head.
>
> Angel Martinez was only eighteen years old when he was shot to death at a friend's house in Whittier last Tuesday. He was looking for a way out of the drug life that seems to overpower all young males growing up on the streets. He thought he had found a way to escape, only to die before his opportunity arose.
>
> Most people are probably thankful that another drug dealer is off the street. But the reality is that for every one killed, two more are ready to take his place. Not because it's a thrilling or prestigious position, but merely because they feel they have no choice. Angel Martinez saw no other choice.

Society discounted him. The education system failed him. The legal system degraded him. But worst of all we ignored him.

Blame it on the economy or the technological boom. Or whatever reason you want to use as the scapegoat. But the young boys living in the poverty of Los Angeles have little opportunity to be successful or to leave the crime-ridden streets where they live. They realize early that money can help them escape, can help them grow up to reach their goals. As young men in Los Angeles, they fall into drugs, gangs, and crime as their only savior.

It is a sad day when an Angel dies. So I have to ask this. How many Angels have to fall before we stand up and take notice? How many more Angels have to die before we realize there is a larger problem that needs to be fixed?

I looked up and found Ward watching me.

"Did you find the girlfriend?" I asked.

"Not yet. But we picked up Mert this morning at the airport. He was planning a quick trip to Vegas. He lawyered up, but I think we have enough on him."

"That's great news. So Spencer can go home?"

Ward rubbed at his red eyes. "He took Mattie's car to the station to give his official statement."

I nodded. "I guess I should thank you for helping him through this."

"I can only do so much, Luc."

I eyed him, wondering if he really was up for a fight. I wrote off his attitude to lack of sleep.

"I advised him to hire the best defense lawyer he knew, just in case."

I smiled. "Bill?"

"He's meeting him at the station." He played with the beer bottle. "Do you need a lift to Mattie's?"

I tossed the paper on the bed. "No. That's the last place I want to go."

He drank his beer and let the room fill with silence. I wondered why he was even in my room.

"Spencer told me the divorce papers would be delivered to her this morning. She could probably use a friend."

I sat on the bed and closed my eyes. I couldn't imagine what Mattie was feeling. She still loved Spencer. I knew that. Having to admit failure and end a three-year marriage would be painful for her. I should have been there for her.

"I think it's best if I just get the hell out of here."

"You think that's best?" he asked. "To give up?" His eyes were focused on the beer. Maybe he really did want a fight.

"I don't have a choice."

"You've always had a choice."

"Says the man that slept with a married woman to get ahead. Nah," I said. "That may be your choice, but that's not mine. I'll deal with the hand I was dealt without stealing an ace from another man."

He laughed, put down the beer, and looked at me.

"You know, Luc, if you're going to use my past against me, then you should have looked further back. You keep saying that you have no choice. That you became a criminal because of the cards you were dealt. Well, that's bullshit. You took the easy way out. Fuck morality or anyone else. You took the route that would get you a quick escape without ever looking at the other options."

"You don't know what you're talking about, Ward."

"Oh yeah? My mother threw me out the window of a car when I was only days old. Said she didn't want to be a mother. After six months of therapy, the state decided she was ready to be a mother again. When I was two years old, I watched as she killed her parents and turned the gun on herself. For the next sixteen years, I grew up in an orphanage, wishing she had just pulled the trigger on me."

"Fuck, Ward." I couldn't look at him. I definitely didn't want to fight with him. "We're not the same."

"The only thing that separates us is the decisions we made. I didn't have money or even a family to care for me," he continued. "They changed my name so prospective parents wouldn't be reminded of the insanity that ran in my family. But it didn't help. I would always be a ward of the state."

I felt my stomach turn as I wished I could've helped the child he once was.

"But I didn't choose crime like you did. I figured if my life was going to be hard, it would be because I chose it. No way in hell would I let anyone else have that control over me. I looked past the easy life of selling death to addicts too weak to reject it and stealing worthless shit from people who worked hard to get what little they had. Instead, I worked two jobs so I could pay for college. And I never slept when I was lucky enough to get accepted. I studied hard instead of stealing grades.

"I chose law enforcement, after watching the Rodney King tape played over and over again on the nightly news. I watched those assholes beat a man just because they wore a badge. I watched the riots after the officers were cleared and realized if the courts couldn't fix the problems then it was best fixed from within. I knew it would be the most difficult job I could do since not even honest citizens respected the badge anymore.

"So I dropped out of college and jumped into the academy. I worked my ass off once I made the force and got where I am because I survived the hard road, not because I fucked up and slept with a superior. So don't throw that shit in my face again."

He got up and moved toward the door. "You have a choice, Luc. It's up to you to make the right one. Stop looking for the easy road. And start fighting for what you want. You got dealt a shitty hand. Guess what? You're not the only one. But it's your choice whether you fold and walk away."

He walked out without another word, and I found myself feeling very sick. I picked up the beer he had left and threw it against the wall. I watched the bottle shatter and the froth slide down the gaudy brown wallpaper.

Ward was right. I still had a decision to make. And I was nowhere close to making it.

I took a taxi to Mattie's house. I didn't know what to say, so I sat in the cab and stared at the house on the cliff. I watched as a light breeze kicked up and carried a paper cup down the empty street. It was quiet.

After twenty minutes, I finally stepped out, paid the driver, and walked slowly up the drive. I took a deep breath and knocked on her door.

There was no answer. I knocked again.

She had to be home. She had no car and nowhere to go. I tried to look through the window but couldn't see through the tint.

Then I heard her yell at me.

I knocked again. Waited. Charlie barked from the backyard.

"Open the door, Mattie. I know you're home!" I yelled.

More yelling. But I couldn't hear what she was saying.

"Damn it, Mattie. If you want to yell at me, open the fucking door."

Debating whether I should pick the lock, I knocked again.

I was relieved when I heard the dead bolt finally give. Mattie opened the door an inch. Her face was dry and red. It wasn't sadness in her eyes. It was anger.

"Mattie, I need to talk to you. Let me in."

"No, Luc. You need to leave. Go away. Now."

"I'm not leaving. I canceled my flight. I'll never leave you again. I can be the man you deserve, if you let me."

I sounded like I was begging and it made me sick. I never begged when it came to a woman. I knew I was already changing for her.

I saw the anger fade from her face. A tear fell. She looked away.

I hated to see her cry, to see her sad. I wanted her to be angry again. I cursed myself and reached for her.

Then the moment passed. Her anger returned as she tried to close the door on me. I grabbed the door and pushed my way inside. She looked behind her as the door slid from her grasp. Edgar Twaine was standing behind her.

"How romantic, Mr. Actar," he said. He moved quickly. He locked the door behind me. Then I noticed the gun pointed at Mattie.

"Too bad it just got you both killed."

CHAPTER 37

▼

Wednesday, November 10, 2004
9:30 AM
Malibu, California

"I am really getting tired of people pointing guns at me," I said.

Mattie started crying. I pulled her behind me.

"I was expecting Spencer, not you, Luc. But this is basically your fault anyway. You just had to come back to play hero. Now you can die, too."

"Put the gun down, Edgar. You're a lawyer, not a killer. Let's talk."

Edgar laughed.

"OK," I relented. "Then put the gun down and we can have a fair fight, just you and me."

He ignored me.

"I couldn't have planned this better. Now I can get rid of all three of you and pose it as a love triangle. That stupid detective will believe anything."

He looked past me at Mattie. He smiled at her. It pissed me off. The gun was now pointed right at my chest.

"Your father always thought there was more between you two. Did you know he talked about that? Years ago, he thought you two would end up together."

I kept Mattie behind me. If he was going to shoot, I wanted him to shoot me first. But I hoped he wouldn't have the chance to get a shot off.

"You know this girl has some balls on her," he said, laughing. "She almost got herself killed trying to get you to leave. You've always been a persistent punk. Now you both can die together."

I needed to stall him. Think. Plan.

"That's not going to happen. The cops are right behind me," I threatened.

"The cops aren't coming."

"The house is bugged." I now hoped it was true.

"They didn't get a chance to bug the house." Unworried, he looked at the couch. "Sit down," he ordered. "Now, we wait for Spencer."

I tried to look relaxed as I turned toward the couch. I put my hands in my jacket pocket reaching for the cold metal. I grabbed the tape recorder. The gun wasn't there. Shit. I had left it in Spencer's room. I held onto Mattie. She buried her head in my chest and continued to cry.

I tried to think of a way to overpower Edgar. I was younger, stronger, and bigger than him. But I didn't have the gun. It hadn't stopped me before, but Mattie was here. I wouldn't risk her getting hurt.

"Spencer's meeting with the sheriff's department."

The information didn't faze Edgar. He still looked confident. I wanted to smack that smug look off his face.

"He's telling them all about you."

"There's nothing to tell. All I did was suggest he take the case."

"Angel talked to Spencer before you killed him. He told him how you promised him a fortune in exchange for a few lies."

"Nice story, but mine is better. Spencer didn't get a chance to talk to Angel. I told him to stop by and see me first. It was the perfect plan. Spencer missed his chance to talk to Angel and I had an alibi just in case Spencer cleared himself. I didn't kill anybody."

"No, you're too much of a pussy to do it yourself. You had to have Ron Mert kill him for you. The detectives are already looking into every single one of his cases."

Twaine turned to Mattie. Anger sprang to his eyes.

"Her stupid father wouldn't let me take any more corruption cases. Said it was bad for business to be so narrow-minded. He didn't realize that was where the money was. Mert was so willing to help. Then Spencer practically begged for a case. But he couldn't handle it."

"Unfortunately for you, the detectives arrested Mert this morning for the murder of Angel Martinez and Lito Figueroa."

I saw a flash of worry, and then it was gone.

"Good for them. He was a lousy lawyer. He deserves to go to jail. I told him I would fix this. All he had to do was leave town. He couldn't even get that right. It doesn't matter. I can find another lawyer to play my games. There are plenty out there looking for a piece of the action."

"It'll be a little tough for you to continue to practice law behind bars, Twaine."

"For a street thug, you sure have an odd confidence in the legal system. I'm not going anywhere. Mert will go down for the murders. You did a hell of a job getting Spencer off—"

"You tried to frame him, didn't you? You told Spencer to buy the gun. The same type you told Ron Mert to use to kill Angel. Then you sent him off to see Angel."

"Just a little safety net. Angel threatened to talk. I told Ron to take care of it. But he wanted to make sure it wouldn't come back on him. We needed a fall guy. Spencer fit perfectly, especially when he decided to take off. I was supposed to find him before you did."

"I still don't see how you're going to get away with this."

"With Spencer killing his lovely wife and best friend before turning the gun on himself, I think I can reverse what you screwed up. The suicide note will show that Spencer was the mastermind all along."

"Mert is going to tell the detectives all about your connection. With Spencer's corroboration there should be no problem convicting you of murder and fraud with or without us."

He lowered the gun as he thought about what I said. He knew he was too late.

"That doesn't mean I can't kill you—" he started to say.

"Shut up, both of you!" Mattie screamed.

She pushed away from me. Her face was dry. The fear gone.

The last time I had seen the look in her eyes, she was eight years old. Staring into the face of Julie Clark.

She stood as Edgar turned the gun toward her. Hands clenched at her sides.

"I don't care about whatever you did. I don't even care how Spencer was involved. And I really don't care if the cops are on their way. The only thing I care about is that you are in my house and I don't want you here. So get the hell out."

My body went into shock. It gripped me by the throat. I was unable to move.

Edgar glared at her. He was going to shoot her. His face hardened. His fingers tightened. And all I could do was watch.

The slight hesitation cost him. Mattie's right fist streaked up and smacked into Edgar's nose. I heard a crack and heard Edgar grunt in pain.

He lowered the gun. Cursing, he grabbed his nose with his left hand. Blood seeped through his fingers as he tried to focus on the woman in front of him.

My fear for Mattie overtook my shock. My body released. I jumped from the couch. Knocking him with the full force of my shoulder in his gut, I forced him to the ground.

Mattie screamed. Charlie barked. But I didn't hear anything. I never heard the shot from the gun. I didn't even feel the bullet tear into my flesh.

Nor did I notice the several men that stormed into the house moments later. All my concentration and anger centered on Edgar's face as I slammed it against the floor over and over. I was going to kill him. I knew I would.

But then I was jerked up and my arms snatched from the man I had every intention of killing. I felt a cold pain jolt through my body. Someone laid me on the floor. Several men held me down as I fought to get back to Twaine.

Surrendering, I watched in silence as men with guns drawn ran all around me. One tried to talk to me but I couldn't hear the words coming from his mouth. I turned from him and tried to focus on Mattie.

My sight was fuzzy and starting to turn gray in the corners, but I saw her screaming. I smirked as I realized she wasn't sad or scared. She was mad at me.

As the cold rushed over me, I felt alive. Every nerve in my body jolted to try to warm me. Being shot hurts. And although I was relieved to feel the pain start to numb, I suddenly realized I didn't want to die.

As the blackness took over, I remembered all the times Mattie had been angry with me. I remembered all the times she had yelled at me or fought with me. And I remembered how I always smiled and told her nice girls don't argue.

I wanted to tell her how sorry I was. Instead, I succumbed to the exhaustion and closed my eyes to the world. I knew she never stayed mad at me for long.

CHAPTER 38

▼

Wednesday, November 10, 2004
5:08 PM
Los Angeles, California

I was dead. My throat burned, my eyes stung. For the first time in my life, I didn't wake wondering how I had survived another day. This time I knew I was dead.

I opened my eyes and looked around the tiny room that housed me. I searched for the gate that would tell me I was going to hell. To my surprise, I saw medical equipment in the corner trying to distribute life to me. I pulled the oxygen mask from my face. I tried to curse but I ended up coughing instead.

The two men in the room turned and stared at me in silence. I focused my eyes and then dropped my heavy head back on the pillow.

"I must be in hell. Either that or God sent the two ugliest fuckin' angels to come get me."

"Damn, I was hoping you weren't going to make it," Carliss said, shaking his head.

I pulled myself up on the bed and took another look at the IVs running into my arms.

"Didn't anyone tell them I hate needles?" I pulled the IVs from my arm and felt the slight sting. I looked at my bandaged shoulder. Something beeped behind me.

"What the hell happened?" I asked, looking back at the two men.

"You got shot." It was Spencer this time. He was smiling at me, amused with my pain. If I had the strength, I would have kicked his ass. Instead, I closed my eyes.

"Why the hell did you let them shoot me?" I asked Carliss.

- 197 -

"Them? It wasn't my guys. Twaine shot you when you decided to bum-rush him. It appears I was wrong. You really do have a death wish."

"I wasn't about to wait for your guys to get there."

My memory was coming back in bits and pieces. I remembered hitting Twaine. I remembered the gun going off. I remembered the uniformed men surrounding me. I remembered Mattie screaming at me.

"We would have gotten there sooner if you had told us you had talked to Theresa Sancliment."

"Who?" I asked, looking at my aching shoulder.

Spencer pulled a napkin from his pocket. "I found it in Mattie's car after you left the hotel."

I looked at the napkin, trying to figure out what they were talking about.

"The girl from the bar? She blew me off." I put my head back down and closed my eyes.

Carliss laughed. "Theresa was Angel's girlfriend. Ward's been trying to find her for over a week now. In the meantime, she found you."

"I don't understand. Why was she looking for me?"

"She was scared when she heard about Angel. He had told her if anything happened to him, she needed to find Spencer and tell him everything. Then Spencer disappeared. She saw you at Angel's funeral. She followed you to the bar. Unfortunately, you were just looking to get laid and she walked."

"Shit." I looked at Spencer. "Did you talk to her?"

"Yeah, I called her when I saw the napkin. John and I interviewed her. She told us about Twaine."

"How did he fit into all this?"

It was Carliss that answered. "Lito convinced Angel to sue the sheriff's department. He told him how easy it was when he did it. He suggested Angel talk to Twaine. Twaine dumped the case on Spencer."

Spencer sat down in the chair beside the bed.

"I had gone to Edgar a few weeks earlier. I needed a pro bono case that would take very little time. Edgar told me he would throw me a civil or human rights case if he had any that looked easy."

"So he told Angel to see you?"

Spencer nodded. "It was supposed to be an easy case. Angel already had a copy of the arrest report and the medical report. It just required me putting the paperwork together. Twaine was positive it would settle out of court."

"What went wrong?" I asked.

"Angel got scared," Carliss answered. "We don't know exactly why, but he decided he didn't want to go up against the department. Twaine threatened him. He was on the line because he had suggested the case to Spencer. And Twaine didn't want Spencer to know about the scam."

"Too close to home. He knew Spencer would tell Bill." I looked at Spencer. He nodded.

"Angel called the police, hoping to get protection, but we didn't find him in time."

"Then Mert had to kill Lito to make sure the scam was never revealed," finished Spencer. "He left Twaine to frame me for it all."

"How did you know where Twaine was?" I asked.

"Twaine's my lawyer. He was supposed to deliver the divorce papers to Mattie," Spencer explained.

"Where is he now?" I asked, looking around the room. I was already plotting how I could escape the room and hurt him.

"He just got stitched up. Had a nasty gash in the back of his skull. Broken nose. He's on his way to jail." Carliss looked at his watch. "In fact, I should go. I have to handle the paperwork." He slapped at my hand. "Get some sleep. I hear bullet wounds can be pretty painful."

I shrugged and felt the pain shoot through my arm. "I like pain," I winced.

Carliss laughed and headed for the door. "See you around, Luc."

"Hey, Lieutenant," I called out.

He glanced back.

"Thanks for saving my life. Again."

The compliment surprised him. He waited for something, then turned back to the door.

"You're welcome," he mumbled as the door shut behind him.

"Where's Mattie?" I asked Spencer. "Is she OK?"

The pain in my shoulder was spreading through my body. I knew it was only a matter of time before I passed out from the pain.

"She's fine. She's outside. She was having a hard time looking at you in this condition. She blames herself. What happened in there?"

"She went nuts. She almost got herself killed. I don't know what I would have done if she had been shot instead of me."

He smiled. "I do. Edgar would have needed more than a few stitches to put his head back together."

The thought only made me angrier. I tried to get comfortable. The pain shot through my arm again. I tried not to cringe, but the pain was getting worse. I threw the pillows off the bed with my good arm and could feel the tears rising in my eyes.

I was frustrated with the pain. I hated to be stuck in a hospital bed. I wanted to kill Twaine for doing this to me, even more for scaring Mattie.

Spencer watched me fight with the bed. "You OK?"

"Yeah. Just hurts like a motherfucker."

Spencer tried to adjust the bed and I slapped his hands away.

"You know, I've only seen you like this once before."

"Like what?" I snapped.

"Angry and in pain. I never asked about it. It was in college, after you disappeared for two weeks. When I found you at that old apartment, you looked like you had dragged yourself out of hell. You had blood on your hands, on your clothes. You were crying."

I looked at my hands, expecting to see the blood that had been there so many years earlier. I looked away even though I knew the tears had dried a long time ago.

"What did you do?" he asked me.

"I went to see a guy named Carl Palfy."

"Mattie's ex-boyfriend?" he asked, surprised.

"Yeah. She had just dumped him. He was an asshole." I looked at Spencer. "I don't know what she ever saw in him." I looked back at my hands.

"It took me two weeks to find him. I'd been sleeping on the streets, and I was tired. I was young and stupid. I was fucked up, high, wasted. Hell, I was angry and depressed. Whatever excuse you want, I was it."

"You hurt him?" It was more of a statement than a question.

I didn't need to answer. Spencer knew me well enough. But knowing exactly what I had done that night wouldn't change anything. It was best he didn't know. It was enough that I had to live with the image of Carl's empty eyes staring back at me.

I couldn't look at him. I didn't want to see the disappointment on his face. Or see the questions I knew he wanted to ask.

"Can I see Mattie?" I asked.

I closed my eyes and heard the door open as he left me alone.

CHAPTER 39

Wednesday, November 10, 2004
5:22 PM
Los Angeles, California

"What the hell were you thinking?" I asked Mattie. I was furious. Not that I had been shot but because I might *not* have been shot. It could have been her instead.

I was surprised when she smiled.

"I'm so sorry you got hurt. I just got sick of waiting for everyone else to save me. I'm sick and tired of letting other people tell me what I should and shouldn't do. I wanted for once to be in control of my own life."

"You just about got yourself killed!"

"But at least I did something!" she yelled back. "I'm tired of being the good little girl that waits to be saved," she explained.

"You do better as the good little girl. It fits you well."

"Only because you refuse to see me as anything else."

I laughed and felt the pain in my shoulder explode through my body. I was now starting to think the IV wasn't so bad.

"Damn it. Fine. You be that tough girl you always wanted to be. You can speed on the freeway. I'll even let you curse when your father's not around. But don't you ever challenge a man with a gun again."

She looked at me. I couldn't read her eyes.

"You really don't think I can be bad, do you? Well, let me tell you some things you don't know about me, Luc."

Then I saw the anger in her eyes. And I knew the fury was about to be released. For some odd reason, I wanted to see it.

"It wasn't John Carliss that kissed me. I kissed him. And I would have taken it further if he hadn't stopped me. Did you know that I slept with Carl on our first date? He took me to the movies and I gave him a blow job in the back of the theater."

"For God's sake, Mattie," I interrupted. "I don't want to hear this shit." I tried to drown her voice out but she continued.

"Too bad. Do you know I have a tattoo? It's a devil's tail with the words 'bad girl.'"

"Wait a second." I held up my hand to stop her from continuing. "You got a tattoo?"

She smiled. "Yes. It's just below my bikini line. Would you like to see it?"

"Oh, dear God," I muttered. There was no way I was going to answer that question. It would only get me into more trouble.

"Have you filed those divorce papers, yet?" I asked.

She continued to smile and moved closer to me. "I'll probably do it tomorrow. Why?"

"Just wondering," I muttered.

"You just wanted to change the subject."

"No, it was the same subject. I do want to see that tattoo, but not while you're still married."

"Then you'll have to wait six months."

"What?" I sat up and felt the shooting pain in my shoulder again. "Six months?"

"That's how long the process takes. Is that going to be a problem?"

"I'll be dead before that." I grabbed my shoulder and tried to ease the pain. I couldn't tell if the dull ache was from my shoulder or my heart.

"Tell me what you're thinking."

I smiled back at her. "If I survive the next six months, I'll tell you everything. I promise. I don't want to make these six months harder by saying it."

She shook her head. The smile had disappeared. She turned her face away from me, and I knew she needed to hear it. I didn't want to hurt her anymore.

"OK," I sighed. "I love you, Mattie. I have loved you my entire life. I just didn't realize it until it was much too late."

I tried to pull her into my arms, but the pain in my shoulder prevented it. She pulled away from me and glared at me.

"You love me? That's it?"

"What do you mean is that it? It's everything."

She laughed but her eyes showed no humor. "This is definitely not going to work. I should've known. Why don't you go back to Washington DC and let me live my own life? I don't need you anymore."

Her chin shot up. Her demeanor had quickly turned from the fragile little girl to stubborn, strong woman. I couldn't keep up.

"Bullshit. What the hell is going on with you, Mattie? I just told you I love you and you ask me to leave?"

"I know you love me. I've known that for about as long as I knew I loved you. But it's not enough. I need more than that."

"What do you want from me?" I yelled at her.

"I want you to want me, Luc. And not like a big brother wanting to take care of his little sister. I want you to want me like you wanted all those other girls— emotionally and physically."

"Jesus Christ, Mattie. I won't be vulgar with you."

"I'm not asking you to be vulgar. I just want you to stop treating me like a princess. Tell me how you feel about me."

"You don't want me to tell you how I feel, Mattie." I raised my voice. This was one fight she wasn't going to win. "You don't want to hear the truth."

"Yes, I—" she stared.

"No. You don't. You don't want to know that when you walk in the room, you instantly make me hard. You don't want to know that I wanted you so bad in high school that I punished myself every time I thought about touching you. That I used to provoke my father so he would beat the shit out of me and make me forget my thoughts of you. And I would find the most available girl around and fuck her, all the while thinking of you.

"You don't want to hear that when I found out John kissed you that I held a gun to his head and was actually going to pull the trigger because the thought of another man's lips on you drove me insane. You don't want to know that after finding out Carl touched you, I made sure he regretted it by pounding his skull into a concrete wall.

"For years I wanted you, but I forced the thoughts out of my head. I didn't know what love was until that day on your balcony. For the first time, I felt it. I wanted you, physically and emotionally. But I knew I didn't deserve it. I forced myself to watch you marry another man, a man you deserved to be with, a man that understood what love really means. And that alone hurt me more than this damn bullet. I couldn't spend another minute looking at you without being reminded of that pain. It was worse than any other hell I had ever lived through. I knew I wouldn't survive. I had no choice but to leave everything behind.

"So, no, I don't want you like I wanted those other girls. I never loved any of them. I want to marry you, and I want to have kids with you. I want to spend every waking second with you and be able to fall asleep with you in my arms. Hell, I need you."

I hadn't realized my voice had risen to a shout. I lowered my voice.

"But that means giving up who I am. To be with you, I have to stop fighting everything I have spent my life fighting. But I am willing to do that for you. I am willing to change and to give up my past for you. Not just because you deserve it but because I would do *anything* to make you happy. I need that just as much as I need you.

"So don't tell me that's not enough. Don't tell me to get on a plane to DC. Knowing I loved you and couldn't have you was hell. Knowing you love me and don't want me is worse. I might as well have let the bastard kill me."

I let the silence fill the room. I couldn't look at her. I was disgusted with myself and I knew she was probably thinking the same thing. I heard her move closer to me.

"I was with John and Carl only to make you jealous," she finally said.

"It worked," I mumbled, not knowing what response she wanted.

"I'm sorry. I was hoping for a different reaction. I was hoping you would come to me and tell me what you were feeling."

"I couldn't do that. You may have known you were in love with me then. I didn't even know what love was. And I definitely didn't deserve you."

I looked at her. I was surprised to see it wasn't the fragile Mattie I was looking at. Even with my shouting, she had remained firm, strong.

"It doesn't matter anymore."

"Yes, it does. I don't want you to change, Luc. I would never ask you to give up who you are or to stop fighting for what you believe. It wouldn't be fair, to either of us. I love you because of who you are and what you are. If you change, you wouldn't be the man I fell in love with."

"I can't fight a system. I have joined."

She smiled at me. "Sometimes the best way to fight something is from within."

I thought of Detective Ward and realized he was doing just that. Maybe I could learn something from him.

"All I ask is that you start realizing I don't want to be that sweet little girl that needs everyone to take care of her. I don't want to be weak anymore."

"So we wait six months," I said, pulling her back into my arms, "and see where this road leads us." Six months was starting to sound like an eternity.

"Since when do you follow rules?" she teased.

978-0-595-37710-7
0-595-37710-6

Lightning Source UK Ltd.
Milton Keynes UK
UKHW010636060621
384988UK00001B/41

9 780595 377107